MW00954927

KISS ME LIKE YOU MISSED ME

TAYLOR HOLLOWAY

Copyright © 2018 by Taylor Holloway

All rights reserved.

No part of this book may be reproduced in any form or by any electronic or mechanical means, including information storage and retrieval systems, without written permission from the author, except for the use of brief quotations in a book review.

TAYLOR HOLLOWAY
ROMANCE

**I thought I could handle seeing Cole after all these years.
I thought I could avoid the temptation of his chiseled
body, cocky attitude, and soulful eyes.
But one look from him and I'm sweet sixteen again.**

My brother's best friend Cole was my foolish, hopeless
teenage obsession. I've never felt anything as intense as my
time with him, and nothing since has measured up. I know
it was impossible for us to stay together, but it still
crushed me.

I can't deny that there's just the tiniest little sliver of my
mind that wonders what might have been.
There's just the smallest, most fragile corner of my soul
that wonders if we could ever rekindle what was lost.
And then there's my body, screaming ravenously and insistently for just One. More. Night.

As my brother's best man, Cole and I will be seeing a lot of
each other.
He's made it clear that he wants a second chance, but all
the obstacles between us are just as real as ever.

With my heart hanging in the balance, I know I'm in trouble.

Kiss Me Like You Missed Me is a full-length second chance romance featuring a bold alpha hero who's about to meet his match in a feisty, smart-mouthed heroine. It can be read as a standalone or as part of a series.

PROLOGUE

KATE

WHEN THE MYSTERIOUS PACKAGE ARRIVED, I had to maneuver sideways to avoid catching the delicate fabric of my full skirt on the ragged screen door. The delivery guy stared at me with wide eyes. He handed me the nondescript cardboard box, stammered "Here's your package ma'am," and stumbled back to his truck in confusion. I could understand his shock. Instead of my usual second-hand clothes, today I looked like I'd stepped off a runway in Paris. Not bad for a girl who lived in a shabby double-wide on the last lower edge of the working class.

With my aggressively nipped-in waist, tea-length, percale-lined, grey taffeta skirt and black silk bodice, my homecoming dress wasn't exactly on trend. I loved it. I knew all the other girls at my fancy high school would be wearing what I saw in the malls.

Brightly colored, sequined, mermaid-style dresses were

everywhere this year. Even with their four-figure price tags, those dresses all looked the same to me: garish, heavy, uncomfortable, and overpriced. Besides, Jessica Rabbit might've been able to keep her dress up with sultry willpower, but my double D's would be straight-up vulgar if I tried to wear a strapless, sequined piece of lingerie.

My demure dress couldn't be more different. Dior's new look rocked Paris when it debuted in 1947. It was an attempt to reclaim the freedom, glamour, femininity, and optimism that had disappeared during the austerity of war. My prom dress didn't have Dior tags, but it was very beautiful, and it made me feel sophisticated and special.

Even though it was older than my mom, the materials and construction were much finer than the mass-produced clothing of today. The dress had been handmade for someone, and she'd conveniently been exactly my size. My dress had still cost *much more* than I could afford, but I couldn't regret buying something so gorgeous. The vintage shop didn't even know what they had.

My ex-boyfriend hadn't known what he had either, and I'd be going to the homecoming dance alone as a result. *Screw you, Travis,* I thought to myself as I collected my heavy, dark hair into a chignon at the base of my neck. *You thought for sure I'd put out on prom night, huh?* The rumors had worked their way back to me just in time for me to dump his spoiled ass in spectacular, screaming fashion.

What really hurt was that he'd both denied the rumors to my face and then spread it around that he dumped me because I was a crazy cheater with an STD. I stabbed bobby pins into my hair with a bit more force than necessary as I thought about stupid, entitled, good-looking, popular Travis and his equally awful little group of friends. I should have known the whole group was only being nice to me because of Travis. The really messed up thing was that if he hadn't bragged to the whole school about taking my v-card, I might've given it to him. *I was dumb enough to believe he really liked me.*

I added a strand of my grandmother's white pearls and my reflection looked back at me from the mirror approvingly. I'd made the right decision. I would go to the dance alone, look like a million bucks, and make Travis very, very sorry. I may have been one of the poorest girls in school, and I certainly wasn't the smartest or the most popular, but I had my pride.

A text from my mom made me jump: *Be safe tonight! Have fun. I've got to work a double, but I'll see you on Sunday. Love you.*

I sent her back a thumbs up, a heart, and a happy face. She didn't know about the Travis situation, and I wasn't going to bother her with it. My mom—a nurse—had been working nonstop shifts at the hospital. The dirt bag she'd just broken up with had cleaned out our bank account and stolen all our electronics (including the laptop I used for school) before disappearing a few weeks earlier. Between him and my deadbeat biological dad, who hadn't paid child support for me or my brother since I was in diapers, my mom had plenty of her own drama to deal with. And that was just in her personal life. Professionally, she dealt with all kinds of crap (most of it literally, well, crap). I tried not to make it all worse for her.

Another text, this one from a blocked number, made me cringe. In the attached image, Travis was standing in front of a black, stretch Hummer with three guys and four girls from our school. In the background, the manicured lawns and sprawling houses of the nice side of town looked like something out of a magazine. Travis had his arm around the waist of one of the girls, a pretty blonde named Ashley. She was wearing a pink and gold sequined gown, and I could see the characteristic red soles of her Louboutin shoes beneath her long skirt. Just *one* of those shoes was worth more than my entire wardrobe.

But money clearly couldn't buy class or good taste. Her dress was a size too small and the straps looked like they were painfully digging into her shoulders. Her bronzer also looked a shade too dark, making her look less sun-kissed and more sunburned. I thought about replying with a snarky comment about her over-aggressive contouring but managed to restrain myself.

For once, I was determined to take the high road. This time I wasn't going to give anyone the satisfaction of seeing me go ballistic when they called me trailer trash. It had taken a long time, but I was finally starting to learn that setting my temper free made situations worse and not better.

I didn't know which one of my eight pictured class-mates had sent the picture, but my money was on Ashley herself. We were on the volleyball team together and she despised me for beating her out for captain. Whether it was her or not, the implication was clear. *You aren't one of us. You'll never be one of us.* Like I needed to be reminded of that. After I dumped Travis, I'd had several snide comments directed my way that I wasn't good enough for him anyway. Someone had also stolen my books out of my locker and written 'trashy bitch' on the inside covers. The casual bullying stung, but I'd had plenty worse treatment than that over the years.

A second photo, this one of Travis making out with Ashley in the limo, lit up my phone. Whoever was sending me this shit was really rubbing it in. They even added a message this time: *He's better off without a crazy, cheap slut like you.* As if sticking his tongue down Ashley's throat was not the equivalent of French kissing a filthy toilet seat? Please.

I tossed my phone down on my bed next to the package and grabbed some scissors off my desk. I needed a distrac-tion before I melted down and lost my nerve. The mystery package would have to do.

Feeling frustrated and helpless, I stabbed into the card-board down to the plastic wrapping beneath.

Like a science project volcano made of vinegar and baking soda, a small-scale explosion issued out from the plastic bag with a decisive pop. Shock and fear slowed the experience, but I was powerless to prevent what came next. A multicolored plume of powder shot up and hung thick in the air. The powder—no, *glitter* I realized after a moment—drifted down like shining snow, settling on every available surface in my room. It adhered like superglue to my skin, my hair, my eyelashes, and my dress. It was *everywhere*. I'd never seen so much glitter in my entire life. There were *pounds* of it, kept under pressure in that plastic bag. Until I punctured it, that is.

Through the salty sting of my tears, I saw nothing but red.

MY NOW-GLITTERY HEELS left a little trail of sparkles through the hunting and fishing mega-store. The girl working the register at eight p.m. on a Friday was about my age. She took in my appearance with a nonplussed expression. I'd pulled one of my brother's hoodies on over my dress as protection against the freak cold front, but I still looked like I'd been rolling around the floor of a glitter factory. It rubbed off on every surface I touched, including the money I slid across the counter to her.

"Did you find everything you were looking for tonight?" She asked me carefully, loading the bottles into the bag and not meeting my eyes.

"Yeah. Thanks. You're out of these ones now," I said, lifting one of the little amber bottles.

She nodded, looking down at the glittery bottle, then at me, then back at the bottle. "Hunting season starts next week."

I nodded back, collecting my receipt and purchases and making as dignified a retreat as I could. My sparkly lips pulled back into a humorless smile. "Thanks."

I was hunting all right, but not for Bambi. Hunting season for my prey started right fucking now.

THE DRIVE from Plano to Austin ordinarily takes about three and a half hours. I made it faster than that, because I never went below eighty-five. In hindsight, that was not a great idea for a sixteen-year-old with a learner's permit, but I was running on frustration, humiliation, Waffle House, and Red Bull.

Interestingly, the package did not originate from one of my classmates in Plano. Instead, its address was from two cities away in the state capital where my brother was going to college. In fact, it was from his next-door neighbor. That was an odd coincidence, since it was one of the few places I knew how to navigate to, having just helped him move in a couple of weeks ago. Still, I could only assume that somehow Travis or one of his nasty friends was behind my glittery predicament.

By the time I arrived in front of the door belonging to Cole Rylander, resident of the men's dorms at the University of Texas, it was almost three a.m. I managed to sneak in the door after a drunk guy—security wasn't exactly tight. You'd have thought my anger-fueled adrenaline rush would not have lasted long enough to see this plan through, but I was special. I had anger to spare, all the time. Right then, I was still trembling with it. I banged on the door with one gloved hand, clutching the squeeze bottle I'd stolen from a Waffle House on the way behind my back.

"Jesus Christ, what do you want?!" The man said when he opened the door. His voice was groggy, like he'd just been awakened, and he was rubbing his eyes as if in total disbelief. I guess it's not every day a walking disco ball knocks on your door in the middle of the night. I wasn't even seeing him at the moment. "Who are you?" He stuttered.

"Are you Cole Rylander?" I confirmed, dancing from foot to foot. The squeeze bottle—the kind that restaurants use for condiments like ketchup—was a cold weight in my hand. I'd put everything in the locked toolbox in the bed of the truck as a precaution, only filling it up in the hallway right before knocking. It had gotten icy cold during the drive.

"Yes, but—urgh!"

As soon as I knew it was him, I whipped out the squeeze bottle filled with chilled deer urine and doused him with it. The man retched when the smell hit him, and I just kept squeezing, exhausting every last drop of the thick, putrid-smelling liquid all over his bare front. I didn't aim for his face, but I wasn't avoiding it either. He probably got a mouthful or two.

"Oh God, oh God, what is this shit?!" he cried in between gags. Guilt pinged through me and I quashed it. This was justice. He was rubbing his eyes again, this time to get the deer piss out of them. *"Why?!"* He stumbled out blindly into the corridor, and I easily escaped his grasp. He collided with the wall in front of him with a loud, painful thump.

"Because fuck you that's why! Fuck your glitter package you fucking asshole!" I screamed at the top of my lungs. "You ruined my homecoming dress. You ruined everything. I hate you!"

Around me, I could hear voices and stomping behind the other doors in the hallway. People were waking up and would want to know what the hell was going on. Before I could be caught, I dropped the squeeze bottle and ran back to my truck. I thought getting revenge would make me feel better, but instead of energized and vindicated, all I felt was exhausted and alone.

* * *

I'D NEVER HAD a hangover before, but I couldn't imagine it felt worse than I did the next morning. Driving for almost eight hours straight made my joints ache and my head pound. I woke up at two p.m., feeling and looking like I'd had a very rough night. It took four showers to get most of the glitter out of my hair and off my skin, and two vacuum bags to remove the worst of it from my room. My dress, however, was irreparably ruined, along with my hairbrush, a lampshade, and a handful of other possessions that couldn't or shouldn't be washed. Even my hairdryer was ruined. The glitter had lodged in the motor, making it smoke.

Feeling defeated, I wrapped myself in a fuzzy afghan blanket and sat on the couch with a cup of hot chocolate while I waited for my hair to dry. There was even an episode of 'Say Yes to the Dress" on that looked promising. The sudden chime of the doorbell made me freeze. I waited, hoping whoever it was would give up and go try to convert the neighbors instead. *Ding-dong!* I gritted my teeth.

"Go away!"

Ding-dong! No way was I getting up. It wasn't Girl Scout season. *Ding-dong!* I just couldn't see the point of getting up. There was absolutely no one on the planet I wanted to see. *Ding-dong!*

"Come back with a fucking warrant!" I yelled at the door, praying that whoever it was would get the message.

Ding-dong!

"Fine! Fine! I'm coming. Don't get your panties in a twist!"

Finally irritated enough to see who it was, I wrapped the afghan around myself like a cape and shambled over to the door. The shotgun my mom kept in case of bad guys was within an arm's reach in the adjacent closet, if needed.

I peeled back the door and glared balefully at.... *Glitter dude?* Cole Rylander was standing on my doorstep.

My irritation drained out of me all at once. In my anger the night before, I'd managed to ignore his physical appearance. Now though, I couldn't deny that he was objectively, well, pretty damn perfect. Tall, with amber-colored eyes, dark glossy hair and smooth tan skin, his even, symmetrical features and athletic body *ticked all my boxes*. The fact that he was older than me, probably my brother's age, twenty, and not from my oppressive Plano high school didn't hurt either. I slammed the door in a panic.

Ding-dong! Ding-dong!

I opened the door much more sheepishly the second time around. Cole and I blinked at each other in the late afternoon sun. My heart pounded furiously.

"I brought you some flowers to apologize for the glitter," he said. His voice was a baritone rumble. I looked in wonder at the delicate bouquet of daisies he was extending. I had suddenly lost the power of speech.

"Ugh..." I managed. *Why was he here? What did he want?*

"I didn't know that Ward even had a little sister," he was explaining rapidly. "I really didn't mean to ruin your night or your dress. It was a prank meant for him, I swear. Ward told me he'd kick my ass if I didn't come down here and apologize to you, so, um, here I am."

My disbelief was complete.

"You don't know Travis?" I could barely believe it.

Cole shook his head. His amber-brown eyes shone with earnestness. "Who? No. I don't know any Travis. I was just messing with Ward. The glitter wasn't meant for you. I really am sorry."

I bit down on my somewhat still-glittery lip. The prank had been meant for Ward?

"You brought me flowers?" I warbled, completely charmed. Nobody had ever bought me flowers before. Not even on a date. Especially not someone so cute.

Cole nodded. He seemed to be searching my face for something, because he was gazing at me intently. It made it hard to keep looking at him, but at the same time, I wanted to keep looking at him forever. Maybe he wanted to see if I was still angry. I wasn't. With hesitant fingers, I reached out and took the flowers from Cole's grasp, feeling a little electric thrill when our fingers touched.

"Thank you. I like daisies." My voice was just above a whisper. I was usually chock full of words (it was sort of my weakness), but at this moment I was unable to think of any snippy comments. All I could do was stare at the apologetic, handsome man in front of me. He didn't even mention the whole deer pee thing. "They're beautiful."

He smiled at me and, just like that, I knew I was lost.

1

KATE

EIGHT YEARS LATER...

Sweetie

Honey

Gorgeous

Darlin'

Sugar

"Come on, *Baby*." The drunk guy's voice somehow managed to be condescending and whiny at the same time. "Don't be like that. I'm not making any trouble."

What is it about working in a bar that makes tipsy dudes think it's okay to refer to grown women like we're miniature poodles? Drunk *women* generally don't do that. Just the men. It's one of life's little mysteries, but it still makes my skin crawl. My job might be to pour drinks and serve them, but I don't have to flirt with my customers or otherwise pretend to have more than a professional interest in them. That's not part of the job. At least, it shouldn't be. After several years working at the Lone Star Lounge, I was fresh out of patience.

"Listen up and listen good. I'm not your baby." How many times would I have to have this conversation? The drunk man in front of me on the barstool looked dumbfounded. "You're sloppy drunk, you aren't listening to me, and I'm cutting you off."

"But I—," he tried to grab my wrist, and I kicked his barstool in response, making him jump and unsettling him enough that he blinked out of his stupor. I knew I needed to make the most of any lucidity he'd scraped together. "What's that, ma'am?" His voice had turned sheepish.

My answer was cold and direct. "My brother, Ward, who owns this bar, is having his engagement party tonight. All the customers need to move to the patio. I told you this when you sat down. Go out there and sober up. Drink this water." I pointed at the glass in front of him.

Drunk guy made his shaky way to his feet, grabbed his water, and reluctantly made his way to the patio. He was the last patron to leave the main room and, now that he was gone, I could finally, *finally* start decorating. I had a lot to do. I rubbed my hands together in anticipation. Behind the bar, our bartender, Willie, smirked at me.

"You really have a way with the drunks, Kate." Willie's sarcasm was a rare gift. I supposed I had been a bit abrasive with the guy. More than usual, anyway. I *could* have been nicer.

I sighed and ran a frustrated hand through my carefully blown-out hair. "I just don't want anybody messing up the party." I admitted. As the sister of the groom and best friend of the bride, I'd put a lot of time and energy into planning this engagement party. Even though I was sure I'd thought of everything, I couldn't shake the feeling that I'd forgotten something important. I started running through the list of tasks in my head: caterers, decorations, music, guest list...

"Your lack of patience is going to have a direct effect on your tips tonight," Willie reminded me. It was a conversation we'd had many times. I generally left the more difficult drunk-wrangling to Ward; he was better at it. Mostly because he was big and scary and male. I usually just came off as a bitch, even if I was in the right. And as the sober party in any conflict, I was pretty much always in the right.

"Patience is for those who wait." My typically short reply was even more halfhearted than usual. Keeping my temper under control was a constant battle but worrying about the party was making it especially hard.

"It'll be fine," Willie promised. I nodded vaguely, and it earned me a grin. Willie could tell that I was anxious, and I think he was enjoying it. "Relax Kate! It's just a party. You planned for everything. Everyone is going to have a great time. Even you."

TWO HOURS and some champagne later and I *was* enjoying myself. Very much so. Emma, my future sister-in-law, had just asked me to be her Maid of Honor. Visions of lace, tulle, satin, and silk charmeuse danced in my head. Emma needed to wear a slinky style. She was built for an old Hollywood dress. Something that Vivian Leigh would have worn to the Oscars. Not white. Either antique ivory or maybe even a light, champagne gold. I could already see it coming together in my mind.

Staring dreamily off into the distance as I weighed the pros and cons of a corseted style, my eyes caught on a familiar face out in the sea of strangers. Cole Rylander's face.

He was staring right at me.

In a dizzy instant, my happiness drained out of me all at once. I felt empty and lightheaded from the sudden shift.

Oh God, why didn't somebody warn me he would be here? My own mind answered back with a snide reply. *Because nobody knows about your weird, fucked-up fascination with him.* Cole was still staring at me knowingly.

"Kate?" Emma asked, following my gaze. "Are you okay?"

Well, almost nobody.

"Yeah, fine," I lied, shaking my head. I needed to get away from her and my brother before I lost it. "I'm going to go powder my nose. Be right back."

I scuttled off and splashed cold water on my face. Who the hell powders their nose? I looked at my cowardly reflection in the mirror until I couldn't stand the sight anymore. Although I was sure I'd just given my carefully concealed secret away to Ward and Emma with my bizarre reaction, at least I was able to breathe again in the dark hallway near the bathroom. I leaned against the wall, counting to ten, then twenty, and then thirty. By the time I got to one hundred and ten, I had to admit that the counting wasn't working.

"Hey there, stalker," a familiar voice called out. Cole had found me. He approached down the shadowy hallway, causing my heartbeat to race with a mixture of feelings I couldn't even try to identify. "If I didn't know better, I would think you weren't happy to see me again."

2

KATE

"DON'T FLATTER YOURSELF, COLE," I told him, adopting the aloof, superior tone of voice I used to deter the drunk creeps who hit on me at the bar. This tone was something I'd picked up in high school, mostly from kids who had used it on me. It was a lie, of course. Inside I was quivering like I was eighteen again. Cole had that unique effect on me. One look at him and I was heartbroken all over again. Our last interaction during my freshman year of college had really done a number on my self-esteem. I wasn't going to let him see how much it still stung.

"That hurts," he replied, touching his chest and looking me over from head to toe appreciatively. I looked him over right back and rolled my eyes for good measure. *What did he know about hurt?*

"What do you want?" I asked, arching an eyebrow at him and wishing I could run away. I didn't really care what he wanted, since I knew it wasn't me. He'd made that perfectly clear.

"Am I not allowed to say hello to my best friend's little sister?" His voice was dripping with feigned shock.

"Hello. And goodbye." I said sarcastically. I even added a saucy little wave.

"Well, I'm happy to see you," he said, his expression softening. The moment stretched between us, heavy and full of unspoken things.

An invisible force pulled me forward across the dark hallway toward Cole. One step, then two. He met me in the middle. He was close enough to touch now, and he lifted a hand as if to touch my face.

I was about to say something I would regret when another one of my brother's friends, Lucas, popped his head around the corner. All the air went out of the room.

"Look what the cat dragged in! Hey man, we weren't sure you were gonna' make it," Lucas cried to Cole, giving me an out. I slunk past them and back into the party.

My heart was pounding out a heavy metal rhythm in my chest. This wasn't how this night was supposed to go. This engagement party was supposed to be a nice night. I was going to dance, drink, be merry, and toast Emma and Ward. *He wasn't supposed to be here.*

Rationally, I knew that I shouldn't care what Cole Rylander thought of me anymore. It had been years since we'd seen each other or spoken. Life had pulled us in very different directions. He'd gone on to have a tremendously successful NFL career. I worked for my brother in a bar. But I still felt helpless and speechless when he was around. It wasn't fair.

The one saving grace of managing this place was that no one could stop me from rounding the bar and pouring myself a double. I went straight for the good stuff and poured like it weighed more than it cost.

"Are you okay?" Emma asked me when she found me a few minutes later. "I'm sorry I didn't warn you."

I shrugged, smiled and faked an unconcerned expression.

"Are you okay?" she repeated, looking at my now-empty double glass.

I grinned at her. "I'm completely fine." My voice, honed by years of merciless teasing and playing it off like it was nothing, sounded convincing—to me, at least.

Emma looked unconvinced. After years of friendship, she knew me too well.

"He's moving here, you know," she said after a second, perching her tiny body next to mine on a bar stool. My wide eyes told her that I hadn't known that fact. "Did you know he was retired?" she asked.

I nodded. "Concussions."

Despite his phenomenal success, Cole had decided not to risk additional head injuries in the NFL. I couldn't say that I blamed him. Four concussions in two years wasn't safe at all. That was something I was grateful for with my brother; Ward hadn't been permanently disabled during his career playing pro, despite his best efforts to wreck his entire body.

"When is he moving here?" I asked, hoping my voice didn't betray anything that was going on beneath.

Emma shrugged. "I think this week. You'd need to ask Ward."

That would happen ten minutes after never. If there was one thing I could say with confidence, it was that Ward had no idea how bad I used to have it for his friend. He was oblivious even at the best of times. I probably could have hired a skywriter to announce my crush on Cole and Ward still wouldn't have noticed. Ward was a great guy in many ways but being emotionally sensitive and perceptive wasn't one of them.

"Did my brother tell you anything about why he's moving here?" I asked, looking down at my hands as if suddenly very interested in my acid green manicure.

When she responded, Emma's voice was dry. "I honestly have no idea."

Emma had lived with me the year after my great rejection freshman year. She probably knew perfectly well that I was brimming with questions, but she couldn't help. She hugged me before returning to the party, whispering "just go talk to him" in my ear before traipsing off.

She made it sound so damn easy. *Just go talk to him.* There was no one else at this party, including all the people I didn't know, that I would have a problem going up and talking to. I could strike up a conversation with a brick wall, but not Cole. Even now, I could feel his eyes on me from across the room. Every time I glanced in his direction he was staring right at me.

"Hi Kate, would you like to dance?" The question came from my left. I swung around to see a friend of Ward's had sidled up next to me.

The guy was about my age. He was of average height, with an average build and average looks. He was wearing a Hawaiian shirt and khakis, which were dreadful, but totally in line with his inoffensive looks. I grasped for the guy's name while I considered his offer. Vincent? Victor? Something like that. I'd had a few casual conversations with the guy in the bar. He didn't exactly make my heart flutter, but he was okay.

Would I like to dance with Victor/Vincent? Not really. But it was a better idea than just sitting around and sulking for the rest of the engagement party. Maybe he'd get my mind off Cole.

"Sure! I'd love to." I said brightly, putting on my happy face and pretending like I'd been waiting for him all evening. His answering smile was enough to make his overbite more obvious, and I felt a bit guilty for leading him on.

But when I looked over my shoulder and saw that Cole's expression had gone blanker-than-blank, all thoughts of guilt disappeared.

Just because you don't want me doesn't mean that no one else will, I thought at Cole as I moved against my dance partner with more eagerness than I really felt. After two songs, we took a break. The guy, whose name was Vince, went to go grab us some water. As soon as he was out of earshot, Cole was at my elbow.

"You can't be serious about that guy," he said by way of a greeting. I looked up at him and frowned.

"I'm sorry?" I asked.

"I know what you're doing," he replied.

"I have no idea what you're talking about."

"Leading that poor guy on for my benefit is just cruel." He shook his head in poor Vince's general direction.

"Well, you would know." Before I could censor myself, the words were out of my mouth and delivered with a lot more anger than I intended. I felt a hot blush cover my cheeks. Cole's eyebrows climbed high up his forehead and his lips parted, but I turned on my heel before he could reply. I disappeared back into the crowd and away from Cole.

I managed to avoid him for almost a full hour afterwards. I'd almost put in as much face time as I thought was necessary to be polite when Ward waved me over to where he and Cole were sitting in a corner. My oblivious brother didn't notice how uncomfortable I must have looked coming over to them, but Cole certainly did. His wide, amber eyes seemed like they were full of secrets.

"What's up?" I asked my brother, pulling up a stool and affecting some semblance of a casual tone.

"I've just popped the question to Cole here," Ward said.

His voice was proud, and the double entendre flew right over his head.

"I've always thought you two made a lovely couple," I replied. My sarcasm level was one hundred.

Ward was smiling his most mischievous smile. "Funny, I was about to say the same thing. Y'all will be walking down the aisle together and all."

My face went blank before I realized what Ward was trying to tell me.

"Cole's gonna be your best man?" I managed.

What did you think he was talking about, Kate? I cringed internally.

"Okay. Why are you telling me this?" I asked Ward, trying to ignore Cole. He was still staring at me. I didn't know what that look meant, but it made me feel like I was sitting there stark naked.

"Because you two will have to work together," Ward replied. "Emma wants a really small wedding party. It's just you two doing all the usual stuff."

Usual stuff? My brother was in for a really rude awakening when the real wedding planning got started. He was going to have to pay attention to things like *flower selections* and *china patterns*. I couldn't wait to see Ward getting all domestic.

The fact that Cole and I were the entire wedding party was a surprise, but it shouldn't have been. Emma was very much a small, intimate wedding type of girl. Actually, I was a bit surprised—but delighted—that I was going to be her

Maid of Honor.

"Huh," I said, because I eventually had to say something. He was right, of course. We would need to coordinate to make sure the bridal shower and bachelorette party didn't conflict with the bachelor party, make sure the travel and accommodations for the guests went smoothly, work on the formal wear for the bridal party, etc., etc. I was already composing a list in my head. And all of this would involve talking to Cole and being close to him. My rebellious, masochistic imagination explored the possibilities...

"Kate? Earth to Kate?" Ward reached out and poked my shoulder.

"What?" I blinked at Cole and Ward, both of whom were now wearing confused expressions. I got the distinct impression my brother had been trying to get my attention for a while.

"What do you mean 'what'? You totally zoned out!" He was looking at me like I was crazy.

I smirked apologetically. "I was just planning out the zoot suits you two are gonna' wear."

"I think we're supposed to wear tuxedos to the wedding," Ward said innocently. Of course, he had no idea what a zoot suit was. I rolled my eyes. Ward never understood my fashion jokes.

"So, can I have your number?" Cole asked, quickly following it up with a glance at Ward and a polite, "so we can coordinate wedding stuff?"

Considering that he asked in front of Ward, and had a

perfectly reasonable reason for asking, I couldn't very well refuse. I was trapped. I frowned and ponied up the digits. The seconds ticked by afterward, excruciating and slow.

My rescue came from Vince. Tonight, he was my knight in shining khaki. He appeared over my shoulder with the glass of water I'd requested more than an hour ago. The poor man had clearly been looking for me all that time.

"There you are," he said breathlessly.

I smiled at him sweetly and drew him by the elbow away from Ward and Cole's table. "Hi, Vince. Thanks for the drink. Where've you been? I thought you lost interest."

Vince blushed. "I thought you lost interest." He looked at his feet, and then up at me in a puppy-dog-eyes way that was probably meant to be endearing, but just struck me as weirdly submissive and sad.

I felt more than a little bit evil, but knowing that Cole was watching me flirt with Vince was an undeniable thrill. I knew jealousy when I saw it, even if it was probably just motivated by disappointment that I wasn't throwing myself after him anymore. When Beyonce's 'Single Ladies' started playing, I knew it was fate. Heading towards the dance floor, I took off the cozy sweater I'd been wearing to reveal my black crop top and pierced navel. Vince looked at me appreciatively, and a glance back at Cole showed he was still equally riveted. If I was going to have to spend time around Cole, at least I could do it in style.

3

COLE

MY UNCLE JIMMY, who was one fry short of a happy meal even when he was stone cold sober, had taught me an expression back when I was a kid. Jimmy said a girl's shirt ought to look like 'two puppies fighting under a silk sheet' when she was dancing. It didn't sound hot at all when I was eight, but it turns out that Jimmy knew exactly what he was talking about. You can take the boy out of rural Arkansas, but you can't take the rural Arkansas out of the boy. Watching Kate dance was torture.

She moved around the dance floor like she owned it. She was as confident and sexy as she'd ever been and seemed to have gotten even more outspoken than I remembered. The guy she had in tow stared at her like he'd just hit the jackpot, and practically every other guy looked at him like he'd just stolen it out from under them. Especially me.

"Be careful," Lucas said to me. "If you aren't, your face is gonna' get stuck like that."

I looked over at him and frowned. Did I look as jealous as I felt? Probably.

Lucas laughed at me. "Are you doing okay?" He raised his eyebrows and glanced back at Kate. "Because ogling Ward's baby sister is asking for trouble, and the whole reason you retired was to avoid head injuries, not invite them, right?"

Lucas was a know-it-all pain in the ass, but he was also my friend. I bit back a snide reply. It wasn't like I could really deny I'd been staring.

"It's not my fault I have eyes," I protested. "Don't pretend you don't see her. I'm only human."

Lucas shrugged his shoulders. "Kate? She never has been my type."

I'd known a few women who had been Lucas' type and they weren't for me. He liked a mysterious, exotic, evil genius sort of woman. His type was somewhere between Pepper Potts and Black Widow (*always redheads, too*). He'd once said that Cake's "Short Skirt, Long Jacket" was written about his true love. What a weirdo. His last girlfriend had been a total nightmare psycho. Thank God they hadn't lasted, although Lucas was still getting over her.

"You have bad taste," I told Lucas. He didn't deny it. He just stared at his beer.

Lucas liked redheads while I preferred a more red-blooded type of woman. The girl next door, but sexier. I liked a woman who didn't mind things a bit wild, and Kate was all that and more. She'd added a few tattoos and piercings to her collection since the last time I'd seen her. She hadn't had those when we first met or even the last time I'd laid eyes on her. I wanted to know all about them, but didn't dare ask Ward or, God forbid, Kate herself.

"At least I don't have a death wish," Lucas added. I pretended he was talking about my football career.

"Didn't you hear? I'm retired."

Lucas laughed. "Retired from sex? Dude, you aren't even thirty yet. By the way, they make pills for that these days."

"Fuck you." I said it without emphasis, and it was received with the intended disinterest.

Lucas made a dismissive gesture. "No thanks. *You've* never been my type, either," he quipped.

"We've already established that you have bad taste." I made a kissy face at him and he flicked me off.

While Lucas and I watched, Ward's future bride, a tiny little pixie of a girl that looked like she weighed ninety pounds soaking wet, cornered Kate. The two took one of those girl selfies in the middle of the dance floor. Next to Emma, Kate looked leggy and tall, but next to me and Ward, she looked positively petite. Why someone Ward's size would go for somebody he could throw for twenty yards was a mystery for another day. A different mystery was more pressing.

"I still can't believe Ward's getting married," Lucas remarked, reading my mind. It was pretty bizarre.

"For real. After he and Jessie broke up, I didn't think Ward would ever get serious again, let alone married." I shook my head.

Ward had recovered from his broken engagement, but it had taken *years*.

"You're the only one of us three that hasn't ever really dated somebody for long," Lucas added as if the thought was occurring to him for the first time. I supposed it could even be true. My carefully designed appearance of being a happy bachelor was generally excellent.

"I'm just waiting for the right girl to come around," I answered, still staring at Kate out of the corner of my eye. I'm not sure what possessed me to come back here to Austin. I could have gone anywhere. I could have gone home to Arkansas. But instead I came here. I told myself it was because my best friends, Ward and Lucas, were here. The inconvenient truth was still dancing away with some jerk wearing business-casual.

She glanced at me over her shoulder then, tossing her long, glossy hair back and flashing her blue eyes in... what? Challenge? Loathing? I probably deserved it. She looked away again before I could decipher her expression and tipped her head back to laugh. The long, slim column of her neck had a blue butterfly tattooed on it, just behind her ear. Like something rare and beautiful, just like that blue butterfly, Kate was always just within my reach while still being totally beyond my grasp.

"Hmm," Lucas remarked, watching our little staring contest with amusement. I'm not sure if he was perceptive or I was letting my image slip, but I wasn't fooling him. "Whatever you say, man. This ought to be entertaining, though. I'm gonna' go grab another beer."

He wandered off in the direction of the bar with a knowing look in his eyes.

I knew it was going to be an uphill battle. But being in the same city with Kate meant the chance to spend time with her. And I had a lot of lost time to make up for.

4

COLE

"COLE—COLE—MR. RYLANDER!" The voice that was calling me was dripping with the loud, smiling, fake-nice enthusiasm that I'd come to associate with reporters. I smiled a tight-lipped, equally false smile at the man who owned the voice. Another pearl of wisdom from my uncle Jimmy drifted through my memory as I took in the man's shiny shoes, staid button-down, and tape recorder: don't ever let your battleship mouth overtake your rowboat ass.

"Yes?" I asked, preemptively committing to one-word answers. I *hated* talking to reporters. No good would come of it. The reporter dropped down into Lucas' recently vacated seat with a gleam in his eye. He smiled at me like a predator looks at its next meal.

"I'm Edward Nassar from the Texas Advocate," he announced like I ought to care. "I thought I might find you here. Heard you were in town. Would you like to give a statement on your recent retirement and plans for the future?"

I looked at him like he'd just grown a second head. Was I really famous enough to stalk to a party? That was news to me. "Nope."

"How about—" Edward began, and then turned a sickly white. His eyes were fixed behind me, and I turned to see Ward approaching from the bar with Lucas. Lucas and I exchanged a smile, and I sat back in my seat to enjoy the show. Nobody hated reporters like Ward. I'd retired from the NFL at the peak of my career, and it had been one hundred percent my idea (well, in actuality, eighty percent my doctor's idea, but whatever). Ward had a much less pleasant exit from the League. As in, he had a career-ending compound knee injury and then his mean, gold-digging fiancée split. Imagine having to answer thousands of questions about that mess, and it's easy to understand his dislike of the press.

"Dammit, Eddie!" Ward snapped, menacing the much smaller man by his tone and size alone. He was still a good six feet away. "How many times have I told you not to come into this bar?"

"I just came in to use the bathroom," Edward—Eddie—squeaked. His voice had climbed a good half octave in fear.

"*Bullshit.*" Ward wasn't buying it.

"And—and then I realized that bathrooms were just for customers, so I bought a beer..." He trailed off when Ward got within striking distance.

"This is a private party. Leave now or I call the police. Then, once you're arrested for trespassing, *I'm calling Nancy*," Ward continued.

Whoever this Nancy was, and I was guessing either his boss or his girlfriend, she put the fear of God into Eddie. The mere mention of her name turned him from white to nearly green. His eyes went huge and round in terror.

"I'm going!" he stammered, rising and making a beeline for the door. I did notice that he left his card sitting on the table. I flicked it toward Ward when he and Lucas sat down. Ward set his beer down on top of it with a decisive clunk.

"Fucking press," Ward said unnecessarily. "Did he bother you?"

I smirked, entertained. "Not nearly as much as he clearly bothers you."

"We've had words in the past." Ward's expression was dark.

'Having words with someone' was Texas for 'I've come close to punching him before but haven't... yet.' Ward didn't let his upbringing in the peaceful suburbs of sprawling Dallas prevent him from using the more colorful southernisms. I liked that about him, even if he was pretty much a city boy.

"At least you got to threaten him with *Nancy*," Lucas added. He shook his head. "She scares me, and I've only witnessed her from afar."

Unlike Ward, Lucas was a true city boy. He grew up in

LA and converted to the southern lifestyle in college. I tried not to hold it against him too badly.

"Okay, I'll bite," I said. "Who's Nancy?"

Ward smirked. "Nancy is the editor in chief of the Texas Advocate. Eddie's boss. *She also happens to be Willie's battle-axe of an ex-wife.*"

"*Willie* had a *wife*?" I asked. Lucas and Ward nodded solemnly. I tried to wrap my brain around it.

I knew Willie from our college days, back when Ward, Lucas, and I were patrons at this very bar. Back before Ward bought it from him. However, I had no idea Willie had an ex-wife. Or a life outside of the bar. I sort of imagined he folded himself up into the broom closet at the end of his shift.

"Willie has a son that lives in Lubbock too. He's even got a grandkid or two as well. Nancy's second husband recently passed away, actually," Ward said conspiratorially. "Willie's been making noise about asking her out again."

That was the best gossip I'd heard all week. My expression must have been as mystified as I felt, because it made Lucas and Ward laugh. I looked around for Willie, but he was nowhere to be found. I'd seen him earlier, but maybe he'd gone home. *Or maybe, he'd gone to meet Nancy.* It was a Friday night.

Willie might be damn near eighty, so if he could go after a second chance, what excuse did I have not to try with Kate?

Ward cracked his knuckles dangerously. "I'd better not

see Eddie back around here again," he growled. "Next time it won't be words."

Oh, right. Her protective, six-foot-four, two-hundred-and-thirty-pound hulking beast of a brother. My best friend.

5

KATE

AFTER THE ENGAGEMENT PARTY, I went on a full-fledged Cole Rylander Googling spree. It was a complete and total relapse to my teenage years. I hadn't fallen so deeply down the Cole-fangirl rabbit hole in years. It wasn't my finest moment by a long shot.

When I emerged from my creepy-stalker psychosis, it was *Sunday morning.* I hadn't slept, hadn't eaten, hadn't done anything really for almost twenty-four hours. I had, however, learned a great deal about what Cole had been up to since I was eighteen.

I knew the general story already. He'd graduated right along with Ward and had been the only other UT player in his year to be drafted into the NFL (not bad considering only 2 percent of college players go on to play pro). He played for a few years, first in Oregon and then in Wisconsin. Then he took a few too many knocks to the head and decided to make a good choice and retire early.

What I didn't know, and what I didn't want to know but still somehow desperately *needed to know*, was who he'd been with when he wasn't with me. My answer could only be determined through careful sleuthing. I started by looking at how many girls he'd been photographed with over the years. There were a lot. Hundreds of them.

I spent hours scouring the photos for repeats. Girls who cornered him for selfies didn't bother me much. What I wanted to see were his *girlfriends*. I carefully pieced together Cole's relationship history through pictures. I was looking for Cole taking the same date to lots of parties in a row or being spotted at dinner over a series of months. Tabloid or society stories helped me to figure things out too. Surprisingly, there were only two real relationships that I could trace.

The first, Delaney Melrose, was a model. And not just any regular catalog model, either. She was a Victoria's Secret Angel. She was drop-dead gorgeous, of course. Tall, toned, and tan, Delaney's face looked like something that had been designed for maximum sex appeal by a super-intelligent AI. I traced their six-month relationship through photos until she suddenly disappeared.

Then, about two years later, Mattie Diaz appeared. The popstar-turned-actress was known mostly for her wild period after a successful Disney channel career, but her time with Cole was during her 'reformation period.' She'd already successfully kicked her embarrassing substance abuse problem before they were together, and they made a pretty couple, although it hurt to admit it. Her petite, delicate, olive-skinned beauty was a surprisingly lovely complement to his tall strength. But like Delaney before her, Mattie only lasted a few months on Cole's arm and then disappeared. It didn't *look* like he maintained any kind of lasting contact with his ex-girlfriends.

Did he love them? Staring at the pictures didn't tell me. In the pictures they seemed affectionate enough, but they also looked posed. Even in the ones that were more personal they looked oddly stilted. Perhaps Cole just didn't like having his picture taken very much. All I could do was wonder.

But all good fugue states come to an end, and eventually I needed to turn off the computer and return to the real world. The real world had been impatiently waiting. I had four missed texts from Vince, two missed calls from Rae, and an invitation to brunch from Emma.

It took every iota of my energy not to call Lucas and try to enlist his tech-genius help to wage an *enhanced cyber-stalking* campaign on Cole. Too risky. I also had more pride than curiosity, but only by a small margin. Instead of humiliating myself, I focused on pulling myself together to meet Emma.

She wanted to meet at a particularly trendy boutique

hotel that had a particularly trendy all-brunch restaurant. Unlike Ward or me, she hadn't yet come to terms with the fact that the vast majority of the food and drink for the rest of her life would come from the Lone Star Lounge. She'd figure that out eventually.

I had to hand it to Emma when I pulled up though, the trendy boutique hotel was super cute. Located on the hip shopping and dining thoroughfare of South Congress Avenue, all you had to do was look north to see the sprawling state capital. On either side of the street, hip vintage shops mingled with fancy coffee joints mingled with art galleries. It was a hipster paradise.

And I'd dressed for the occasion. I was wearing one of my favorite vintage outfits, a two-piece tweed skirt suit from the sixties that looked *just like Chanel*. It might even be Chanel, but someone had cut the tags out, which was the only reason I could afford it. In order to keep from looking like I was wearing a Mad Men Halloween costume, I paired the cream suit with an edgy black bustier, messy modern hair, punky combat boots, and dramatic dark eye makeup. I may have been sleep deprived, but at least I looked fantastic. Some people might say that my look was a bit much for brunch, but some people are stupid and wrong.

"Oh my God! I love your outfit!" The hostess squealed immediately when I arrived at the restaurant, instantly restoring my faith in humanity. She was wearing a very adorable 90's floral dress a la Winona Ryder in 'What's Eating Gilbert Grape.' She even had the whole heroine-chic-waif look going on, complete with the pixie cut and black cherry lipstick. We chatted happily about vintage clothes as she led me back to where Emma was waiting. For whatever reason, Emma had requested a table way at the back of the restaurant, next to the hotel elevators, so it was quite a walk. All the better, since I wanted to ask about the hostess' gorgeous tattoos.

"You really can make friends with anyone in two seconds," Emma said in wonder when I settled in after exchanging numbers with Diane-the-hostess.

I shrugged. "She likes clothes too."

Emma sighed. "*All women like clothes.* Not all women can just strike up a conversation like it's no big deal." Her voice was wistful.

I'd realized a long time ago that Emma was extraordinarily shy. I didn't think of myself as an extrovert, but she definitely did. Little did she know, I'd overdeveloped my people skills to try and make friends at my snobby-ass high school, and had still been the weird, friendless loner until college.

"What can I say, it's my superpower," I answered with a sly grin, then adding, "and also my tragic flaw. I honestly can't avoid talking about whatever pops into my head. I've just got a big mouth. At least you've got a smart one."

She didn't contest the point, but she did grin. "Okay," she said after a short pause where we ordered mimosas, "if you're so honest, tell me how you're feeling about the whole Cole-is-moving-to-Austin thing."

I took a deep breath, put both my hands flat on the table, and looked her square in the eye. "I don't know."

"Did you Google stalk him yet?" she asked, raising a delicate golden eyebrow at me that said she already knew. I nodded in shame. When I didn't elaborate, she let almost a minute elapse in silence before she followed up. "Well, did you at least find out anything good?"

That was a much better question.

"Not really. He had a good career in the NFL. His ranking as a wide receiver was extremely respectable but didn't win any rings for his teams. He can jump like six feet straight up in the air like a cat..." I trailed off and Emma stared at me until I continued. "He also dated a couple of super-hot girls. He's clearly single now." I chose those words carefully and tried to keep my voice neutral.

"And?" Emma pushed.

"And it's driving me fucking nuts!" My attempt at not sounding like a crazy person had already failed. My mimosa had appeared on the table, and I chugged it in one go. "Why did he have to move back here? I was doing fine, and now it's like I'm right back to where I was when you met me: a pathetic, moping mess."

Emma rolled her eyes, scooped up her flute with her tiny fingers and took a delicate *sip* of her own drink. She made me look like Godzilla, and that was only when I compared our manners. "You weren't a pathetic moping mess when I met you," she said. Her voice was gentle.

"I wasn't exactly functioning normally either."

"It's not a crime to be heartbroken." Heartbroken was putting it mildly. I almost flunked out of college.

"*He never even liked me.*" Even now, it hurt to say it out loud.

A little line formed between Emma's green eyes when she frowned at me. "Listen up, *sister*. You don't know that," she said. "You especially don't know that's still true. I know I wasn't there during our freshman year, but I saw the way you two were giving each other fuck-me eyes all during the party."

My jaw dropped open. "Oh my God, we are going to be *sisters,* aren't we?" Somehow, I hadn't connected those dots. I'd always wanted a sister, although knowing my dad, I probably had a few half siblings off somewhere. But before I could fully digest the prospect of having a real sister, Emma's other statement sunk in. "And I wasn't making fuck-me eyes at Cole."

"*Oh, you so were,*" Emma corrected. "If looks could fuck, you'd be pregnant right now."

"No. I'm on the pill." It wasn't the best comeback by any means, but it was all I had.

Emma rolled her eyes at me once again, but then, instead of returning to my face, they stayed fixed in the distance.

"Cole!" she yelled.

I was now deeply confused. "Huh?"

"Cole!" Emma repeated, using a tone and volume that was totally inappropriate for a brunch conversation. My head whipped around behind me, looking back toward the hotel elevators to see who was now walking toward us: Cole Rylander.

Sweet little Emma, my beloved future sister and dear friend, had just set me up.

6

KATE

"GOOD MORNING, ladies. Fancy meeting you two here," Cole said suspiciously as he came up to our table. He was dressed casually, just a pair of what were obviously Levi's 501 jeans, a plain black T-shirt, and what looked like a green waxed canvas jacket (maybe Filson?). He looked like he ought to be on a billboard. Just the right amount of rugged, but still classy. I even liked the checkered Converse Chucks he was wearing, but only because it was him.

"Yes, what a nice surprise," Emma said unconvincingly. I wished I could melt into my chair and disappear. My face must have been glowing beet red, because it felt tingly and hot. "Join us?" Emma was saying, "We were just about to order brunch."

Cole looked from Emma to me several times in quick succession. "Sure." He sunk down next to us on the other side of the four-top table. "Did Ward tell you I was staying here?" he asked Emma.

Cole's reactions proved that he hadn't been in on Emma's plan to play matchmaker. I couldn't imagine that Ward would have been either. Emma blinked at Ward in faux confusion.

"What? Oh, no, Ward didn't mention it." She looked like she was trying very hard not to laugh.

Once my initial shock and confusion had worn off, I realized that this was totally in line with Emma's general MO. She may seem shy, but she was clever and generally got what she wanted. Emma wasn't too good for a little old-fashioned deception if she thought it would do the trick.

The waiter came around just then and took orders for Cole and me. When he asked Emma what she'd like, she threw a wrist up to her forehead dramatically. Seriously, it was like Scarlett O'Hara faking a fainting spell.

"You know," she said in a strangely high voice, "I'm feeling a bit dizzy all of a sudden. I think I'll head home. You two have fun without me." Then she winked. *Emma actually winked.* I hadn't realized she even could.

Cole and I were probably giving her identical disbelieving stares. This was the worst acting of all time, and she was barely even trying. Emma seemed not to notice or, at least, not to care that no one was believing her act. She slid a few bills across the table to pay for her drinks, gathered her coat and purse, and sauntered off. She didn't walk like she was ill. Instead, I detected a certain *triumph* to her steps.

Cole and I were left looking at each other in stunned silence.

"Ward said she was the quiet, careful, studious type," Cole remarked after Emma was gone. He shook his head. "He actually told me to rein it in around her. He was afraid I'd scare her off."

"Well, Emma is actually all of those things, but she's also got Ward wrapped firmly around her tiny little finger." I smirked. "And she's not nearly the retiring little flower she pretends to be, although sometimes even I forget that."

Cole grinned. "I can't believe he ended up with someone like Emma."

I bristled. "What's wrong with Emma? She's my friend, you know."

His expression turned apologetic. "Nothing's wrong with her! She's just Ward's total opposite. That's all I meant."

"I guess that's true," I admitted, relaxing. "But they work."

Cole nodded. Silence descended once again.

"That's a great outfit," he said eventually. "You look like Parker Posey in 'House of Yes.'"

The idea that I looked like a deranged, murderous psychopath who was obsessed with Jackie-O might have been insulting to some women, but that was pretty much exactly what I was going for. I also *loved* that movie. "I'm going to take that as a compliment."

He flashed his white smile at me for a second and my heart skipped a beat. "It is a compliment."

Then, more awkward silence, followed by more uneasy, excruciating staring. I wracked my brain for words to say but couldn't find two to rub together. Was this how Emma felt all the time? No. My pounding pulse proved that this was more than regular shyness. The waiter brought our food, read the mood at the table, and took off as soon as he could. We ate our first few bites without making eye contact.

Eventually it all became too much. I dropped my fork as a hysterical giggle escaped me, and Cole raised an eyebrow.

"What?" he asked, touching his face and looking down at his shirt to make sure he hadn't spilled food on himself. "What did I do?"

Seeing Cole looking self-conscious, even in such a small way, only made me giggle more. "Nothing," I replied, shaking my head and basking for the briefest moment in his relief. "This is just way too awkward. So much for Emma setting us up, huh?"

He smirked at me. "I've been on worse dates."

Were we on a date? Before I could let myself think too deeply about that, I replied. "Worse than our first date?" Even after six years, I still winced when I thought about it.

Cole looked guilty for a moment, but then his small smile returned. "Unfortunately, yes. Much worse."

"Tell me about one."

Cole's smirk turned into a full-blown smile. "One of my other bad dates?"

"Yeah."

"Only if you reciprocate."

I thought about it for a second and shrugged. "Sure." I certainly had plenty of lousy dates to choose from.

"Okay," Cole began, "so one time my publicist set me up with—"

I interrupted with an unladylike noise of disbelief. "Excuse me? Your *publicist*?"

He at least had the good manners to look vaguely embarrassed. "Yeah, it was actually Ward's idea to get a publicist, and it's becoming more common."

"Why?" Knowing how much Ward disliked press in general, it was hard to believe.

"He said it was good protection, and he was right. A good publicist goes a long way to keeping your public image and your private life separate, for one. And they can help you build your brand, find opportunities for endorsements, that kind of thing." He looked a bit sheepish about the whole thing, but it honestly did make sense. I decided not to give him any shit about it.

"I guess that makes sense. Sorry, I got us off track. So, your publicist set you up?"

"Yes. She set me up on a date with a girl whose job was,

and I quote, '*Instagram influencer, cultural anthropologist and tastemaker.*'" He shook his head in what looked like disbelief.

That wasn't ringing any bells from my cyberstalking binge. "What exactly does an Instagram-blah-blah-blah do?"

He shrugged. "Your guess is as good as mine. We never got that far. Apparently, she'd seen me online, liked the look of me, and had her people reach out to my people. I looked at her pictures online and said okay. Normal enough so far, right?"

What a bizarre world he lived in. That was not normal at all, but he seemed to have forgotten that. Just once in my life, I would like to tell someone 'have your people call my people' and mean it. What a delightfully powerful feeling that must be.

"Then what happened?" I asked.

"I still don't know. Despite having hundreds of thousands of followers, she was totally and completely phony."

"What do you mean?" I was imagining a girl so conceited she couldn't raise her face up from her screen long enough to hold a conversation.

"I mean she was literally not a real person. She was a computer program. Specifically, she was an experiment that some grad student programmed and then forgot about."

I blinked at him. "I'm honestly not following you."

"Her photos were composites of other people. And the

locations were taken from other accounts. She'd been made so that her program looked around on the internet and learned what people liked from other Instagram personalities who were popular. Then she would paste her image into their photos and repost them."

"How does a bot account fool a professional publicist enough to ask someone out?"

"She isn't a bot," Cole corrected. He seemed to have a begrudging respect for this...creature. "She's incredibly sophisticated. She's not an artificial intelligence exactly, but she had been programmed for maximum exposure. One of the things she could do was find other Instagrammable public figures and request to... collaborate with them. She had a whole social media presence that coordinated to look real, a backstory, friends, everything. She sent believable emails and texts. It wasn't until she didn't show up at the restaurant that I started to get suspicious."

"So basically, you dated Skynet." That was pretty bad. He was successfully catfished by a trolling robot.

"Sort of. Yeah." He sighed.

"Are you sure it wasn't a prank Lucas was playing on you?" It sounded a little bit like something he might do.

Cole laughed. "Lucas doesn't have the skills to pull that off. It was some serious international espionage-level fakery. The FBI was interested in her; she was that good. They called a few months later and asked me a few questions about the whole thing. Lucas is smart, but I don't think he's that smart."

"It does seem like a lot of effort just to embarrass you." Lucas was also generally committed to using his powers for good—or, if not good, money. This wasn't really his style.

In truth, thinking about Cole being fooled in this way made me feel even guiltier for my cyberstalking. I was really no better than Ms. Skynet, only I hadn't been programmed to deceive him. I just looked. Still, I consciously and knowingly chose to invade his privacy. I had free will.

"Your turn," Cole said, looking at me expectantly.

I smiled my sweetest smile. "One time I punched a guy in the throat and got arrested for felony assault."

"Jesus Christ!" Cole's eyes were wide.

"He was asking for it," I told him. To this day, I was utterly remorseless about the whole thing. "I was on a *first date* and he tried to put his hand up my skirt within five minutes of sitting down to dinner. It was horrifying. I think he was on drugs or something. We were in full public view."

Cole looked properly outraged on my behalf. "Sounds like a good throat-punching was exactly what he deserved."

"Oh, that's not the half of it. So, like any rational person, I told his ass off and stormed out of the restaurant to wait for my friend to pick me up. He followed me outside and started calling me names, and then, when he grabbed my elbow, I punched him again. The problem was, his buddy, who just *happened* to be an off-duty cop, was walking by *at that exact moment.*" Only I could have such rotten luck.

"I assume the charges were dropped immediately?"

"He didn't even get done handcuffing me. One of the waitresses from the restaurant—this grizzled, lunch lady type—came outside and screamed at him. It was like something out of a movie." That moment cemented my commitment to grow up to be like that grizzled lunch lady. She knew what was what. No one else was saying anything, and we'd made a huge, loud scene inside. But only that one lady stood up for me. She was a total badass and had singlehandedly restored my belief in human decency that day.

I was grinning at the memory of my savior. Cole looked a little disturbed. "That's awful on many levels. I'm so sorry."

I shrugged.

"No really," Cole said. His tone was insistent. "I remember hearing something once. I don't remember where it came from, but it was something like this: the thing a man fears the most about a blind date is that the woman will be ugly, while the thing a woman fears most about a blind date is that she'll be murdered."

"Jeez, that's bleak," I replied. "Accurate, but bleak. Usually it's not that bad for me, thankfully. I've only had to throat punch that one guy. And let me tell you, that asshole went down like a rock, and then stayed down."

"I'll keep that in mind," Cole said. His smile was oddly approving. "You don't need Ward sticking up for you, do you?"

I rolled my eyes. "Please. I can do my own throat-punching, thank you very much." Then I paused. "Don't tell Ward about any of that, okay?"

Cole blinked. "He doesn't know you got assaulted and almost arrested?"

I shook my head. "No. I was still in Plano—that was right after I graduated and before I moved here. Ward was in Austin and it would only make him upset if he knew."

My brother labored under the misconception that I needed him around all the time, and just knowing about this incident would only reinforce it. In reality, he was the one that needed constant supervision. Between me and Emma, it was still a fulltime job to keep Ward from playing in traffic.

Cole blanched at the request, but then nodded after a moment. "Okay."

"I should have told you a milder story, sorry. I'm not trying to make you keep secrets from Ward." I bit my lip.

"No, it's okay," he replied. "Really. There are plenty of things Ward doesn't necessarily need to know about." My heart did the little fluttery thing again, and I dropped my gaze. When I looked up again, there was a look in his eyes, a heat, that hadn't been there a second before. I'd almost convinced myself that I had imagined it, until he added, "Do you want to go for a walk with me after this? It's a pretty day and I'd rather not enjoy it alone."

7

KATE

FOR MAYBE SIX weeks of winter, the weather in Austin is cold enough to demand a coat, and during about ten weeks of summer, it's too hot to want to do anything outside. The rest of the year, however, it's beautiful and sunny almost every day. But Cole was right, today was especially lovely. I stole excited little glances at his handsome profile as we walked down Congress Avenue. Perhaps it was just the company.

I'd be happy to walk through falling snow, an earthquake, or even a meteor shower as long as Cole was by my side. I wasn't going to admit it to him or to Emma, but I had it bad. This was almost worse than when I was a teenager, because now it really seemed like he wanted me back. I kept waiting for the other shoe to drop.

The second the thought crossed my mind, Cole asked, "Want some new shoes?" making me momentarily concerned that he *actually* could *read my thoughts*. Instead, Cole was just pointing jokingly in the direction of a trendy shop that had an impressively hideous selection of bowling shoes in the window. It was only an artistic display and not what they actually sold inside. I'd been in there before, and they actually had some great stuff. I looked down at his shoes, which were honestly not much better than the bowling shoes in the window.

"Will you throw away those hideous Converse sneakers if I can find something you like better?" I asked. I meant it teasingly, but there was some hopefulness mixed in.

Cole looked down at his shoes as if surprised to find them attached to his person. "My shoes? Chucks? Are they ugly?" My face must have told him the answer, because he nodded with more enthusiasm than I expected. "Okay," he said. "You don't like my clothes? Dress me up." He held his arms wide. "Fashion is your thing, right? Give me a Kate Williams makeover."

"Oh. My. God. Really?!" I couldn't believe this was happening. This was officially the best day ever.

Cole flashed his smile at me again. "Really." He took in my excitement with an expression that looked only the slightest bit afraid, but *he'd asked me*. It would be bad form to back out now. I quivered with excitement when he grabbed me by the hand to lead me into the store. I tried not to look crazy or squeal with glee. In reality, there are few things I like more than playing dress-up, and now I was going to get to play dress-up with Cole?

And he was holding my hand? I felt like I'd died and gone to heaven.

"Don't be scared," I told him as we walked the aisles. "I won't put you in a dress or anything."

"I'm not scared."

"You look a little bit scared," I teased.

"A little bit," he admitted. "To be honest, I was holding an ace when I made that suggestion though. I don't think you're going to find a single thing in this store that will fit me besides shoes, ties, and cufflinks." Cole's smile was smug and confident, like always. He flicked through a rack of flannel shirts. "This stuff looks like it was made for elves. I usually have to get extra extra length on everything. One of the many, many reasons I don't like shopping."

Ward had stopped letting me buy clothes for him long ago, well before puberty, and none of the men I knew were exactly lining up for me to style them, nor were they as tall as Cole. I turned him around and held one of the shirts to his back for reference. He complied with my manhandling like a pro, letting me manipulate his arms this way and that as if he was a gigantic doll. I frowned. He was right. There was no chance.

"Aww, this is no fun," I griped, putting the shirt back down. "You're going to be as hard to find clothes for as me."

That got me a raised eyebrow. "You?"

I blinked at him. "Well, yeah. I mean, look at me. I'm a giant." I'd come to terms with my unusual height long ago, and some men did genuinely like it, but most of the time it sucked. Most of the time I didn't mind standing out, but sometimes I felt like Big Bird in a world full of swans.

He shook his head at me. "If you're a giant, what does that make me?"

I rolled my eyes and turned away, embarrassed. "A man. Men are supposed to be tall."

"You're not a giant," Cole told me seriously. He put both hands on my shoulders "You're gorgeous, and you know it."

He was only inches from me, and just breathing his air felt unreal.

"Why are you being like this?" I asked. My voice sounded frightened, even in my own ears.

"What do you mean?" he asked, still gripping my shoulders.

I pulled out of his grasp, backing away and looking anywhere but at him. I wasn't even sure if I knew how to put an answer into words. Not any answer I wanted him to hear, that is. I turned around, suddenly not sure if I wanted to run away or stay and risk something to gain something even better.

"Kate?" His sexy low voice was soft but urgent. I couldn't very well resist a voice like that. I never could. Steeling myself for honesty, I turned back around.

"Cole, do you like me?" I asked.

He looked me straight in the eye and his answer was confident. "Yes." The smile he aimed at me a second later was pure sex.

I shifted uncomfortably from foot to foot. "You know

I've *always* liked you," I told him, the words coming more easily from me now that he'd opened the door. "Ever since you showed up with those damn daisies after the, um, glitter incident. You let me think that you liked me back when we were in college, but you were just being polite because I was Ward's little sister. I get that. I do. *Really.* It took a while for me to come to terms with it, but I just don't want to misread this situation."

Cole looked like he was fighting some sort of battle with himself. "You aren't misreading anything right now. I like you."

I should have been happy. This was what I'd wanted. I'd fantasized about this exact moment—when Cole told me he wanted me—in emotional, visceral, photo-realistic detail for years. But even though my heart was pounding, my face felt flushed, and I was vaguely out of my body, it wasn't with joy; it was with fear.

Terror, actually. I was terrified. Even though I was holding the prize I'd dreamt of in the palm of my hand, all I could do was marvel at how fragile it was. Most of my friends think that because I'm extroverted, I must also be brave. I'm not. That isn't how it works at all. I'm a great big coward when it comes down to it.

"Kate. You aren't misreading anything. I like you a lot," Cole repeated, more quietly this time. "Say something... maybe? Um... Kate?"

"I can't do this," I mumbled. "This is a bad idea."

I turned to run away, but Cole was faster. Whether he

was using his crazy football skills or I was just distracted by my own emotional state wasn't clear, but he was suddenly in front of me. For all I knew, he teleported. But there he was.

"No running," he told me seriously. "I've been trained for decades to try and catch you." Cole pulled me against his chest in a heartbeat, tipped my chin up, and kissed me.

My body surrendered in an instant. My fearful heart and second-guessing mind might have opinions, but my body only had needs. I kissed him back, savoring the soft press of his lips and eagerly parting my own when his warm tongue sought entry. His hands buried in my hair, pulling me closer, and I went willingly, twining my arms around his hips. His hold on me was gentle, but still firm enough to promise passion in addition to affection. I could see myself spending lifetimes in his arms. I've had plenty of good kisses and a couple of great ones, but until that moment I'd never had a perfect kiss. Cole gave me a perfect kiss.

It was just too much all at once. When we broke apart to share a breath and stare at one another in wonder and surprise—and there was enough surprise in his amber eyes to tell me that he hadn't expected to do that either—the fear in me came flooding back.

"Kate?" Cole asked again, reading my face and maybe guessing that I was about to bolt.

"I'm really sorry. I gotta' go," I said, hanging my head

and walking around him and out of the store without a backward glance.

Despite his teasing words, Cole didn't pursue me. Perhaps my story about throat-punching had convinced him that it wasn't a good idea. Perhaps he'd changed his mind after the kiss. Or—more likely—I just wasn't worth the fight. Either way, he let me go and I went home in a dizzy blur. All the sleepless Googling, the shock and surprise, and *that kiss* had overwhelmed my senses. I was all out of energy. I collapsed on my bed and slept solid for almost eighteen hours.

8

KATE

Six years earlier...

When I arrived at UT as a freshman, there was one thing on my mind: Cole Rylander.

Yes, I was there to obtain an education, but let's be real. I was a raging cyclone of hormones and anticipation over Cole. I'd spent two long years waiting, but finally, *finally*, we were living in the same town. Like a hurricane hitting the Texas coast, I was on a crash course with absolute disaster. It didn't take long for me to find it.

Cole was a senior by the time I arrived and had been absolutely killing it on the field. Just like my brother, Cole was showing every indication of having a shot at a professional career after graduation, and it meant that he spent every spare moment in the gym. So, if I wanted to find him, that was where I went to look. Ambushing him on his way out of the locker room was easy.

"Hi, Cole!" I said, surprising him and falling into step beside him as he walked out. "Remember me?"

Cole looked over at me in shock. He was wet from his shower and looked so much like my ultimate fantasy come to life that I could barely contain myself not to throw myself at him.

"Kate? Were you stalking me?" His voice was stunned, and appreciative.

For this long-awaited meeting, I'd pulled out all the stops. I was wearing a pale pink, strapless minidress that exposed much more than it concealed. It was August, so it was hot, and I therefore reasoned that less was more in the clothing department. My hair was super long back then, almost down to my waist, and I'd braided it into two long pigtails.

"Maybe. Didn't Ward tell you I was starting at UT?" I asked, batting my false eyelashes at him.

We'd kept up an intermittent texting conversation over the years. Nothing serious or explicit, but enough banter and joking on both sides to keep it interesting. We'd also run into each other a few times during the intervening years, but always with Ward around. Today, however, my meddlesome brother was nowhere to be found. What he didn't know couldn't hurt him, anyway.

Cole nodded and flashed his bright smile at me. He looked happy to see me, and it was making me vaguely delirious. I walked alongside him, glad that my legs were long enough to keep up. "Yeah, he did mention it. How do you like it here so far?"

"It's a really big campus," I said honestly. "I get lost a lot! The other day I think I interrupted a Board of Regents meeting looking for my English 101 class." There was a reason they called the campus bus the 'Forty Acres.' This place was enormous.

Cole's grin widened, and he held the door open for me as we walked outside. "Is that why you're here? You're lost? I don't think you have access to the athletics men's locker room. I can show you where the gym for students is if you want."

My answering grin over my shoulder was sly. I was well aware that the gym for regular students was across campus in the other direction. Not that I needed to use it. I was on the volleyball team and had every right to use the nicer facilities for student athletes. "Oh no, right now I'm not lost." My confidence was high, spurred on by two years of dreams. "*I was looking for you.*"

Cole blinked his big, amber eyes. His grin grew wider. "Oh, really? Well, you found me. What can I do for you?" His tone was sweet and teasing, like his texts always had been. His eyes sparkled in the afternoon light.

"What are you doing this Friday night?" I asked. My heart was pounding in my chest at a rate that felt just shy of 'heart attack.' But I wasn't about to lose my confidence now. I'd waited far too long for this moment. Two long years. "Do you want to go out on a date with me?" I felt proud that the words came out smoothly, at a consistent volume, and without stuttering.

Cole's grin faded. He drew us to a halt. "Kate, you're my best friend's little sister." He said this like it should affect my feelings.

I held my ground. "So what? Don't you like me?"

He looked at me like he was trying to find the right words and pulled a hand through his damp hair in frustration. My confidence drained out of me as the seconds ticked by. Finally, when I was afraid that he'd just stare at me and never answer, he looked around carefully and then shrugged.

"Can I pick you up at eight?" he asked. My exhale of relief was transcendental. I felt like my dreams were all coming true. My heart leapt up in my chest like it was threatening to escape my rib cage entirely. When we started walking again, each step at his side felt like I was growing taller. *He wanted me back.* I *knew* that he did, and I was *right*. He was so much better than the guys back home that it wasn't even funny. And now I was going to go out on a date with him.

"Sure!" I said, smiling widely and hoping I could get through the next five minutes without making him somehow change his mind. "You've got my number, right?" He nodded, still looking vaguely stunned but still happy. "I'll text you my address. I managed to avoid living in the dorms, thank God. I've got an apartment over in west campus." It wasn't a nice apartment or anything, but

I had half a room and one quarter of a bathroom to myself.

Cole nodded, looking both torn and delighted. He kept looking around like he expected Ward to appear out of the bushes with a machete or something. Ward, however, was home in the apartment that he shared with Cole and their friend, Lucas. I'd just texted him to make sure, so I knew for a fact that he wouldn't be getting in the way.

"Sounds like a plan," Cole said after a beat. I couldn't stop smiling.

"See you then." I traipsed off in a dream. "Bye, Cole," I called over my shoulder. He waved, smiling at me.

Cole was almost mine already.

9

COLE

I'd been on worse dates, sure, but after I kissed Kate and she ran off, it was safe to say I'd been on a few better ones, too. I was left standing in the shop with a bunch of curious clerks and the ruined remains of my pride. The walk back to my hotel room was lonely.

The plan I'd hatched during brunch had ended with inviting Kate back to my hotel room, but, when I arrived there alone, I knew I'd gone much too fast. I'd rushed her, and she wasn't the same impulsive person she used to be. She'd grown up, and she'd grown wiser. Kate didn't trust me, that much was clear. I would have to prove to her that my interest—and my feelings—were real.

I considered calling up Ward and telling him the truth but suspected that would not end any better than my date with Kate. In fact, it might even end violently, depending on the mood I caught Ward in. So, instead, I called up Lucas. We ended up meeting at his loft.

"This place is really nice," I remarked when I saw the view. Austin was sprawled out beyond his windows. We were so high up—the thirty ninth floor—that even the hill country beyond the city limits could be seen rolling outward to the west.

"Have you started looking at places yet?" Lucas asked, handing me a beer and then settling across from me on his couch. "Or do you just plan on living in hotels forever like a travelling salesman?"

I cringed. "I do feel like I've lived in hotels my entire life at this point. I guess I'm used to it." I'd seen literally thousands of hotel rooms, in nearly every state in the union. They were all the same after a while.

"Well, unless you want to make that a permanent arrangement, I'd suggest calling a realtor. It took me eight offers to snag this place. The struggle in this town is real."

I knew, rationally, that he was right. The housing crisis in Austin was well known. The number of well-paid tech people, academics, and government workers was more than enough to exceed the amount of available land. The fact that new people just kept coming, and coming, and coming compounded the issue. Multiple all cash offers on even modest properties were the norm in Austin. After San Francisco and New York, Austin was quickly becoming one of the most unaffordable real estate markets in the nation. But that wasn't why I was sitting in Lucas' overpriced loft.

"I have an issue. A Kate Williams issue," I told him.

Lucas smirked, which told me he'd already figured me out. Typical. The guy was too smart.

"If you're asking me for assistance, I may not be super helpful. Despite seeing her all the time, I don't actually know her that well. She's not a huge fan of me."

"What did you do?"

Lucas looked offended at the question. "*Do?* If you recall, *I did exactly what you asked.*"

I remembered. We drank in silence for a moment. I didn't like the beer he had on hand but was too polite to refuse it. Each mouthful was more bitter than the last. Then again, perhaps it wasn't the beer at all. Perhaps it was the reason for my visit that put a bad taste in my mouth.

"I made a mistake," I admitted, staring at my bottle instead of Lucas. When I looked up, he was staring out the window.

"Yeah, you did." His voice was soft, but I'd known him for long enough to know that was because he pitied me. Generally, I disliked being pitied, but in this case it might work in my favor.

"So, now what?" I asked. It didn't seem like one bad decision that I made at twenty-two ought to have so much lasting impact. Surely Kate could see past what I'd done so long ago.

Lucas shrugged, still not looking at me. "Maybe tell her the truth about why you were a dick back in college?"

It wasn't like I hadn't considered it, but telling Kate the truth was even more frightening to me than telling Ward. I shifted uncomfortably atop Lucas' ridiculously cushy club chair.

"I sort of did, already. But the whole truth could seriously backfire," I finally mumbled.

Lucas looked over at me at last. His expression was unimpressed, and his voice was dry. "If telling the truth was easy, everyone would do it. I have faith in you, though. You can do it if you try."

He was right, of course. He was almost always right, and he knew it. That was the frustrating thing about Lucas. Of the three of us, Lucas was by far the smartest. He was easily smarter than Ward and I combined, which was saying something, because despite being dumb jocks, neither one of us was actually dumb. Ward was good at practically everything he attempted, and although I lacked verbal skills given my down-home upbringing, I'd gotten a perfect score on the math section of the SAT.

"Is that all your advice for me?" I pushed, hoping he had something better than telling the truth. I wasn't sure I could handle that just yet. "Because I could use something a bit more... useable."

He yawned condescendingly before answering and I resisted the urge to snap at him. "You could give up on Kate and date someone else. You know, someone who is not related to Ward? I could even introduce you to a few perfectly nice women, if you're interested. This town is full of them."

I'm sure the look on my face told Lucas that I had no interest in that. He blinked at me. He'd just realized something, and it surprised him.

"Were you always this into her?" he asked, his hazel eyes narrowing. He didn't wait for me to answer. It must have been all over my stupid face. "Shit, you really are an idiot," he continued. "I'm not helping you. Not this time. I shouldn't have helped the first time. Either go tell her the truth or leave her alone. She deserves that much."

I paused. Lucas. Sardonic, sarcastic Lucas had just given me some tough love. Being direct wasn't really Lucas' general MO. He tended to find other ways to make his meaning known. Even Ward, who was probably the most difficult roommate ever when it came to food stealing, had never earned himself an ultimatum from Lucas. And one time he'd *literally* eaten Lucas' birthday cake—the German chocolate cake his mom made and mailed to Texas, and that she'd conspired with me to surprise Lucas with. Lucas had simply smiled and then gotten even. That was Lucas' way.

"Well, this has been a fun and informative visit," I said, setting my beer down on the coffee table and rolling my eyes.

"Because I want you to tell people the truth? What kind of friend would I be if I didn't?"

My reply was instant. "The same kind you were six years ago."

Lucas had no reply to my reference to my first date with Kate back in college. He shifted uncomfortably for a moment. He obviously felt guilty, too. "Say, what are we doing for Ward's bachelor party? I'm guessing you're going to veto The Usual."

The change of subjects was welcome. Anything to avoid talking about our goddamn feelings any more than absolutely necessary.

'The Usual' used to refer to a night spent down in the seedier clubbing district downtown on Sixth Street. Lucas, Ward, and our larger group of friends had spent many a Friday night doing The Usual, and I think I was still nursing a mild hangover all these years later. There were still certain drinks that I couldn't touch because of The Usual. I'd never drink another shot of Jägermeister for as long as I lived.

"Do you really want to do shots? Aren't we a bit old for that?" The median age in most of those clubs was all of about twenty-two.

"I'm not," Lucas replied. "And speak for yourself. I'm still young and cool." He looked like he actually believed that.

"You're older than I am!" By a couple of months, but it still counted. I was the youngest of our trio, and they never let me forget it before I could legally buy alcohol and was forced to mooch off them. Now that we were all old enough to acknowledge that being young was a good thing, I had no intention of letting Lucas forget.

He merely shrugged his shoulders at the reminder. "If partying on dirty Sixth Street is out, then what do you want to do?"

I hadn't really given the bachelor party a ton of thought. Most of my mental effort recently had been spent on thinking about Kate. Inspiration came to me spontaneously.

"How about a party barge?"

Lucas raised an eyebrow. "That could be promising." I could see the wheels beginning to turn in his head as he considered the idea. Party barges on the lake were rarely a bad choice.

"Oh, wait, doesn't Ward still have that boat?" I vaguely remembered him purchasing a small fishing boat a few years ago.

"I think so, but he *never* uses it. We'd definitely want to rent something bigger anyway."

I nodded. "I want to get something big enough to put a band on." And secretly, I definitely wanted to get one that had a slide.

"How about a stripper that pops out of a cake?" Lucas was obviously kidding, but I felt it was worth mentioning Ward's ground rules for the party anyway. Just in case Lucas got any ideas.

"Ward said that Emma said no strippers are allowed."

Lucas smirked. "Why am I not surprised? Can a man be whipped before he's even married?"

"You don't even like strippers," I countered. "Isn't the industry exploitative or something?" Lucas had taken a few women's studies classes in college. I think the initial plan had been to pick up the cute feminists, but they'd indoctrinated him rather than the other way around. The funny thing was that feminist Lucas got a lot more action after his conversion than before, so it was really a win-win.

"It definitely can be," Lucas said, warming to the topic. "But it's more complicated than just that. Stripping reinforces the sexual objectification of women even if the strip club itself is a feminist enterprise. That's not why I don't like strip clubs though."

"Me either," I agreed. I didn't know jack shit about feminism, but I knew the entire thing made me uncomfortable. The older I got, the more uncomfortable strippers made me. What had seemed fun at twenty-one now seemed creepy, seedy, and gross. "I just hate the idea that a woman would only give me the time of day because I have money she wants. It's not sexy. It makes me feel dirty." If there was one thing being a professional athlete had taught me, it's that a certain type of beautiful, manipulative woman is never far away.

"And speaking of dirty, strip clubs are always *really sticky*. Like, the whole place is just a sticky, glittery mess. I just don't want to think about why that would be."

We exchanged a disgusted look until the mention of glitter just made me remember Kate again. This meeting with Lucas may have been productive from a best man perspective, but I was no closer to figuring out what to do about Kate. If only I hadn't been such an idiot back in college.

10

COLE

SIX YEARS EARLIER...

When I got home from the gym, I found Lucas exactly where I'd left him two and a half hours before—in front of his computer. I would have thought that he hadn't moved a single muscle, except that the cereal bowls sitting next to him on the desk had multiplied. There had been only one before, and now there were three. Lucas shoveled the last bite of Lucky Charms into his mouth and waved his spoon at me in greeting. Couldn't the man reuse a damn bowl? He was the reason we always had so much dishwashing to do.

"How's the weather out there?" he asked, peering out the window and then wincing away like the pasty vampire he was. "It looks hot, and I need to go to the post office."

I smirked. I'd been meaning to buy him a parasol and a fan like a proper Southern Belle. Lucas and Ward both burned like babies. Whatever my racial makeup was—and it was a true mystery, since I was adopted and just looked permanently tan—it was a lot slower to sunburn than those two. Ward was used to the long summers of Texas and learned to love sunscreen, but Lucas had grown up in California and hadn't adjusted well. He turned lobster red almost every weekend.

"It's really nice out there," I lied. It was so hot that I was 'sweating like a whore in church' from just a five-minute walk. "Not too humid or anything." I'd been in drier steam rooms. "There's even a nice breeze." There wasn't.

"Why do you look so weird then?" Lucas asked. He looked suspicious.

Did I look weird? Well, I felt weird. The prettiest girl I'd ever met just asked me out. That didn't exactly happen every day.

"Ward's little sister just asked me out on a date." I felt like I needed to tell someone immediately, since the idea was so unbelievable, and so wonderful, that I needed to prove it was true.

Lucas set his spoon down into his cereal bowl with a little clink. "Katie?"

"Kate," I corrected, grinning like an idiot.

Lucas giggled. "What did you say?" Then he paused. "Oh no. You idiot. Did you say yes? Are you really that dumb? Ward's gonna' kill you and make it look like an accident."

"Hey, I'm not a bad guy," I argued, "and Kate is eighteen. She's an adult." I'd kept careful tabs on her age over the years. In fact, I'd had every intention of tracking her down on campus myself. She'd just beaten me to it.

"Both of those things are totally irrelevant."

"Look, I know Ward is protective of his sister, but—"

Lucas made a dismissive noise. "But nothing. Let me walk you through this from Ward's point of view. Pretend that Kate is your little sister. You two grew up in a trailer park, with an overworked single mom and an asshole absent father. Are you with me so far?"

"Yes, but—"

"Hush," Lucas said, continuing, "now Kate is your only sister, and she's a couple of years younger than you. She had a really tough time when you went to college because the only person who had the time and interest to look out for her disappeared. You were really worried she wouldn't even get into college, but she managed to get a sports scholarship. You know that she needs to get an education, or she'll end up just like your mom, pregnant at twenty with some asshole's baby. Still with me?"

I'd fallen silent at this point, stunned by how well Lucas seemed to have Ward pegged. Did he have me this thoroughly psychoanalyzed, too? I nodded at him in astonishment.

"Now your sweet, virginal little sister has come to college and the first guy she's gonna' go out with is your friend, Cole. Is that a problem?"

"No," I argued, "because Cole is a decent human being and Kate is an adult."

Lucas shook his head. "Cole is an extremely spoiled rich kid that might go on to play in the NFL next year but is definitely going to graduate and leave next year. He has a trust fund and a future that will lead him far away from Kate. Meanwhile, she will be left heartbroken, deflowered, and possibly with herpes."

"*I do not have herpes.*" That was just plain old rude.

"Ward doesn't know that."

"Ward doesn't know about my trust fund either." I tried to keep my family money to myself. Apparently, Lucas had figured it out. He probably hacked into my email or something. Maybe while he was freaking profiling me and Ward like some kind of science project.

"Wrong. Ward does know about your trust fund. He told me about it."

"What?" I was learning so many new, disturbing things today.

"Your mom told him when the toilet overflowed that one time you were home for the weekend, and we weren't sure how we'd pay for the plumber." *Thanks, mom.* Now my friends think I'm a spoiled brat.

I rolled my eyes at him and received a grimace in return. "You're getting me distracted. Who cares about my trust fund?! Why would I break her heart?" I countered. "Why can't we just go out on a date and see what happens?"

"Remember, in this scenario, Kate is your virginal little

angel of a sister. Stop seeing it from your perspective." His hazel eyes were bright. *He was actually enjoying this conversation.*

Virginal little angel of a kid sister? That was pretty much the last way I wanted to think of Kate. Based on some unkind things the girls at her school had posted to her Facebook page (I had checked her Facebook on the walk home), I was also fairly certain the ship had sailed on her virginity sometime back in high school. Nevertheless, Lucas was still wrong.

"If Kate were my sister, I feel like I'd want her to do what made her happy."

"But what if what made her happy temporarily was falling for some dumb, rich jock who was just bound to abandon her? What if you knew from personal experience how much it sucked to see a single mom struggling to put food on the table because a guy split on her? What if you knew that your sister only *pretended* to be tough as nails? What if you were the one person that looked out for your sister when you were kids, and you feel guilty that you haven't been around as much? Wouldn't you want to spare her from that pain even more? And wouldn't you be extremely angry at your friend—*whom you've known to sleep around more than once before*—for even going near her?"

Reality came crashing into me when I saw his frown. Lucas was right. All roads led to Ward ending me. I might be bigger by a little bit, but he was faster and more motivated. It was well known that Ward adored his little sister, despite the fact that she irritated him in a typical little sister way.

I was an idiot. A doomed idiot.

"I'm picking her up at eight on Friday. You have to help me. I have to, I guess, fake my own death or something." My voice was desperate, and conflicted. It didn't look like Lucas picked up on the conflict. He seemed too amused by the desperation.

"I have to do what?" Lucas' giggle turned into a full-blown laugh. "No way. I want no part of this." He shook his head emphatically. "I remember the whole glitter thing."

Ward had threatened me with *an actual tire iron* for ruining his sister's dress (after Ward, Lucas and I finally figured out what had happened, that is). I'd never driven down I-35 faster than when I went to Plano to apologize to Kate. Ward, when angry, was absolutely terrifying and twice as cunning. Underneath his dumb tough guy act was an even tougher, not-as-dumb reality.

"Come on. You have to help me figure this out," I pleaded. "I have to figure out some sort of a plan."

"Nope. I'm too smart to get involved with this. Ward is going to fucking murder you." Lucas looked like he was already picking out the flowers that he would lay on my grave. Maybe some nice daisies like the ones I gave to Kate would look nice. I swallowed hard.

"Why exactly am I going to murder Cole?" The voice in

the hallway was light and pleasant, but it made my blood run cold. *Ward was home?* I wasn't remotely ready to talk to him. Had he been listening from the other room?

Lucas returned to laughing, and I huffed at him in frustration. Lucas could have warned me that Ward had come home. But no. It was much funnier for him this way. Lucas was having a literal laughter fit in his desk chair. I kicked the back of his chair repeatedly until he shut up and glared at me.

There was no lying to Ward now that he was staring at me from two feet away. Just like before the start of a game, adrenaline spiked in my bloodstream and time seemed to slow down. I took a deep breath and turned to face him. Ward looked vaguely amused.

"Oh, um, it's about your sister," I ventured carefully.

The smile disappeared. "Come again?" he asked.

"Your sister." I repeated. My voice had no inflection. I kept my face as neutral as possible.

Ward frowned deeply. "Kate?"

"What? Do you have another one lurking around?" Lucas asked, peering around himself like a second Williams sister might appear and threaten *his wellbeing with her sexiness*. I nodded in answer, and Ward ignored Lucas' question. Ward's attention was entirely on me. It felt like a physical weight on my chest.

"What about Kate?" Ward asked cautiously. "Have you seen her? Is she okay?"

In the next two seconds, my life flashed before my eyes.

I'd never been so sure that I was about to be beaten up as I was in that moment, including the time I backed up over my uncle Jimmy's favorite dog's tail (after an amputation, Rattail the coonhound was rechristened Stumpy and recovered just fine). Lucas was silent, and his gaze shot between us, back and forth, like he was watching a particularly riveting table tennis match.

"Yeah. She's fine. Uh, I saw her today on campus," I stuttered. Did I dare to tell him the truth? Maybe it would be better? Maybe he would be understanding? That could happen, right?

"Why would that make me want to kill you?" Ward seemed genuinely, and rightfully, confused by our conversation. My words flowed out of me in an unthinking rush, spurred on by horniness and stupidity.

"Well, anyway, I saw her today. She was wearing this super tight, strapless pink dress and it was really..." I trailed off when his eyes narrowed and his shoulders tensed. His hands balled into fists, and my hands, which were tracing the outline of an hourglass, dropped to my sides like they'd been turned into lead. *Bad move, dumbass.* I shrugged and tried to look casual, although I was suddenly afraid that he might charge me. He wasn't a linebacker, but I could bet it would still hurt. "It's not my fault!" I protested when he continued to glare.

The tense seconds dragged by as Ward stared at me. His left eye twitched in a way that would have looked somewhat comical if it didn't also look vaguely psychotic. "Let's just pretend this conversation never happened," he finally grumbled, looking at me with what could only be described as a clear and unambiguous warning. He picked up his water bottle and left, sending a final, parting glare at me. "I don't want to hear you talking like that about Kate *ever again*." Then he glared at Lucas. "You either."

Lucas spread his hands in innocence and his eyes went wide. "What? Me? I didn't even do anything. I was just sitting here minding my own business!"

Ward slammed the door to his room in answer. Once he was gone, I looked at Lucas in a panic.

"You're screwed," Lucas pronounced. He picked up his cereal bowl to drink the milk, seemingly unconcerned about my fate.

"I have to figure out a way to get out of this date," I told Lucas, scared shitless. "I think she has a serious crush on me, man." I said nothing of my feelings for her. My need for self-preservation was too strong in that moment.

Lucas drank his cereal milk—a revolting habit if there ever was one—and then put down the bowl to stroke his nonexistent beard thoughtfully. "Shit," Lucas eventually said, shaking his head. "This is going to be complicated." Which meant he was going to help. He liked complicated. Lucas rose from his desk chair and slumped down onto our tired, secondhand couch. It groaned under his weight. I knew how the old couch felt. "We need a plan."

Even though I hated what I was about to do, I couldn't figure out another way to deal with my current predicament. It was this or murder. In the second that I had to decide, I made the only choice I had available to me. And I truly didn't want to be murdered by my best friend. So, Lucas and I sat down around a pizza and a six pack and we came up with a plan. Project Kate Date was born.

11

KATE

I was glad I had to work the following evening, because it gave me something to do other than dodging texts from Emma or obsessing over the kiss. I threw myself into work and let it carry me through the next four hours. The good thing about working in a bar is that no amount of work ever really feels like enough. There's always something that needs doing.

By the time I surfaced again around ten, it was only because Ward texted me while I was working on our tax returns and asked me to come meet him in the main room.

Predictably, Ward was behind the bar with Lucas sitting in front of him. Less predictably, Cole was right there as well. I swallowed hard, put a smile on my face, and told myself to act normal.

"What's up?" I asked in a too-high voice. Cole looked

especially good tonight. His hair was pushed back from his forehead and it looked so soft and shiny. I wondered for the one millionth time where his family was from. His smooth, tan skin was too olive to be Irish like Ward and me, and his handsome features were ambiguous enough that he could be almost anything from Hawaiian to Turkish. His people, wherever they came from, were hot.

Ward grinned at me as I approached. "Can you hook Cole up with your girlfriend Tiffany?"

I blanched. My friend Tiffany was beautiful, single, smart, and bound to jump at the chance to meet a hot, successful guy like Cole. I'd rather gargle glass than see her have him. "What?"

"Cole needs to find a place to live," Ward added. "Isn't Tiff a realtor?"

My brain caught onto what Ward was actually saying. "To buy a place to live?" I asked dimly.

"Or maybe rent," Cole interjected. "I haven't decided exactly what to do yet, but I'm determined to figure it out. I'm here to stay and need to find the right fit." He was looking at me intently, and I wondered if his words were a double entendre. My heart skipped.

Lucas, who was watching this whole exchange, was smirking into his citrusy beer like he knew something. Ward was as oblivious as ever. I frowned at all of them.

"Tiff only works with people looking to buy in east Austin, that's her specialty," I managed to spit out. "Do you want to live there?"

Cole shrugged. "I don't know. I was thinking that I should probably look all over."

"Okay, well, I can text you her number. She can hook you up with somebody good." I shifted uncomfortably as he smiled appreciatively.

"Thanks," he replied politely. He was a better actor than me, or else he didn't have any trouble pretending that we hadn't passionately kissed the last time we saw each other. I could feel a blush spreading over my cheeks already.

I didn't think I could hold together for much longer. Standing here having a regular, boring conversation was making me feel lightheaded. Just twenty-four hours ago, *Cole had kissed me*. Even now, all I could think about was the feeling of his lips on mine. The weight of his hands on my body. His intoxicating scent. The way he felt like he belonged to me...

"Is Tiff the hot Latina girl with the red hair and all the tattoos?" Lucas asked, ripping me out of my daydream.

I nodded at him and frowned. "Yeah. Do you want her number, too?" That would be an interesting pairing to say the least. Lucas did have *quite the documented preference* for redheads. I couldn't actually recall him dating women with any other hair color.

He looked like he was giving it serious consideration, even though my voice had been entirely sarcastic. "Nah, I'll let Cole have the first shot at her. Once he strikes out, I'll swoop in all gentleman-like and ride off into the sunset with her." He was doing an impression of Cole's lilting

Arkansas accent, and all three of them laughed. Ward and Lucas also fist-bumped at this declaration of strategy.

I rolled my eyes at them. Lucas had no game whatsoever, and I knew for a fact that he was still sobbing into his pillow about his ex-girlfriend. Little did Lucas know, Tiff could eat him for breakfast. She was nobody's rebound fling, either. She was the woman *men needed to rebound from*. She went through men's hearts like I went through sunglasses: the ones I didn't misplace, I crushed to smithereens.

"Okay, well, I gotta' get back to the office," I told the trio, backing out of their conversation. "I'm doing our quarterly taxes."

"How'd we do?" Willie interjected from down the bar. He'd owned this bar for a good thirty years before Ward bought it, and still acted like it belonged to him when it suited him.

"Ward did well," I said sweetly. "You and I had less impressive revenues."

Willie shook his head and grinned. "You don't know what I pulled in last year. I don't report my cash tips. Besides, *I've got investments*."

"Yeah," Ward teased, "Willie's been putting a lot of capital into the bank of Nancy lately. He's excited to start collecting *dividends any night now...*"

Willie's cheeks turned a darker color where they emerged from his whiskery beard, but he didn't deny it. The fact that he was seeing his ex-wife again was something of a running joke in the bar these days. Unlike Ward, I actually liked Nancy quite a bit. She was an old, crazy hippie, just like Willie. The last time I'd seen her, she had orange and green streaks in her hair.

"I think it's sweet that you and Nancy are reconnecting," I told Willie. "How's she doing?"

"She's got it in her head to move back to Lubbock," Willie admitted, looking saddened and confused. "We barely got out of that godforsaken town with our sanity intact. I don't know why she'd want to go back."

Whether Willie and Nancy actually escaped west Texas with their sanity intact was up for debate, but the answer was still fairly clear. "Doesn't your son's family still live there?"

Willie nodded. "Yeah." His voice was stubborn. "God knows why."

"That whole town smells like cow shit," Cole remarked. Ward nodded in disgusted agreement.

"That's only when the wind is from the southeast," Willie explained, "since that's where the feedlot is for the dairy. Forty thousand head of cattle don't smell nice, but that's not even the worst of it. When the wind blows from the other direction you get the hell-on-Earth sulfur smell off the oil fields. You do get used to it after a while."

Lubbock sounded like a delightful place to live.

"Perhaps someone just used a bit too much polish on the 2008 Big 12 South Division Co-Championship trophy,"

Lucas offered, earning him a look of treasonous disgust from the other three.

"I think you mean the smell of Aggie defeat," Cole corrected. The rivalry between Texas A&M and the University of Texas football programs was strong.

"Well," Ward added, "you know what they say: Lubbock or leave it."

I used the moment of ensuing laughter to make my way back to the office. Not fifteen minutes later, however, a knock on the open door made me look up. Cole was looking at me expectantly from the hallway.

"Can I come in?"

I nodded. "Um, sure." My voice sounded shaky in my own ears.

"I have a proposition for you," he said, settling into the chair in front of the desk.

There was probably a really snappy answer I could have given right then, something clever and witty, but I couldn't think of it. All I could do was stare. Eventually, Cole blinked at me and continued.

"I think we should go out on a date," he said confidently. "A real date. We need a total reset on the past. What do you think?"

My stubborn heart screamed gleefully, but I looked down at the tax documentation in front of me and tried to play it cool. A very real part of me still hadn't forgiven him for what happened in college.

"I think you give yourself a lot of credit," I said. "What

makes you think I even still like you? You had your shot back in college."

"I was an idiot back in college," he replied. His voice was earnest. "Forgive me?"

I didn't know what to say.

12

KATE

SIX YEARS EARLIER...

He picked me up at ten past eight on Friday, and every second that he was late took a bite out of my self-esteem. I answered the door in a blue and white striped dress with a hi-low hemline and a halter neck that I thought treaded the perfect line between sexy and cute. In addition to the dress, I was wearing kitten heels, my one strand of real pearls, and the world's biggest smile.

Cole looked like he'd spent the afternoon doing yard work. He was wearing cargo shorts and a stained wife beater tank top. He had on crocs. Fucking crocs! I looked at him in silent dismay. This was how he'd dressed for our date? He'd texted and said to dress nicely. I'd tried, so why couldn't he?

He'd also asked if I still liked daisies, so I was half expecting some. But he was empty handed. I swallowed my disappointment. He certainly didn't have to bring me flowers.

"You look beautiful," Cole said wide eyed, and then looked like he regretted the compliment. He dropped his gaze to my feet and stayed there for some time.

"Thanks," I said tightly, not understanding what was going on. He seemed so standoffish and uncomfortable all of a sudden. It seemed like he didn't want to look at me. I followed him out to the truck and let myself into the passenger seat when he didn't move to open the door. His truck was filthy inside and out. It smelled like something had died in it.

We drove in almost complete silence to our destination. Every time I tried to make conversation, Cole would start to engage with me like usual and then trail off and frown. Eventually, I gave up and stared out the window in confusion. This wasn't going well so far.

The easy chemistry that had always been there between us was gone. The way he was behaving was like he was *trying to be rude* and couldn't quite manage to pull it all the way off. The result was excruciatingly awkward.

Cole drove us to a part of downtown that I'd never been to or seen before. It looked okay. The restaurant was just your average, boring Applebee's. I wasn't particularly impressed, but we were starving college students, right? Money was tight. I wasn't disappointed, either. I'd grown up poor enough that any restaurant where the food didn't come in a big paper bucket felt like a fancy restaurant.

The restaurant was okay inside, and we sat down in a booth. I mentioned that I'd eaten Applebee's a lot as a kid when my dad came around and decided he wanted to be 'cool dad' for a few days, so it actually had a special place in my memory. Cole shot me a pitying look, ordered a beer, and then pulled out his phone.

I blinked at him for a moment or two before shaking my head. If it had been anyone but Cole, I would have snapped at him. This date would have ended right there. I would have told him off for ignoring me like this on a date, but I just couldn't. I still believed that somehow this date would turn out okay. I ate my very mediocre chicken tenders in relative silence while Cole continued to ignore me. He barely even looked at me the entire time. He seemed more focused on his beer, of which he drank three during our thirty-minute meal.

After dinner, I paid for my own food without Cole asking. I was ready to go home, but he said we were going to meet up with Lucas and his date for the evening. I almost demanded to be taken home but couldn't make myself snap at Cole. He almost seemed disappointed that I wasn't protesting. We walked a few blocks to a bar I'd never heard of. The hulking doorman asked for my ID, and when I produced it, he looked at me like I was an idiot.

"You can't come in," he said slowly, articulating every word so I would be sure not to misunderstand. "This is a twenty-one and up club." He pointed at a sign to his right that announced the age requirements in English and Spanish, just in case I had some sort of hearing impairment or language barrier.

I looked over at Cole in confusion, who pulled me aside.

"Do you have a fake ID or something?" he asked me. "I forgot that you were only eighteen."

I didn't see how he could have forgotten that since he knew I was a freshman. He'd known my age for years. I shook my head in disbelief. "What? No. I don't have a fake ID." I wasn't really a hard-partying type, and I wouldn't even know where I'd buy one. "There are lots of places we could go that are eighteen and up..."

"Look," the bouncer said grumpily, "get out of the line or produce an ID. No ID, no entrance to the club." He paused and looked me up and down, "Unless you're working, I mean. Some of the girls are under twenty-one. Are you a stripper?"

Cole brought me to a strip club?! I was too stunned to be angry. This entire date had been totally surreal, and this was just the fucked-up cherry on top.

"N-no. I'm not," I managed to stutter out. *"I'm not a stripper."*

The beefy guy shrugged. "Well then, you can't come in. Sorry."

Just then, Lucas arrived with his date. "Hi, Cole. Hi, Katie," I winced at the nickname. "This is Amy." His date was a small, somewhat scary looking redhead with a lip ring and a lot of very poorly inked tattoos that looked like they *might* have been done in a prison somewhere. She smiled to reveal one of those weird, split tongues that people get done at tattoo parlors when they're—presumably—on drugs.

"Hi, Cole. Nice to meet you, Katie. Are you two ready to get totally trashed?" she asked us. "I've been pregaming a bit," she admitted with a wink, "but I'm sure you can catch up."

"It's Kate," I corrected softly, but I didn't think anyone heard me.

"Kate's got an issue," Cole said. He looked at me and I felt like it was my fault. "She's underage."

Amy rolled her eyes and tugged at her fishnet stockings. "Well, I'm going inside. Since I work here, I get half price drinks. You two can go to Chuck-E-Cheese with baby Katie if you want." The way she twitched her ass back and forth as she stomped off made me suspicious that she was doing it on purpose.

Lucas and Cole both stared at me as Amy walked inside.

"Dude," Lucas said to Cole in a stage-whisper, "I'm trying to seal the deal here with Amy. Don't cockblock me with your jailbait date."

Cole looked at me, then at Lucas, then back at me. He didn't say anything. I sighed. Even now, I didn't want to disappoint him. I ought to be angry, but I was just stunned and sad.

"I, um, I'll just call an Uber and go home," I told him. "Go have fun with your friend."

I made it only halfway down the block before Cole caught up with me. He grabbed my elbow and swallowed hard when I turned to look at him. There were tears in my eyes, and I couldn't very well hide them now. He stared at me, shook his head, and then grabbed my hand.

"I'm so sorry, Kate. I thought this was a good way to push you away," he said. "But I don't want to. Not like this. I've got to tell you the truth."

13

KATE

"Oh, please. I forgave you a long time ago," I admitted. I chewed on my bottom lip for a moment in indecision before continuing. "Call me crazy, but I just don't want to be humiliated again."

Cole sighed and shifted in the chair like it was poking him in the back. "I never meant for you to be humiliated."

"Are you sure?" I challenged, arching an eyebrow at Cole. I'd found my anger for the way Cole had treated me way back when, although it had taken a while. At least he had the good sense to look ashamed when called out.

"I'm sorry. You're right." He hung his head and stared down at his hands. He ought to be sorry for taking me on the world's crappiest first date.

I nodded. The anger evaporated again the moment I saw his unhappiness, just like it had years before. I couldn't

99

ever seem to stay angry at him, even when he deserved it. "I know you are." I sighed.

"Will you give me another shot, Kate?" Cole asked hopefully. He leaned forward in the chair and looked at me eagerly. My heart beat faster.

"Why?" I asked. There were so many reasons we shouldn't be together.

"Because I like you, Kate!" he replied like it was the most obvious thing in the world. His amber eyes reflected the light in a way that made it look like they were glowing from the inside. "Because you like me." He paused, and when he spoke again, his voice was soft and vulnerable. "And because I really think we've got a shot at something pretty amazing, and I don't want us to miss out on it this time."

"You might not like me once you get to know me," I warned.

"That's a chance I'm really very willing to take. I'd say it's not very likely. I know I'm going to like you more once I know you." His eyes sparkled mischievously, and that heat that made me feel breathless was back in them again.

"I might not like you," I whispered, trying to remember what I was doing.

"But you like me now, don't you?" He was challenging me to say I wasn't attracted to him and God knew I couldn't deny it. He knew I wanted him. He'd known for ages. "Or do you want me to kiss you again to make sure? I'm more than happy to, you know. I'll happily kiss you for as long as it takes until you make up your mind."

I felt a hot blush burning my cheeks. My pride was at war with my heart. When the two sides fell silent, I'd reached an odd compromise with myself. I knitted the raw edges together and hoped they'd hold. My plan wasn't perfect, but it would just have to do. The only thing I could think was that I'd be kicking myself for the next eight years if I said no, but that an unqualified yes was even worse. I had to protect myself.

"I'll give you a shot, but only on one condition: don't tell Ward," I said to Cole. "*Promise me you won't tell him or anyone else.*"

"Why not?" he asked. His voice was confused and surprised.

I drew myself up to my full height in my desk chair to try and scrape together a bit of dignity. "Because I don't want him to know. I don't want anyone to know."

"But why?" Cole looked like he was fully willing to march into the other room and tell my brother that he wanted to date me, consequences be damned. Since that was exactly what he wouldn't do six years ago, it *should have made me feel good*. I never seemed to feel the way I should where Cole was concerned.

"I don't want people to know because *I'm not sure about you,*" I told Cole. "You seem so convinced that we're perfect for each other. But you don't even know me, and I sure don't know you. And if you go tell Ward right now, and it doesn't work out, then you can't un-ring that bell. We share friends. You know I'm right." I stared down my nose at him, waiting for an answer.

He looked at me and I could imagine what he was thinking, at least a little. He was seeing the logic, even though he couldn't guess that this was my way of protecting myself. As long as no one knew, I could pretend that this wasn't real. If he changed his mind again, I wouldn't have to suffer explaining things to Emma, or Ward, or anyone. It could be my secret.

"Tell me you won't tell," I pushed when he said nothing. "Promise me."

He looked genuinely conflicted and perhaps a bit offended. Maybe it didn't feel so nice to know that I wanted to keep it a secret, but this was the only way. Eventually, by the time I was wondering if this would be a deal breaker for him, Cole nodded. I exhaled in relief.

"One day you'll let me tell him," he said and sounded sure that he'd win me over.

"No, I won't," I corrected. "But, maybe, I'll tell him myself."

"Good enough," Cole replied, smiling happily and clearly deciding the secrecy was something he could deal with. "I accept your conditions."

"Promise me." Until he promised, I wouldn't be satisfied. I might be reduced to a silly school girl when he was around, but I was smarter than I used to be. I needed that promise.

He didn't roll his eyes at my stubbornness, but I could sense that he wanted to. "I promise I won't tell anyone until you let me."

I smiled at him hesitantly. This was something. This was real. This time, finally, maybe, I would get to be happy.

And if I wasn't, then this time, nobody needed to know.

14

COLE

Six years earlier...

Kate's big, beautiful blue eyes were full of unshed tears, and although she tried to blink them away, one crawled down her flawless cheek anyway. I felt ill watching her cry and knowing I'd caused it. She looked at me like I'd just ripped her heart out.

My fingers twitched to touch her, but I resisted the impulse. It wouldn't have been welcome at this point. That much was obvious from her expression. I also knew enough about Kate to suspect a swift right cross would be headed my way if I tried to touch her at that moment.

"I'm so sorry, Kate. I thought this was a good way to push you away," I said. "But I don't want to. Not like this. I've got to tell you the truth."

She frowned at me and shook her head. It looked like she wasn't quite ready to say anything, so I just rushed forward with my half-assed explanation before she stormed off.

"This was a dumb idea Lucas and I had. We figured if you hated me it would be better."

"What?" My plan clearly wasn't the best, so it was no surprise that she looked confused.

"I thought it would be better if you didn't like me anymore," I tried to clarify.

"What would be better?" she warbled, brushing the fallen tear away like it had betrayed her. Maybe it had. But not as badly as me.

I cleared my throat uncomfortably. This was already harder than I had anticipated. This whole night had been godawful, and I wasn't even the one being subjected to the world's crappiest date. It was the least I could do to come clean now. At least, as much as I could.

"It's obvious you like me," I told her. "And I'm about to graduate and you're too young. Plus, you're Ward's sister."

"You don't like me?" she asked, searching my face for the truth. I hid it from her, staring away and down at my shoes. My non-answer was enough to convince her that I didn't.

"You could have just told me you didn't like me," Kate said, a small spark of her personality showing back through her disappointment. "You should have just, like, let me down easy or something. It would have been kinder."

Perversely, it made me happy to see her get angry. Not only because I deserved it, but because I knew that if she was angry, she would be okay. She'd recover just fine without me. She was strong, I knew that. After all, she'd proven that before I even knew her name. The vision of her with that squirt bottle was seared into my memory forever. This time I actually *deserved* to be doused with deer piss.

"I didn't want you to keep hoping there was a chance with me," I told her. "Sometimes girls get really clingy with me." It wasn't just that, of course. It was that I knew that if I left any chance, I wouldn't be able to resist her. Just looking at her now was almost too much. She was flushed, passionate, and so beautiful it drove me half out of my mind. I wanted nothing in the world more than I wanted to see Kate spread out and flushed in my bed, to touch her lush tits, to see those pink lips part when I kissed her neck, and feel her warm hands grip my shoulders when I took her...

"You really don't like me at all?" she asked again, staring at me in confusion. "But you've always been so nice to me."

"Kate... I was just being polite," I lied. "You're just a kid. I'm not interested in you that way." It didn't feel like she should believe me, but of course she did. A good woman's heart is a fragile thing. Easily broken by an asshole like me. I'd never felt as evil as I did at that moment. It was made worse because I was breaking my own heart at the same time. She hung her head in defeat.

"Oh." Kate was no longer looking at my face. She must have figured out whatever it was she needed to know. She focused her eyes somewhere down on the ground between us. "Well, thanks for being honest, I guess. It's better than the alternative."

She was braver than me. I wasn't willing to be honest with her, not really. But there she was, listening to me tell her that I didn't want her, and still displaying more poise than I ever could. I didn't deserve her anyway.

"I should have been honest from the start," I told her, and then followed it up with a half-truth, "but I wanted to show you such a lousy time that you never wanted to see me again... anyway, it wasn't fair. I shouldn't have done it."

Her bright blue gaze flipped back to me. "It was a lousy date, but it wasn't any worse than hearing you don't want me. If you ever change your mind, let me know. You know where to find me."

I dragged a hand through my intentionally ugly, unwashed, messed up hair as she walked away. Nothing could have prepared me to deal with those being her parting words. They cut me like a knife and were delivered with just as much sharpness. She might have been younger than me, but she was worlds more mature and infinitely classier. Trailer park upbringing notwithstanding, Kate was living proof that money meant nothing when it came to what really mattered about a person. The fact that Kate could have been mine, and never would be, wounded me in ways that I didn't think it even could.

I sent her daisies the next day to apologize again, but the flower shop called and said she wouldn't sign for them. They had to leave them on her doorstep. I didn't doubt that she threw them in the dumpster. It would take a lot more than a handful of daisies to win Kate's forgiveness this time.

My remaining year at college was spent playing football and avoiding Kate like the plague. When I saw her on campus, she immediately went the other way, so it wasn't exactly hard work. Then I graduated and spent the next few years meeting woman after woman who couldn't begin to hold a candle to Kate Williams.

15

COLE

Present day...

 I'd never put more effort into planning a date than I put into my first real date with Kate. The first time around was just a mulligan. This time it was going to be absolutely perfect.

 When I picked her up from her little condo in west Austin on the following Friday night, I had a bouquet of yellow and pink daisies in my hand. She grinned when she saw them.

 "You remembered!" Kate said, taking them from me and ushering me inside so she could put them in a vase before they wilted. I followed her into her little kitchen.

 "Of course, I remembered," I told her, looking at my surroundings with interest. "I don't think I could ever forget."

Kate's kitchen was as eclectic and quirky as her fashion sense, but just like her clothes, it totally worked. Her kitchen cabinets were painted bright red, and the appliances were the minty green color that was popular during the 1950's. The countertops were white tile and the floors were stained concrete. Dozens of little prisms hung from the window, filling the whole room with late afternoon rainbows. It was dazzling, and almost tacky, but too charming to be anything but wonderful. Just like Kate.

Tonight, she was wearing a black sheath dress that was nothing like her usual vintage look. It hugged her every perfect curve but was otherwise completely simple. Her hair was free and loose, and she was wasn't wearing any makeup I could see at all. The look was a stark but lovely departure from what I usually saw her in. Any time I thought I had her figured out, she surprised me.

"Perfect," she said, setting the glass vase down and smiling at it. The delicate flowers did fit right in on her kitchen island. She'd clearly mastered her look. Everything around us was very Kate.

"Do you cook in here a lot?" I asked, wondering about Kate's life away from the bar. She shook her head.

"Almost never," she admitted, looking the tiniest bit embarrassed. "I don't cook very well and it's hard when I have all the free food I can eat from the food trucks by the bar."

"I don't know how to cook either," I admitted. "Ramen, sure, but that's about it."

"Your mom didn't teach you?" She looked somewhat wistful. I wondered if her mom didn't have time to teach her. From what I understood from Ward, before she had the alpaca farm, Ward and Kate's mom worked her ass off as a nurse. I'd never met her, but anyone who could raise *both Ward and Kate* must be quite the woman. I could only imagine she had a personality the size of Texas.

I frowned as I considered her question. "We had a cook," I admitted. The only thing I could actually remember my mom cooking were grilled cheese sandwiches and cookies. However, both were delicious.

She arched an eyebrow at me. "Well, aren't you fancy? I didn't know you had a cook."

"Well, I mean, our housekeeper cooked. She wasn't just a cook." I didn't deny my privileged upbringing, but I generally didn't advertise it either. Usually people assumed that a guy who grew up in rural Arkansas with a weird Uncle Jimmy and a pack of coonhounds lived in a shack in the woods rather than a sixteen-room antebellum mansion, and I was just fine with that. Better that they think me simple than spoiled.

That made her giggle and shake her head. "Okay, rich boy. Let's go before I decide your privilege is too much for me to stand."

There was the sassy, mouthy Kate I knew. I grinned at her. "Don't you want to know where we're going?" I asked as we drove.

"Is it a strip club again?" Her tone was suspicious, but her eyes were smiling.

I cringed but simultaneously laughed so hard I nearly choked. "No," I managed when my fit subsided into coughing. "It's not. In all fairness, Lucas and I had no intention of ever actually going to that strip club. Amy was a friend of Lucas' from his women's studies class. She went along with our plot because he described it as some kind of weird performance art."

"Oh, yeah, that makes it all okay." She pouted her full, pink lips at me.

"I only bring my dates to the classiest of strip clubs," I asserted confidently, still feeling internally mortified. Bringing her to a strip club had been a real stroke of asshole genius, but not one I could take credit for. No, that had been all Lucas.

In reality, I was taking her to Uchi, a particularly well recommended local sushi place. According to the internet, it had won practically all the awards a restaurant was eligible for. It was like the EGOTs of sushi places. Kate grinned when we pulled in and she realized where we were eating.

"I've always wanted to come here!" she said excitedly. "They have a really good vegetarian menu."

I looked over at her in surprise. "You're a vegetarian? Since when?"

She made a face and rolled her big blue eyes. "Since

living with Emma sophomore year. She *ruined me* with her whole sappy but well-reasoned 'meat is murder' thing. Now I can't even enjoy a hamburger without feeling oodles of guilt."

I briefly reflected on the fact that Ward, Mr. Medium Rare Steak himself, was marrying a vegetarian. His children would grow up eating *salads*. I couldn't actually remember ever seeing him eat a vegetable, let alone an entirely meatless meal. It must be absolute torture for him to marry a woman who subsisted entirely off what I'd heard him refer to condescendingly as 'sports candy.' I made a mental note to give him shit about it at my earliest opportunity.

"Do you at least eat fish?" I asked Kate hopefully when we settled in at the intimate table. She nodded.

"I eat fish sometimes," she said carefully. "But I'm *not* eating *any raw fish*. That's an absolute no-go, so don't even ask."

"Have you ever tried it?"

"Yes, and it was totally revolting." The expression on her pretty face was firm.

I swallowed my disappointment and tried to look charming. She couldn't be more wrong. Raw fish is the best type of fish. But seeing Kate happy was more important than my need to shovel fatty tuna into my mouth. "Okay, deal," I told her. "No raw fish."

If this date went well, and I didn't blow it, maybe I could

slowly ease her into enjoying proper raw sushi. Really, there was nowhere for us to go but up. Even now, I could see distrust and skepticism in her eyes. If I could convince Kate that I wasn't just a douche-canoe who led girls on to break their hearts for fun, it would be well worth every bite. Even if those bites weren't full of delicious raw fish.

16

COLE

The after-dinner bat cruise was a risky move for a first date, since it set the bar high, but I was glad I took the gamble when I saw how Kate's eyes lit up. As the one and a half million Mexican free-tail bats came streaming out from underneath the Congress Avenue Bridge where they roosted, they formed great, black rivers in the evening sky above our boat. They went out hunting every night during the summer months, feeding off mosquitos, moths, and any other unlucky insects they happened to find. And yeah, *I did read the bat cruise pamphlet that came with the tickets.*

"Did you know a person who studies bats is called a chiropterologist?" Kate asked me as the flow of bats tapered off from a massive flood to a trickle.

"I definitely did not know that," I replied, impressed. Kate's smile was sheepish.

"I learned that word from Emma," she admitted. "She's really good at pub quizzes."

"They ought to just call someone that studies bats, a Batman," I told her, pointing to the four or five young kids all dressed as the caped crusader for the occasion. They were running around the boat's deck like a tiny, chaotic, masked army of bat-children. "I feel like it would increase youth interest in the sciences."

Kate squinted at them. "You know, I think I recognize one of those Batkids..." she said, right as someone called her name from behind us. We turned around to see a woman approaching from the stairs.

"Cameron!" Kate cried, embracing the woman happily when she got close. "You didn't tell me you were in town."

The stranger grinned, snagging one of the smaller bat-children toddling past and scooping him—no her—up into her arms. "Janey and I are just here for the weekend to visit with my grandparents. She's doing stuff with her friends tonight, so I thought I'd show Maya the bats."

Maya, who looked somewhere between one and two years old, squealed happily in her mom's arms and warbled something unintelligible while pointing at the last few straggling bats that were flying out. Her pudgy fingers reached up for the bats eagerly and then towards her mom's face. Cameron looked at me interestedly from between her daughter's stubby digits. She looked about Kate's age.

"This is Cole," Kate told Cameron, introducing us.

"Cole, this is my friend Cameron. We met through Emma's old roommate, Rae. She even worked at the bar for a little bit a couple years ago."

"Nice to meet you," I said politely. It wasn't that Cameron didn't seem nice and all, but I didn't want to share Kate. Lucky for me, Maya seemed like she didn't want to share her mom, either. She immediately began fussing when Cameron shifted her into Kate's arms to shake my hand.

The picture of Kate holding the little girl seared into my consciousness like someone took a tattoo gun to the inside of my corneas. All of a sudden, a vision of a different life, a life that included Kate and kids that looked just like Kate but smaller, played out in a millisecond. I found myself thinking how much fulfillment it would bring me to protect and cherish *our children*. That was new. *And terrifying.*

"Likewise," Cameron was saying, instantly reclaiming her kid, who was now fussing loud enough to make Kate pout. The dream-version of my future vanished, and I found myself missing it and being simultaneously very relieved it was gone. "I think it's time for Bat-Maya to go eat a snack," she said apologetically.

"Call me!" Kate called after Cameron, and she grinned and nodded over her shoulder, trying to wrangle her red-faced baby at the same time. "Babies always cry when I hold them," Kate told me a second later. "I'm cursed. I think I must be scary or something."

"Me too," I admitted. "According to my uncle Jimmy, a baby can sense fear. If you're scared, it makes them scared."

Kate smirked at me and then laughed. "Well, that explains it!" She bit her bottom lip. "I like kids a lot, you know, but I'm secretly always terrified I'm gonna' drop them on their little heads or something and they'll just explode like eggs," she whispered. Her eyes were wide like she was telling me some deep, dark secret.

"I like kids, too," I told her honestly, "but I like them a lot better from a distance at this point in my life."

"Do you have any siblings?" she asked me, looking at me as if she should have already known the answer.

I shrugged. I'd never really considered my family as being different or incomplete, although objectively I knew my situation was a bit *unique.* "Biologically? Maybe. But no, in every way that matters, I was an only child."

"That must have been nice," Kate replied wistfully, but I could tell it was facetious. She and Ward got along well enough to successfully run a business together, and although neither wanted to admit it, they were close friends in addition to being siblings. I couldn't help but envy their family and its closeness. Still...

"I was really lucky to be adopted by my mom," I told her as the bat cruise began to turn back towards the dock. "She wanted to be a mother so bad, and she was great at it." My mom didn't let her lack of interest in romance or husbands get in the way of her maternal instinct. Single women didn't have the easiest time with adoption agencies, either. But she fought them until she won me, and I was sure she did as good a job or better than any couple.

"Your mom raised you all alone?" Kate asked, looking at me with an expression that made me wonder if she was trying to avoid poking any sore spots that I might have about my family. She didn't need to worry. My upbringing was fairly idyllic.

"Yep. Well, not really. We lived with my uncle Jimmy, who was actually my mom's uncle and my great-uncle. He raised her too since her parents died when she was little, so if you want to get technical about it, you could say my uncle Jimmy *is my uncle, my great-uncle, my dad, and my grandfather.*" Kate looked at me for permission to laugh and I nodded, joining in, and then adding, "I know it's weird. Trust me. I know."

"Very Arkansas," she said.

"Yep. The only place a rich, adopted kid can also sound like he's an inbred hillbilly."

"But you grew up with a cook?"

"A housekeeper who cooked," I corrected, and she rolled her eyes at the distinction.

"Where did the money come from?" she asked. "Your mom?"

"My uncle Jimmy made a fortune in the eighties. He invented a type of industrial insulation and patented it."

"An *industrial insulator*?" She arched an eyebrow. "How come I can't invent something lame that's worth a bunch of money? I have weird ideas all the time, but none of them are for stuff that people would want to pay money for."

"If it makes you feel better, he didn't invent it until he was almost forty."

She brightened. "That actually does make me feel better. I've still got time."

There's always time, I thought. Side by side with Kate on the boat, I watched the last sliver of sunlight disappear over the water and I remembered something else that Jimmy once told me. Unlike his usual hillbilly-isms, this was real advice. It was during the most awkward of my middle school years, when I was growing at a dramatically uneven rate. I looked like a giraffe-human hybrid at twelve: I'd grown out of my baby fat blubber, but suddenly my limbs and neck were too long, and I had no bulk whatsoever. My looks would all change for the better in a few years, but at the time I was human birth control: girls found me repulsive.

Jimmy found me sobbing and rejected in my room one afternoon and sat next to me in silence until I told him what happened. It wasn't a remarkable story. Boy meets girl, boy likes girl, girl tells boy she'd rather kiss a toad. I went home and cried like a baby for hours.

Jimmy listened to my sob story and told me not to worry. He said that no matter the problem, no matter its complexity, everything was fixable as long as I had time. Since I was only twelve, I had plenty of time. Time is the only real independent variable in any problem, he said, proving that he'd once been an engineer.

Looking over at Kate, I knew Jimmy was right. We still had time to fix whatever needed fixing. We still had time to build whatever trust needed building between us. She caught me staring at her and smiled back at me, still wearing a guarded expression, although I thought it was at least slightly less mistrustful than it had been. I knew that I was making progress.

"Do you want to go have a drink after this?" Kate asked, cocking her head to the side and shifting closer to me until I could feel her body heat and smell her light perfume. My heartbeat sped up. "I don't want to keep you up past your bedtime," she teased, although her voice was also hopeful. Her vivid blue eyes caught the lights from the city. They flashed passionately.

"Are you sure?" I teased back, rising to the challenge. "Because there's nothing I'd like more than to have you keeping me up until dawn. Don't you threaten me with a good time." My voice was hopeful, too. Maybe too hopeful, because Kate blushed bright pink.

Go slow, I reminded myself. *We've got time.*

17

KATE

THE BAR at the Driskill Hotel was busy on Friday night. I hadn't been here in ages, years actually, but it looked just the same. Since the place was built back in the eighteen hundreds I supposed it made sense that they wouldn't feel pressured to frequently redecorate. Cole and I sipped lovely, fashionable cocktails in cushy armchairs and I felt ridiculously fancy.

In my teenage fantasies, Cole and I hadn't talked as much as we did on our date. We were always busy doing... other things. Naked things, mostly. I found myself surprised by how much I enjoyed just talking to him.

It was even more than just enjoyment, too. I was *voracious* for information about him. Starved for it. I felt like I'd never get enough.

"Why did you move back to Austin?" I asked, thinking it

would have been easy for him to go anywhere with the money he'd made in the NFL. Unexpectedly, he shrugged.

"I don't know," he said. He looked a little bit self-conscious about the decision. "I didn't really think it through as much as I probably should have. It just seemed like a good idea to go where I had friends." His smile seemed to hint that I was one of his friends, and it made me feel warm inside.

"Plus, you know where all the good bars are," I offered.

"That too."

"Did you end up calling Tiffany?" I probed, both because I was curious and because I felt like I needed to know that she wasn't going to be a threat to me.

Cole nodded. "Yeah, but she won't take me on as a client. I'm too indecisive about what I want, probably. She said she'd talk to the other agents in her office and that someone would be reaching out to me soon to look at places. Do you want to come look at properties with me next weekend?"

I blinked in surprise. "Really?" This wasn't quite as good as when he'd offered to let me dress him up, but it was close.

He misinterpreted my shock for reluctance. "I mean, only if you want to..."

"I want to!" I said it so enthusiastically he laughed.

"It's a date then," he replied after a second. The heat was back in his eyes again, and I was starting to wonder where this night would end up. We were already at a hotel...

"Do you like working at the bar?" Cole asked, shattering my sexy daydream.

I thought about his question for a moment before answering.

"I guess so," I told him with a shrug. "I mean, it's not exactly my dream job, but I'm pretty good at it, the work isn't difficult, and I make enough money to do the things I want to do." There were a lot of people that didn't have it as good as I did. Sure, I wasn't a professional football player or anything, but I'd done well for a millennial. I didn't have to wear a nametag at my job or sit in a cubicle. Was it perfect? No. But I knew I should be grateful for my opportunities, not resentful of them.

"What is your dream job, then?" Cole followed up. He seemed genuinely interested in the answer, and for some reason, I wanted to tell him the secret I didn't even trust Ward with. The alcohol may have also contributed to my bravery.

"I want to run a boutique," I whispered excitedly.

"What kind of boutique? Clothes?"

"No, lingerie. You wouldn't believe how many women are out there wearing ugly lingerie. Bras that don't fit them. Shapewear that doesn't flatter them. Hosiery that makes them uncomfortable instead of sexy. Victoria's Secret is selling women trash. Horrible, cheaply made, overpriced trash. The right lingerie is more important than the right

clothes, believe it or not. Well-fitting, well-made foundations make a woman look ten years younger and twenty
pounds lighter. I'm not even kidding. It does. And that says
nothing of the struggle that some women have just finding
their size. I want to make women look better in all their
clothes, not just the clothes they buy from me. It should be
a *positive experience to buy lingerie,* and my store will be
inclusive of different styles, body types, and price ranges. I
like the idea of selling people that sort of glamorous experience that people used to have when they went to their
local department store. That they could walk in looking
like one sort of person and walk out looking *like their best
self...* it would be awesome!" I ended my monologue and
instantly felt a hot flush creep over me. That was quite a
pronouncement I'd just made.

Cole looked mystified by me. "You want to open a
lingerie shop?" he asked. When I nodded, he smiled and
shook his head. *"That's so you."* When I just continued to
look at him wide-eyed, he added, "You should do it. It
sounds cool."

I shifted uncomfortably. "It's just a dream. I won't ever
have the money to open a big store like that right off the
bat, but I've put some money away and I'm saving. In a
couple of years, I'll hopefully be able to have a little shop
somewhere. Everyone's got to start somewhere, right? I
don't expect everything to happen overnight. I need to
make sure the market can support it first."

"If any market could support something like that, it

would be Austin," Cole said. I nodded.

"I think so, too," I told him. Looking around the Driskill bar right at that moment, I could see the women there shopping in my store. There was a brunette to my right that was wearing a lovely pair of clearly vintage, bright blue pumps. She was wearing fishnets, but she ought to be wearing a pair of silk stockings and a garter belt that complemented her 1940's pin-up aesthetic better. She'd be more comfortable too. Sitting at the high-top tables to my left, a woman with blond to bubblegum pink ombre hair was carrying a new, trendy Fendi purse. I bet I could sell her a French lace negligee or fine damask boned corset. And of course, all women needed bras and panties. I *knew* it would work. I would make it work.

"If anyone could do this and find success, it would be you," Cole told me. His confidence made me feel like I was more capable than I probably was, but I didn't mind. It was nice to be validated.

"One day," I said, smiling. "I'll do it one day."

"Have you thought about getting Ward to fund you?" Cole asked carefully.

I grimaced. "I don't want to ask him for money."

"What about getting investors or a business loan?"

I shook my head. "I don't want to owe money to anyone." Student debt was the curse of our generation. There was no way I'd willingly go into debt. I didn't even have a credit card. I was so paranoid about it that I paid for everything in cash.

"I get that," Cole said, nodding. "After seeing so many NFL players wreck their lives after living beyond their incomes when they retire, I definitely understand."

I'd seen what Ward went through when his NFL career ended before he wanted it to, and so I knew that Cole wasn't kidding.

"I'm glad you retired on your own terms," I told him. The idea of Cole suffering the sort of injury that my brother had endured was bad enough. But it was the psychological gut punch of losing both his livelihood, fiancée, and passion simultaneously that had plunged Ward into a yearlong depression. When he came out of it, almost all that was left was his bar. We were both lucky that Willie and I had managed to keep it out of bankruptcy.

"Me too," Cole said, and then paused. "I know it was the right decision, but I have to admit, I feel sort of aimless now."

"What are you going to do?"

"I think I'm going to buy a car dealership," he said, and then his lips parted in surprise. "You're actually the first person I've told about that." Those lips curved up into a smile. "But that's what I think I'm going to do."

"A car dealership?" I tried to picture Cole doing one of those terrible television commercials and failed. "What kind?"

"BMW. There's a guy selling his franchise locations right now. He wants to retire, and I think I'm going to buy them."

"More than one?"

"There are eight in total. All in central Texas."

"No financing, no problem! Call Cole and get in your sweet new ride today. Cole Rylander, BMW dealer. Rylander BMW," I mused aloud while he watched me with an uncomfortable look on his face. "Can I have a free convertible?" I asked, and then immediately added, "Just kidding." I didn't want him to think that I was only dating him for the free luxury vehicles. He just shook his head at me and laughed.

"Maybe I'll barter you a nice lease on a new convertible if you'll be the model in my ads," he teased.

"Do I have to wear a bikini and lay all sexy-like on the hood?" I did my best, clothed impression of the pose in my armchair.

"Yes. Definitely," he joked, framing me in 'the shot' with his fingers. "I want to go full Playboy Magazine with it."

I arched an eyebrow, arching my back more and pushing out my tits. "Full Playboy? Wouldn't that be, well, topless?"

His excited gaze dipped to my chest as if it were an involuntary reflex, and then back up to my face with embarrassment. "Um. Maybe not full Playboy. I don't think Ward would be too pleased with that."

I sighed at him. That comment totally ruined the moment. "Let's not talk about my brother," I pleaded, "he's no fun. *I want to have fun.*"

He flashed his white smile at me. "Sorry. You're right. I want to have fun too."

A thought had begun pinging around in my head and the more of my drink that I sipped, the more it sounded like a good idea. "Maybe we should just go upstairs," I said, looking around and locating the staircase on the other side of the hotel lobby. "If we both really want to have some fun."

Cole didn't seem like he knew what to say to my proposition. A number of different emotions crossed his face in quick succession. None of them stuck around long enough for me to figure out what they were or what they meant. Finally, his face settled on a carefully neutral, totally blank look. "I shouldn't have bought you that third martini."

I rolled my eyes at him. "Please. I work in a bar. I drink more than this on a typical shift." That was a lie. I never drank when I worked; that was beyond stupid—it would be irresponsible. Not only did I work with money, but I was responsible for the safety of our patrons. I could never live with myself if someone left our bar and killed themselves or someone else because they were drunk. But at that moment, I wasn't drunk. Tipsy, but not drunk. I reached out a hand and touched his, seeking heat and comfort, and finding it. "I know what I want."

Cole examined my face carefully. He didn't pull his hand away from underneath mine. If anything, he seemed to be considering my proposition with great interest and seriousness. "Don't you think we should take things slow?" he asked.

I shook my head. "Why?" I'd never thought much of going slow. About anything, but especially about attraction. Life was short, right? Better to live it up while it lasted. "Carpe Diem," I told Cole.

I leaned forward and kissed him like I missed him. Unlike our first kiss which had caught me by surprise, this time I could savor the sensations better: moving in closer to brush his lips with mine, touching the side of his neck with my palm, teasing his tongue with my own and having him steal my breath in return. My emotions swirled and coalesced into desire, pooling between my thighs and setting me alight with anticipation and need. I'd waited a long time for this, and I didn't want to wait any more.

He pulled me closer and kissed the side of my neck, making me bite back a little moan. I tightened my grasp on him and breathed in his scent like the aphrodisiac it was. Was this even real? I wanted it to be real.

When he pulled back, he looked ready to seize the day for a moment, but then his expression flickered, faltered, and hardened. "I think we should wait."

"You don't think it would be better to, you know, just get this out of our systems?" I asked, feeling lighter than air and dreamy. The persistent, needy ache between my legs was making me feel desperate. Maybe once we slept together, I'd be able to think clearly again.

Cole seemed like he was thinking clearly already, but

not the way I wanted him to. He shook his head. "Trust me, I'd love to go rent a room with you. *There's no one more surprised that I'm saying this than me.*" He paused, and I could almost see him change his mind and then change it back. His lips settled into a firmer line. "But I'm not sure this is a good idea yet. You don't even want Ward to know about this date, but you want to go upstairs and sleep with me? I'm just not sure I feel comfortable with that. I don't want to be your one-night stand. I don't want you out of my system."

My heart leapt and then fell and then leapt again. It was getting a workout. I hadn't considered... that. I hadn't considered things from his perspective. Cole didn't want to be my secret. He wanted more. I swallowed my feelings and nodded. "Okay." Although my body was aching for him, I still knew he was right. We wouldn't benefit from rushing anything. I wasn't a teenager anymore. I could be mature if I tried really, really hard at it.

And if I was being honest with myself, I didn't want him out of my system either. We didn't go upstairs. Instead, Cole took me home, kissed me senseless at the door, and left. I caressed the petals on one of the daisies as I drank a glass of water before bed that night and found myself wondering if my system, such as it was, hadn't already become hopelessly addicted to Cole. It was fun now, but I worried what would happen if my supply of him ever ran out. I'd (mostly) quit smoking cigarettes after college, but I knew withdrawal could be a real bitch.

18

KATE

COLE CALLED me the next morning. We settled into a flirty texting routine: morning, noon, and night. Every time my phone buzzed, it was a little zing of pleasure and anticipation. If I thought I'd been like a teenager before, this was a thousand times worse. I was so glued to my next text from Cole that I almost forgot to pick up my friend Rae from the airport a few days later. She was coming to town for the weekend to help Emma and me go dress shopping and I would have totally forgotten to pick her up if she hadn't texted from her connecting flight to say she was delayed.

"God, it's nice here," she said, shrugging out of her sweater and staring around herself as if surprised to see sunshine. Her pale skin, even whiter than mine given her ginger coloring, practically glowed. "I forgot how long the New York winters are when I lived here."

I smirked. "It's June, Rae."

"I know that. You know that. But New York does not seem to know that." She shook her head and her orangey-red hair danced around her ears. "Seriously, I think I might be developing a vitamin D deficiency since moving home. It's so dreary and rainy all the time."

"You could always move back," I suggested.

She shook her head. "Don't tempt me. I just finally got a job."

Rae was originally from New York. She'd come down for her MBA and ended up living with Emma, which was how I met her. She and her British boyfriend, Ivan, had moved to New York after they both graduated, but it hadn't gone so well for them after the move. Their breakup had been nasty and ended up costing Rae both her apartment and her job. He'd been a prick though. She was better off without him.

"You got the job?!" I questioned excitedly. I knew that she'd been interviewing all over Manhattan.

Rae grinned. "I got it! The one I wanted too, with the firm uptown. Ivan can kiss my ass."

"Congratulations!" I told her, genuinely happy to see that she was recovering. Rae had moved up to New York with the intention of working for her ex-boyfriend's family's firm, a prestigious venture capital group with dual headquarters in London and New York. Both the boyfriend and the job ended up falling through for her. He'd told her she wouldn't be able to find another job in her field. He'd been dead wrong.

"Tell me all about it," I ordered.

Rae flashed her straight, even smile at me. "It's another venture capital group. The firm is called Azure Group," she explained, launching into a long-winded explanation of their funding and investment strategy that only barely made sense to me. Rae was one of those people who, like Lucas, just seemed to find professional success wherever they went. She'd been temporarily set back by her relationship with her ex-boyfriend, Ivan, but I was not surprised to see that she had landed on her feet. Unlike me, Rae was born for the cut-throat corporate world. She was tenacious, intelligent, and very hard working. I hoped Azure Group appreciated what they were getting with her.

"So, what will you be doing?"

"Due diligence investigations, at least to start with," she told me excitedly. She was practically vibrating out of her seat. "I'll be travelling around the country and helping to evaluate prospective acquisitions." I didn't have even the slightest idea what that actually meant.

"You'll be travelling a lot, then?" That sounded exciting. I hardly ever travelled anywhere. Come to think of it, other than going home to Plano to visit my mom and the alpaca farm, I hadn't left the state in almost a decade.

She nodded, grinning. "Yeah. I'm already scheduled to be in three states in the next three weeks. I'll even be in Austin soon for business. The only downside is that I'll probably have to give my dog to my brother. I don't think the new schedule will work with pet parenthood." Her face fell. "I know it's better this way, but I miss Tootsie already." She shook her head. "I'm ready to be working again, though. Being unemployed seriously sucked."

"You can always come back to Austin and get a job at the Lone Star Lounge," I suggested facetiously. Rae was not a customer-oriented personality type. "It's messy, but there's less stress and zero travel." I knew there wasn't a chance in hell of that happening. Rae had worked hard for her MBA and was determined to use it. There was no way she'd lean out on her career now, and goodness knows she'd be a terrible waitress. Part of me seriously envied Rae for her work ethic, ambition, and success. She never let anything slow her down, not even her scummy ex-boyfriend, Ivan.

"How did the office reveal for Emma go?" Rae asked. "Was the engagement party fun? I'm sorry I missed it."

I told an enthralled Rae all about the recent Emma and Ward wedding news. Rae had taken a long time to come around to Emma and Ward's relationship, but he had been brilliant to include her in the pre-engagement party surprise office since it went a long way to convince her that Ward really just wanted to make Emma happy.

"...and of course, Ward *forgot* to take the video of her reaction when she finally saw the finished project," I finally fell silent.

Rae, however, was all smiles to hear that everything had

gone so well. She'd finally warmed up to my brother. And she also wasn't jealous that Emma had selected me as her Maid of Honor and only bridesmaid.

"It makes sense," she told me when I asked if she was okay with it. "After all, you've known her longer. And I've got the whole new job to worry about." She shook her head as if to shake out her busy life. "What have you been up to?"

I shrugged my shoulders, playing it cool. "I started sort of dating somebody," I said. My voice sounded just a smidge too tight to be casual. Rae zeroed in on my act like a heat-seeking missile. Her eyes narrowed. Emma, I could sometimes fool. Rae? Never.

"You like him, I can tell," she said. "Tell me." She wasn't requesting.

"He's a friend of Ward's, from college. He just moved back to Austin," I started, and then trailed off. I had resolved not to tell Rae or Emma about Cole and me. I had decided to keep this whole thing a secret to protect myself. That meant not telling Rae the whole truth, and I hated keeping secrets.

"And you like him?" When I couldn't suppress my smile, Rae squealed happily.

We pulled up in front of Ward and Emma's place, and Emma exploded from the doorway to greet her. The two women hugged, and we were all momentarily distracted. It wasn't until I was leaving that Rae texted me and I looked over my shoulder to see her standing in the doorway.

Rae: Are you going to see him again?
Kate: Yes, definitely.

I got into my car so she couldn't see me but continued texting her.

Rae: I'm happy for you. I hope he's your great white buffalo.

Rae, Emma, and I all love the movie 'Hot Tub Time Machine,' but for very different reasons. Emma likes movies about time travel. Rae likes anything about the eighties. I just have a very serious thing for John Cusack.

Rae: Have you sealed the deal yet?
Kate: Someone once told me that a lady never tells.
Rae: That means no.
Kate: We had our first date two days ago.
Rae: Are you in love with him?
Kate: I don't know. We're trying to take things slow. Promise you won't tell anyone I'm seeing someone? I'm not ready for the world to know.

I drove home before she replied again. Part of me had expected her to go sleep off her jetlag, but I underestimated her curiosity. Her text popped up right before I ate my lunch. I reluctantly set down my veggie sandwich to see what the message was.

Rae: Of course. I'll keep your secret. I'm happy for you. But be careful.

I knew Rae, I'd known her for years. She was the one who always told people to be careful. If humans had slogans, hers would be 'be careful.' She was protective to a fault, but I also knew she wasn't wrong. It was Rae who discouraged Emma from dating Ward (although I would have discouraged her from it too, if I'd known). Rae didn't do it out of malice, though, she never did. She cautioned us because she didn't want to see Emma—or me—get hurt.

Neither Rae nor Emma had been around during my freshman year to witness my descent into mopey madness over Cole. I'd had no real friends during that period at all, and it had been a very dark time in my life. Ward was busy with his blossoming football career, and Cole was right alongside him, winning every game. Meanwhile, I was skipping my classes, smoking and drinking too much, and making out with every loser that looked my way. Risky behavior became my escape, and I was damn lucky that nothing bad ever happened to me besides a tanked GPA and academic probation. I snapped out of my funk eventually, but I also had no desire to return to that side of myself.

I considered her warning to be careful and knew it was smart. I chewed on my sandwich, which suddenly had become tasteless, and texted her back the biggest lie I'd ever told her.

Kate: I'm being careful. You don't need to worry about me. I know what I'm doing.

19

KATE

THE FOLLOWING EVENING, I received a Skype call from Cole and had to hustle to make myself halfway presentable before answering. I'd been sprawled out in bed binge watching the new run of Queer Eye (not as good as the old Bravo show) with my laptop on my tummy. I was wearing just a pair of my old, nasty sweatpants and a UT T-shirt and did not look presentable enough for the pizza delivery guy to see me. There was no way I'd let Cole see me like this.

I shot him a text to call back in five minutes, then flew around my room like a tornado. I'd never moved so fast. I was simultaneously brushing my hair, smearing on some makeup, and putting on my one pair of matching pajamas (a Christmas gift from Emma) all at once. They were long-sleeved, pink with white piping, and made of filmy, insubstantial silk. Wearing them made me feel just like Lucille Ball in 'I Love Lucy.'

"You put those on just for me, didn't you?" Cole asked when I answered the video call a moment later.

I frowned, busted. "What gave it away?" Growing up poor had taught me never to throw things away and to get as much use out of a garment as possible, so having dedicated pajamas was actually something of a new development for me. As a kid, Ward's old clothes became my sleepwear. Even as an adult, buying matching pajamas— even for a clothes horse like me—was hard. My nicer casual clothes eventually became gym clothes when they became shabby. Gym clothes inevitably became loungewear when they couldn't leave the house. Even loungewear then got cut down and became kitchen rags or dust rags. Only when the scraps were literally disintegrating did they hit the landfill.

"Your buttons are all off," Cole replied with a small slip of white teeth. He pointed, and I looked down to discover that I'd buttoned the shirt all wrong. The top was comically wrinkled and bunched as a result.

I sighed dramatically. "So much for the elaborate fantasy I was trying to weave for you of me being one of those glamorous, classy women who don't lounge around in their discarded gym clothes," I told him irritably, fiddling with the buttons self-consciously. I couldn't fix it without unbuttoning my entire shirt.

He didn't look remotely disappointed. "Kate, I honestly couldn't care less what you wear to sleep in. You're always beautiful."

Aww. Sweet. So very wrong, but sweet.

I arched an eyebrow at him. "I never said I slept in these. I practice the Marilyn Monroe approach. My sleepwear is two drops of perfume," I purred.

His small smile became a grin, and even through the poor resolution of my laptop webcam, I could see the pupils of his eyes dilate. "Even better." Cole wasn't wearing striped pajamas. He was wearing a checkered button-down shirt, and he looked nice, although I could only hope he wasn't wearing those awful checkered shoes with it. "I'm calling because I wanted to tell you something face to face," he continued. My heart sank, and I held my breath. *He wouldn't break up with me on a Skype call, right?* That would be horrible. Almost as bad as a text. "I bought the dealerships."

Relief so powerful that I felt like a literal weight had just been removed from my chest flowed through me. "That's wonderful!" Not only did that mean that Cole would have a stable thing to do with his life now that his football career was over, it meant he'd be sticking around. "Congratulations!"

Cole grinned at me. "Thanks! It feels really surreal right now, but I wanted you to be the first person to know."

I smiled back at him. "I can't imagine what it must be like to throw down that much cash. Was it scary to write the check?"

"Absolutely terrifying," Cole replied. "It was really

messed up. I've never had to put so many zeros at the end of anything coming out of my bank account."

"Closing on my condo was the scariest day of my life," I admitted. "I'm gonna go out on a limb and guess that the down payment on my condo was a lot smaller than whatever you paid for BMW dealerships, though."

"I didn't realize you owned your condo," Cole said. He looked impressed.

My answering smile was proud. "Yep, it's mine, all mine." Then I remembered. "Actually, it technically belongs to the bank, I guess, but in about twenty-five years, it *will be mine*. Not bad for someone who's just a glorified bartender."

"You're the manager," Cole corrected. "Ward's the bartender."

Yeah, but it wasn't my bar. I let it slide. "I'm really happy for you, Cole. I know it's scary to spend a lot of money, but it's great that you've got such a good opportunity. Have you told your folks about your plans yet?"

Cole nodded. "Yeah, I told them all about the dealerships. They're probably sick of hearing about it at this point. Plus, our family lawyer helped with the deal."

Of course, the family lawyer. How silly of me. Why didn't I know that?

"You have a family lawyer?"

He blinked. "Is that not normal?"

I shook my head and frowned. "Depends on your definition of normal, I suppose. We had a family pawn broker."

Cole's eyes were wide, and he looked embarrassed. "I'm sorry. I didn't realize it wasn't normal to have a family lawyer."

I smirked at him. "It's not your fault you were born into a better financial situation than me."

"I know," he said, but still looked uncomfortable. "I just —" he trailed off, seemingly not knowing what to say. He spread his hands wide. "I guess I just wish it hadn't been hard for you and your family."

I shrugged. "It's not like that now. But yeah, my mom's jewelry went in and out of that pawn shop so often that it basically became her jewelry box. The last time she took her things home because Ward bought her the ranch and she was going to move, she called me and cried because she was so happy. Just knowing that she wouldn't ever have to hock another piece of jewelry made a huge difference for her. Honestly, I think it was a bigger deal for her than quitting her nursing job."

He smiled. "I still have a tough time believing that your mom is an alpaca farmer."

"She's an alpaca *rancher*," I corrected. "But yeah. It's totally bizarre."

"Do you like the alpacas?" he asked me curiously. "Are they friendly?"

"Hell, no." My answer was emphatic. "They're the worst. My mom will say that they're so cute and so sweet, but don't listen. They're a bunch of long-necked, snaggle-toothed stink demons."

He raised his eyebrows. "I sense a story here."

Oh, there was a story. Stories. Plural. I shifted in my bed. "Maybe some other time. I'm not ready to tell you all my humiliating secrets tonight." I picked at the buttons on my top unhappily. "I've embarrassed myself enough today."

"Impossible."

"For me to ever embarrass myself enough?" I smirked. "Yeah, you might be right. My capacity for embarrassment is a deep well."

"For you to ever tell me anything that would make me think less of you."

My mouth fell open in shock and then closed into a smile. *Who says things like that?* Cole had the uncanny ability to knock me off my game, but in the best way possible. He made me feel like I was more than I was, and it ratcheted up my confidence in a way that filled me with lightness and joy. And also, desire.

"Does that mean you wouldn't mind if I fixed this little buttoning issue?" I purred, sliding one hand up my top from beneath and pushing my assets together around it. I was cross-legged on my bed in front of the camera.

His breath caught, and his permission was the look he was wearing. It was a heavy, heated stare.

"Kate, there's nothing little going on there," he said. His eyes were locked on my chest.

I flicked the little pearl buttons open, one by one. The light silk fabric was soft, but stiff, and my nipples hardened against it as much from Cole's riveted gaze as from the cool air coming in my open windows as I slowly pulled it apart just an inch at a time.

"When did you get that piercing?" Cole asked, staring at the bar in my navel.

"About a month after the last time you saw me freshman year." I measured everything that happened that year around his bombshell. "Do you like it?"

He nodded. "I like it. It's sexy. Like your tattoos." His voice was soft and appreciative. I wanted to show him everything. All my tattoos. I pulled the shirt off and halfway down my shoulders, baring my chest—and my under bust lace tattoo that extended up to my sternum —to him.

"Fuck," Cole whispered, transfixed. "You're gorgeous."

"Do you really think so?"

Cole tilted the camera in answer. Beneath the loose, pale blue fabric of his pants, his erection strained, long, hard, and thick. *Fuck.* My breathing had become shallow and quick, and my hands felt empty. My whole body felt empty. I'd never wanted anything as much as I wanted Cole.

"Do you want to come over?" I asked, cupping myself for him to display myself better. "We could celebrate your new business?" The invitation was almost a plea.

He ripped his eyes up higher, to my face. Cole's cheeks were flushed, and his voice was a breathy, wicked whisper. "You're gorgeous, but you're trouble," he told me. "If you let me come over right now, I'm going to make you mine in every way possible. If you're not ready for the whole world to know it—including your brother—don't invite me. Because he's going to hear you screaming my name from clear across town."

I hesitated, and then shrugged my top back on. My body felt alight, and I wanted him so badly I was almost ready to, but I was scared. I shook my head at him.

Cole's smile was disappointed. "That's what I thought." Now that I was covered again, his voice sounded more normal. "We've got time, Kate. It's okay. Besides, you've given me plenty to dream about tonight. See you soon."

I knew what I'd be dreaming about, that was for sure. I smiled a sad little smile at him, feeling like a coward. This wasn't what I wanted. I thought I could spare my feelings, but now it felt like Cole wanted everything or nothing from me. I'd worked myself into a corner and now I didn't know how to fix it. I wasn't typically a commitment-phobe, but the look on his face a moment ago had been intense and the last time I'd felt something this strong for Cole, it had been intense disappointment. That disappointment had been so deep I'd almost drowned in it. "Sweet dreams, Cole," I whispered.

20

COLE

I'D NOW SAID no to sex with Kate twice and I felt like I deserved a fucking medal for my forbearance. Self-discipline was something I'd developed for football, and I'd slowly gotten used to the grueling workout, diet, and practice requirements over the years, but this was on another level. This was torture. By the next day, I was ready to trade eating carbs forever for just one more glimpse at Kate's perfect rack.

Pretending that things were normal with Ward was also torture, although of a totally different and nonsexual type. I'd all but started avoiding him over the secret. An invitation to celebrate my acquisition at the bar the following evening made me feel guilty and jumpy. It showed.

"Why are you being so weird tonight?" Ward asked, looking at me with obvious worry. "Are you having buyer's remorse or something?"

I shook my head. The only remorse I was feeling was over not fucking his sister six ways from Sunday the night before. "I think I'm just having a small case of life whiplash."

That at least was true. Ward nodded understandingly. "It feels weird not to go to practice, doesn't it?" His voice was earnest.

"God, yes," I replied. My voice sounded as stunned as I felt. My nutritionist and doctor had helped me figure out how to go from playing sports professionally to a less active life without gaining three hundred pounds and getting sick, but it was still bizarre not to depend on my body's physical performance for my livelihood. "It's like I can feel myself losing muscle tone just sitting here. Like I'm just wasting away." It was three in the afternoon, and I was sitting on my butt in a bar with my buddies instead of sweating in a field. It was just bizarre.

Ward got it, but Lucas, who was seated at our table with us, rolled his eyes dismissively. "Oh, for God's sake, just go to the gym and lift some weights. That's what I do." His voice was skeptical. Lucas had initially gone to UT to play football as well, but a heart murmur had eliminated him early in our freshman year. It had ended up being entirely harmless to him, but by the time he got the definitive diagnosis a few years later it was too late. Luckily for Lucas, he was smarter than he had been talented at football in the first place (although I wouldn't say that to his face, either).

"It's just not the same without the team," Ward replied,

looking sad. I knew it still bothered Ward that his career had been cut short, and it was hard not to wonder where he'd be now if he hadn't been injured. Of the three of us, he was the most talented. The fact that I'd end up being the most successful at the sport was pure luck.

"At least Cole can go cry into his piles of new BMWs now," Lucas replied, smirking at me. "Have you decided what you want to drive yet? I assume you get a discount or something?"

"Yes, an i8 coupe," I replied instantly. I'd thought about this more than I probably should have, mostly because it distracted me from thinking about Kate. "With a one-point-five-liter Twin Power Turbo 3-cylinder engine. Fully charged in three hours and zero to sixty in four-point-two seconds. Three hundred and sixty-nine horsepower and four hundred and twenty torque." An affection for fine automobiles was a longstanding thing for me, so it worked out that I was now in the business. Plus, the fact the car was electric was just cool.

Both men sat back appreciatively in their seats. Lucas whistled low before saying, "Nice choice!"

"What color?" Ward asked.

"I haven't decided yet, but maybe silver?" I shrugged. I hadn't thought about the color yet, although that was a very important decision.

"A nice burnt orange or white would look nice," Ward suggested. Of course, he'd suggest that. The University of Texas' colors were white and burnt orange. I had plenty of pride for my alma mater, but I wasn't sure I wanted to drive an orange car. It was a bit flashy for my taste.

"White would look nice," I admitted. "Especially with the black interior."

"Don't get a white car," Emma said, coming up from behind us with a second pitcher of beer. "They look like rentals." She kissed her future husband on the cheek, and he pulled her half into his lap. Their easy affection made me feel lonely. Kate was nowhere around, but even if she had been, I couldn't touch her in front of Ward.

"I'd like to know what Enterprise rent-a-car has a fully tricked out i8 coupe in their lot," Lucas joked.

"Oh? Is that a very nice car?" Emma asked, adding a quiet, "I don't know about cars."

Ward hugged her closer, obviously charmed by her automotive innocence. "It's a very nice car," he explained to his fiancée. "A very expensive, very fast electric sports car."

"Well, then never mind," Emma said seriously. "In that case, *you should get a white car*. I read a study once that said white and silver cars were the least likely to be involved in an accident or pulled over for speeding."

I was about to reply to Emma when I noticed that she was waving over my shoulder. I turned to see Kate approaching.

"Hello. Working hard, I see," she teased, looking around at Ward, who was supposed to be behind the bar, and Lucas, whose laptop had gone dark on the table in front of us.

"We're talking about what kind of car Cole is going to get now that he owns the BMW empire," Emma said. She smirked. "What work could be more important than that?"

"He should get an i8 roadster," Kate answered instantly. Lucas and I probably looked stunned, but Ward grinned. His influence on his sister was clear, and he was proud of it.

"He wants the coupe," Ward said.

"He's too tall for the coupe," she replied, frowning at me while she talked to him. "The roadster is much sexier anyway."

"A roadster usually pays a weight penalty against a coupe for its flashier looks," I challenged.

"Usually, yeah. But the i8 did away with that weird, tiny back seat no one could use," she replied with a grin, "so it's almost the same. Plus, the range is longer on the roadster, and let's face it, no one drives an i8 because of its understated looks. That thing looks like a spaceship."

"She makes a good point," Lucas said.

"I do like the Roadster," Ward mused.

Poor Emma looked completely lost. We might as well all have been speaking Greek. Her gaze pinged from face to face in confusion.

For once in my life, I was not confused. I'd never been more certain of anything. The only thing I was thinking at that moment was how sexy Kate was, and how much I wanted her. A woman that looked like Kate and who knew as much about futuristic, electric sports cars as she did about beer and football? It was like God designed her special for me. Especially her tits...

Ward slapped me companionably on the shoulder. "You look stunned, man. Are you sure you're doing okay?"

I ripped my eyes away from Kate's face and shook my head at him in frustration. He totally misinterpreted my expression.

"Don't worry," he told me in a low, sympathetic voice, "you will get used to doing something else. It'll just take some time."

I'm sure my answering smile was thin. Keeping a secret from Ward when he was trying so hard to help me didn't make me feel any better. Ward was a good friend; he always had been. Yes, he was fiercely protective of his sister, but he was also fiercely protective of his friends. I knew that he'd do just about anything for me if I asked him. The promise that I'd made to Kate was beginning to eat at me.

For her part, Kate was doing a much better job of keeping it together than me. She rolled her eyes at her brother but turned businesslike a moment later.

"Say, did you see the contract for that corporate Christmas party come back?" Kate asked Ward. "I wanted to make sure they accepted the changes we needed to make on their decorations. I don't want them bringing in anything."

Ward looked confused and shrugged, but Emma perked up.

"It came back," Emma replied. "I talked to the client on

the phone and confirmed that they won't take anything off the walls or put anything permanent up. I figured the Christmas lights they want to put up won't be a huge issue, so I okayed it. I'm just waiting for them to email the final copy back."

"We already have white strings of Christmas lights we can put up," Kate said. "I usually don't allow people to bring their own, because it can look super tacky." The frustration in her voice was veiled, but I could hear it. Lucas and Ward carried on a conversation about another topic, oblivious to the drama playing out right next to them.

But Emma was clearly fully aware that Kate was annoyed. "I'm sorry," she said with a shrug. "I figured it wouldn't do any harm to let them bring their own lights. You aren't mad, are you?"

Kate paused, shook her head, and her eyes slid back and forth between Emma and Ward a few times. Now that I knew Kate better, I could almost read her mind. She loved Emma, but this was *Kate's job*. Emma was encroaching on her territory and making decisions. Design decisions no less.

I could nearly guarantee that anyone except Emma would get a stern talking to if she stepped on Kate's authority in the bar. But what could Kate do? This was going to be Emma's bar as well as Ward's in the near future. All Kate could do was smile politely and pretend that it didn't bother her.

Poor innocent Ward bore the brunt of her frustration

instead. She glared at her brother, pointed at the bar, and barked, "Get back to work!" Ward reluctantly obeyed. The afternoon was wearing off and soon the happy hour crowd would be in.

"Slave driver," he grumbled with a bemused smile.

"Someone has to make sure the lights stay on around here," Kate snapped back.

"What's got your panties in a twist?" he asked her.

Kate stomped away without answering. She made the rounds to refill water glasses with a frown on her face. Patrons thanked her meekly. Emma stared guiltily at her beer. A moment later, Emma followed Kate off toward the office with her metaphorical tail between her legs.

"Are you sure you want to mess around with that temper?" Lucas asked me, low enough that Ward couldn't hear. He arched an eyebrow at me. He hadn't been as oblivious as I thought.

My answering grin must have been all the answer he needed.

"You really do have a death wish, don't you?" he asked. "If Ward doesn't do you in, Kate will."

But as I watched Kate's flawless hourglass figure stomp back to the office and thought about our video call from the night before, all I could do was think that it'd be a hell of a way to go.

21

KATE

I WANTED to sulk in the office for a few minutes, but Emma wasn't going to let me. She knocked almost instantly after I shut the door and swung it open before I could even answer. She walked in like she owned the place, which of course she nearly did. I blinked at her, feeling both conflicted and cornered.

"You're mad at me," she asserted, flopping down in the chair in front of me and not giving me a chance to cool off. "Why are you mad at me? Is it really because I said okay to the Christmas lights for that party?"

Her voice was concerned and frightened, and I frowned more in annoyance than anger. I sighed as my irritation drained out of me at the sight of her expression. I couldn't stay mad at her. "I'm not really mad at you," I replied after a moment of playing uselessly with the papers in front of me. I shoved them away across the desk and met Emma's big, green eyes. "*Not really.* I'm just being an insecure jerk."

She cocked her head to the side like a confused, blonde puppy. "Insecure?"

I nodded in defeat. "Yeah. Insecure. I feel like I'm just spinning my wheels. My whole life is just stuck on repeat. I'm not going anywhere. Especially compared to Cole, Ward, Lucas, Rae, and you. All of you have your careers figured out, except me. I'm afraid I'm going to get left behind while you all become real adults. I'll probably be managing this bar for the rest of my life."

Emma's wide eyes got even wider. "I can only speak for myself, but I definitely don't have my career figured out! Teaching is much harder than I expected it to be. I like it, but it's hard. I'm not sure I'm cut out for it long term. Every day in the classroom is still really, really challenging."

I sighed. "That's not what I meant. I... I know it's not all sunshine, lollipops and rainbows for anyone. But at least you have a trajectory. An end goal. You may not have a perfect plan, but you have *a plan*. You at least sort of know what you want. I'm just drifting aimlessly through my twenties like plankton."

"You know what you want. You have a goal. You have a plan. You've been talking about opening a boutique since we were in college. Doesn't that count for something?"

I swallowed uncomfortably. "But I'm not any closer to doing it than I was back then." My voice was small, and I felt vulnerable and weak. It wasn't something I was used to feeling, and I didn't like it at all. Seeing Cole, just seeing him sitting in the bar next to Ward, made my stress level go up to level one billion. I wanted him more than I wanted anything in my life, and it was amplifying all my other worries.

"That's not even true. You've been diligently saving up money for years," Emma argued.

"Sure. And in approximately forty years I'll have enough." My voice was bitter. More bitter than I expected, actually. I'd never really been concerned about money much until recently. My bank account was healthy enough to support me, which used to feel like it was all I ever wanted, but it wasn't enough to finance my goal. I was safe —which given my background, I knew was still an achievement—but I wasn't exactly rolling in the dough.

I knew that if I asked Ward for money, he would probably give it to me. Or find a way to give it to me. But I couldn't—didn't dare—ask him to do that. There were no guarantees in business, and certainly not in retail. I would not be able to forgive myself if I crashed and burned on someone else's dollar. Better that I wreck my own finances.

"You could sell your condo," she replied confidently. "You should have a lot of equity in it by now. You've done a lot of improvements over the years."

She was right, of course. That had been my entire plan all along. I bought the condo with the intention that I would fix it up and flip it, and then use the money to start my boutique. Based on my current calculations, I would have nearly enough if I sold it for top dollar. Austin's real estate market had gone completely nuts in recent years. My condo would probably sell in just a couple of days. But then I would have nowhere to live.

"I love my condo," I admitted. "And it's scary to spend all that money."

Emma nodded understandingly. "I'd be extremely scared too," she told me, "but being scared isn't the same as being aimless. No one has it all figured out. Least of all me."

My sigh was embarrassed. "I know. I'm sorry. It's just hard. Being around Cole and seeing his dealership thing come together. Lucas is too smart to ever fail at anything. Ward has his bar. You have your PhD and your teaching. I feel like everyone else gets to have their dreams come true but me."

"Does that mean your date with Cole didn't go well?" Emma asked gently. Her voice made me suspect that this is what she'd wanted to talk about the entire time we'd been discussing other topics. This is what she thought I was really upset about. And she was right.

I shook my head. "I don't think I want to talk about it." In reality, I did want to talk about it. I wanted to talk about it so badly that it was driving me crazy, but I couldn't. I was just too much of a coward. "I don't think it's gonna' work out."

"Are you sure?"

"Yeah," I lied, "I'm sure. I just need some time to process things."

Emma wasn't used to me keeping things from her. Usually we shared all the gory details of our dates (although the fact that she was about to be married to my brother meant that she thankfully didn't share *everything* anymore). I could tell she wanted to ask questions, and I knew if she did, I wouldn't be able to lie to her. But after a moment she nodded, and I saw the moment where she decided to be respectful of my request. I almost wished that she hadn't been. It was becoming harder and harder for me to avoid screaming from the rooftops that Cole Rylander wanted me. But even though I was over the moon that he wanted me, I wasn't sure that I could trust that it would last. After all, I'd been burned before.

Better for me to put the brakes on this flirty non-relationship while I still could. If I didn't, my heart was going to get crushed to smithereens. Cole and I were just not to be.

"Okay, well, if you change your mind, I'm here," Emma said eventually. We stared at one another for a long second before she rose and left. Once she was gone, I put my head down on the desk and closed my eyes. I felt like I was in freefall.

How had everything in my life spun so suddenly out of control? I needed to protect myself before it was too late.

22

COLE

I STEPPED OUTSIDE to take a call from my lawyer about the deal, and the moment I hung up I was instantly cornered by none other than Eddie Nasser of the Texas Advocate. He must have been stalking me and waiting outside. What a little creep.

"Mr. Rylander!" he exclaimed, "do you have a moment to give a statement to the Advocate on your recent business acquisition?"

"No, I really don't," I replied, staring coldly at him with my best impression of Ward.

It didn't seem to have any effect. "Are you sure? I'm sure our readers would love to hear about your purchase of several car dealerships in the area."

I'd already said more than I felt comfortable saying. I handed him my lawyer's card and went to step back inside. I was relatively confident that he'd stay outside the Lone

Star Lounge. Ward had put the fear of God into him the last time I'd seen him.

"What about your relationship with Kate Williams?" Eddie said to my retreating back.

"Excuse me?" I paused, frozen. I spun around to find him showing me a photo of the two of us kissing in the Driskill bar. In the photo, her eyes were closed in bliss as I kissed her neck. My hands were tangled in her hair. The angle of the photo showed the curves of her body much too well, and she looked like a woman who knew her night was going to end in sex. It hadn't—thanks to me and my big mouth—but the photo was much more candid and passionate than anything that belonged in Eddie's collection.

In an instant, my heart was in my throat. The very last way that I wanted Ward to learn about our relationship was by *reading about it the fucking newspaper.* My fingers twitched into fists at my side. Violence wasn't really my thing, but I was reconsidering. I advanced on Eddie two steps, but he held his ground.

"Perhaps you'd like to make a statement now?" he crowed. His smug smile was about to get knocked clean off his face. I wanted to hurt him. Taking pictures of me when I was out in public was fair game. But taking pictures like that of Kate? No fucking way. Eddie's smile wavered when he looked at the change in my expression. He took one uneasy step back.

"Eddie?" An unfamiliar voice called, surprising us. Both

of us turned to see Willie approaching from the parking lot with a well-preserved blonde in her sixties. She was wearing a motorcycle vest and four-inch heels. She had pink streaks in her hair. *Oh shit,* I thought to myself excitedly, *that's got to be Nancy. I didn't even have to hit him! Eddie's fucked.*

And Eddie knew it too. He didn't seem capable of forming a greeting. His mouth worked up and down comically like a dog eating peanut butter. No sound was coming out but a thin, frightened whine. It was really an entertaining thing to watch. He'd turned that unhealthy puce shade again, too. Nancy's carefully penciled-in eyebrows rose up her forehead as she approached. She looked very unimpressed. "Did I not make myself clear about staying away from the Lounge?" Her voice was dry, and her southern drawl was even thicker than mine.

"I, um, well," Eddie stuttered. Nancy snatched the phone he was still brandishing at me out of his grasp and sighed when she saw the photos.

"Well, that's just not very sporting," she said to Eddie after thumbing through the shots. "You know better than this." Her tone was scolding.

Willie looked over her shoulder and then at me with wide eyes. "Kate?" he mouthed soundlessly. I shrugged. He shook his head at me like Eddie had a photo of me kissing bigfoot. He was that shocked.

"Would y'all excuse us for a moment?" Nancy asked Willie and me. We stepped a few yards away and watched what could only be the tongue lashing of a lifetime take place in hushed tones.

"Kate, huh?" Willie asked me in a near whisper. I nodded my head, watching Eddie's face grow more forlorn as Nancy laid into him. "Interesting choice."

I arched an eyebrow at him. "Why is that?"

He didn't immediately answer. We both watched Eddie scurry off to the parking lot away from a still-irate Nancy. Her face changed from angry to pleasant as she approached us like the sun breaking through after a rainstorm.

"Hey there, you must be Cole," Nancy said amiably, shaking my hand with both of hers. Her nails were long and pink, and they matched her hair. "It's so good to meet you. I followed your football career with great interest. And I just fired Eddie, in case you're wonderin'."

"It's nice to meet you as well. Thank you, ma'am. And thank you for sending Eddie on his way." Her timing had been extremely lucky, both for me and for Eddie's face. It was almost instant karma for him. I'm not sure what I did to deserve such good fortune, but I wasn't about to question it.

She smirked and winked at me. "No problem. A man shouldn't have to look over his shoulder when he's just trying to have a drink."

I liked Nancy. Even if she hadn't run Eddie off, she reminded me a bit of a more grown up Kate. She was clearly a bit wild. I would bet money that the vintage

Indian motorcycle that I saw parked next to Willie's Harley belonged to her.

"Well, I appreciate it," I repeated.

"You go on inside, honey bear," Willie said to Nancy after we exchanged a few more obligatory get-to-know-you pleasantries. "I need to have a word here with Cole."

"Sure thing, honey bear."

Honey bear? Jesus Christ.

At least Willie had the good sense to look embarrassed about the nickname. They kissed and then Nancy headed inside to leave Willie and me alone. I was about to tease him until I saw his expression. He regarded me seriously over the top of his half-moon glasses. "Kate's got a lot of friends around here," he said slowly, "and I'm not just talking about Ward. Nobody wants to see her get hurt."

"Are you threatening me now too, old man?" I wasn't really in the mood for Willie's teasing. I'd just had to put up with attempted blackmail from Eddie.

With his typical mildness Willie just shook his head and smirked. "I don't need to threaten you." He paused again, presumably to let his threat sink in. "I just thought you might appreciate a warning. If any harm comes to that woman, every single patron in that bar is going after you with torches and pitchforks. And Ward will be leading them."

I sighed. "I don't need your warnings, *honey bear*. Hurting Kate is the last thing I want to do."

"Word is that you've done it before."

Where the hell did he hear that? I grimaced. I shouldn't even be surprised. I should have known. Willie might be old, but he wasn't deaf (yet). He knew practically everything about everybody, just from listening. It was no surprise he'd learned the story from Lucas or Emma at some point. Hell, maybe Kate told him herself.

Kate. The woman who had singlehandedly turned my life upside down and inside out. Like a bomb had gone off in my brain, I'd reached some sort of breaking point with Willie in the parking lot. I was done keeping secrets, and with Willie, Nancy, and Eddie now knowing, there wasn't much chance of us staying on the down low much longer. But even if that wasn't true, I couldn't wait another second. All my good intentions about going slow were about to go out the window.

I needed to see her. I needed to touch her. I needed to claim her and make it one hundred percent clear to both of us that *Kate was mine*. It was time to cut bait or fish, as my uncle Jimmy would say. I never actually figured out what that one meant, but it sure sounded good.

23

COLE

BACK INSIDE THE Lone Star Lounge, I tried to make a beeline for Kate, but like so many of my plans with Kate, fate blocked my path. Actually, this time it was Lucas, and he was literally in my way. He dove into my field of vision before I'd made it three steps inside.

"She's here," he whispered urgently, reaching out to grab my shoulders and shake me. "Ward didn't tell me *she'd be here.*" There were equal measures of panic and pain in his hazel eyes, but I had no idea why.

"Dude, what are you talking about?" I winced out of his grasp. I'd picked up calling people 'Dude' from California-born Lucas. It seemed only fair to use it on him. I didn't want anything but to get to Kate, although leaving my friend when he was so upset would be unthinkable. I attempted to focus. Lucas didn't do the touchy-feely emotional stuff, so the fact that he was reaching out to me like this was disturbing.

"*Victoria is here*! Right now!" He jerked his head in the direction of the stage to our right where a band was beginning to set up. It was a Friday night, which meant live music. Sure enough, Lucas' ex-girlfriend was there, tuning up her guitar with her bandmates. She shook back her long mane of curly hair and laughed with her bassist, utterly ignoring (or perhaps just not noticing) Lucas.

Shit.

Victoria Priestly had returned to Austin like a razor-edged boomerang. The red-haired she-devil dumped Lucas because he wasn't cool enough when her band got a record deal. She claimed that he didn't understand or appreciate her artistic temperament, which was really just her way of saying that she cheated on him. Constantly. Unapologetically. I couldn't stand her.

But by the look on Lucas' face, he still wanted her back. Bad. Really bad. He stared at her like someone lost in the desert stares at a mirage of an oasis. It was painful to see. I ground my teeth in secondhand frustration. His attachment to this woman was as unhealthy as it was irrational.

"Why are you still so hung up on her, man? It's been months." Years, actually. I knew it wasn't the most sensitive thing to say to Lucas, but it was true. If their break-up was a child, it would be almost two years old by now. Their break-up would be walking and talking and thinking about potty training. He should be over her.

Lucas didn't seem to have a good answer for me. He shook his sandy hair. "It's not a thing I have any control over," he finally said, looking guilty. "I don't want to feel like this. I just..." he trailed off and I thought he wasn't going to finish his sentence, but then managed, "I still love her." It sounded like a confession of something shameful. I bit back a snide comment. He was dead serious.

Lucas stared up at the stage longingly. Seeing him staring at Victoria that way made me hope she'd literally break a leg up there. I'd met her a handful of times during their three-year relationship and she'd become progressively more stuck-up and unlikeable as time went on. Victoria clearly thought she was born to be a star, and her talent was very real. She was pretty okay looking too; I'd give her that. Not nearly as hot as Kate, but still objectively not hideous. But no amount of beauty or talent gave her the right to hurt my friend.

And no amount of intelligence on Lucas' part could prevent her from not just breaking his heart, but then burning the pieces and launching the ashes into a black hole. He was one of the smartest people I'd ever met, perhaps the smartest person I'd ever met, and he was still just as fucked over by love as anyone else. There's no accounting for taste, I suppose.

"Go home, Lucas," I told him, shaking my head and wondering what he thought he was going to do. There was no winning her back. Victoria had made her true character and desires abundantly clear more than a year and a half ago. She'd moved out of their shared apartment in the middle of the day when Lucas was working, letting him come home to bare walls, no couch, and a goodbye text message letting him know she was going on tour. At least he got to keep their two cats, Moxie and Bob.

"I guess the tour is over," he was saying, clearly not listening to me. The gears had started turning in his head, it was obvious. He was looking for some way, anyway, to get Victoria back. His scheming knew no bounds. But even for someone as clever and resourceful as Lucas, it was going to be a tall order. Victoria was semi-famous now, and I couldn't imagine that being worshipped by fans had made her humbler and more personable. Her narcissism would have only been fed by it.

"Don't talk to her. Don't look at her. There's no way interacting with her tonight is going to end up making you happy. Go home," I told him, reaching out to poke his shoulder when he didn't react. He jumped in surprise.

"Huh?" His hazel eyes were confused.

"You aren't even listening to me, are you?"

"I don't feel very well." If I didn't know Lucas well enough to know that he wasn't drunk, I would have thought he was trashed. His already pale skin was ghostly white. This woman was an actual plague.

"Well, you look awful. Go home."

"Do you think she missed me while she was on tour?" His voice was hopeful.

No. She was too busy banging groupies and anyone else who

would give her the attention she wanted. I didn't say it. I didn't need to. I'm sure my face said it for me. "Lucas, please go home," I pleaded.

I caught sight of Ward near and waved him over. I needed backup. Ward looked almost as panicked as Lucas. He practically sprinted over, which was something, since his knee had been acting up again and it probably hurt.

"Shit, Lucas," he said apologetically when he got close, "I didn't know we had a last-minute change with the band. I would have warned you. I'm so sorry." His eyes were wide with concern.

"I didn't even know she was back in town," Lucas replied to Ward. He still sounded totally mystified that she was back within striking distance. "I wonder how long she's been here?"

"Too damn long," Ward mumbled. I nodded in agreement. Hopefully there was another tour planned soon.

"I think I'm gonna' go home now," Lucas replied, proving that he hadn't been listening to either of us. He dreamily made his way around us both, casting a final, wistful look at Victoria before making it to the door. I guess he couldn't bear to hear her sing.

"Was he like this after they broke up?" I asked Ward, feeling suddenly guilty that I'd left Ward to deal with Lucas alone. Unexpectedly, Ward shook his head.

"No, not like this. He was just really quiet," he answered. "You know how Lucas is. There's a lot going on under the surface. I mean, I knew it was bad, but I think

the shock of seeing her now brought everything back..."
Ward trailed off. We exchanged a worried look on Lucas'
behalf. If sarcastic Lucas was being sincere and vulnerable,
you knew it was bad.

"I really just don't get it about her," I told Ward, as we
both watched the band begin to play their opening
number. Victoria's alto voice rose above the noise of the
crowd and the instruments, melodic, strong, and powerful.
Her beautiful singing voice wasn't enough to fool me.
Inside she was rotten. Lucas deserved so much better than
Victoria.

"Yeah, me either," Ward agreed. He ran a hand through
his hair in apparent confusion. "But I guess it's true what
they say. We don't get to choose who we love, do we?"

"No. I guess we don't."

His words struck me to the core. Lucas still had it bad
for Victoria and although I sympathized, I also found
myself bizarrely jealous and frustrated. Lucas wasn't hiding
or skulking around when it came to his feelings for Victoria. She might be an awful human being, but he loved her,
and it was definitely no secret. And why should it be?
There's no shame in loving someone. Ward was right,
Lucas didn't choose to love Victoria or to keep loving her—
it just happened.

There was no choice for me either. Kate and I were as
inevitable as the rising sun. So, I nodded at Ward, hoped I
had him fooled, and went looking for his sister.

24

KATE

THE DOOR to the office swung open unexpectedly for the second time in ten minutes and I raised my forehead up from the desk with reluctance. Cole walked in purposefully, leaning the chair against the door to 'lock' it. I'd been about to start leaking tears and I'm sure I looked freaking terrible. He didn't look like he cared.

I think we need to stop seeing each other. I was about to say it, but before I could, he had grasped my shoulders and kissed me. The words dissolved. Doubts dissolved. My need to protect myself dissolved. Meaning dissolved. All I could think about was him. The tears I'd been considering crying vanished along with all my inhibitions.

His tongue sought mine insistently, far more insistently than our other kisses. After an initial, surprised clash of teeth, I yielded to him and he took and took until I was breathless. It was a fierce, I-own-you type of kiss. When we drew apart, panting, my heart was pounding, and I wasn't even thinking about where this would go.

But he was. And what was on his mind was not a mystery. His hands gripped my hips, pulling me up out of the chair and onto the desk like I was weightless. He set me down again, facing him on the desk, and drew my legs apart to scoot me closer to him. His amber eyes never broke their gaze from mine. My heart was hammering in my rib cage. I'd never been with a guy so much taller than me that I could be manhandled in such a way, and I found myself absolutely loving feeling small and delicate by comparison.

"What are you—" I managed to stutter, and then he was kissing me again. Anything that I wanted to say was lost in the promise of his warm arms, soft mouth, and insistent tongue.

"I'm done with slow," he murmured into my mouth. His hands left my hips and found the hem of my skirt. I was wearing a knee-length, black circle skirt and a prim white blouse with a Peter Pan collar. The feeling of his searching fingers on my thighs had me spreading my legs wider in an instant.

"I'm going to fuck you right here, right now," he promised in my ear. "Tell me you want it too."

I kissed him back in answer, but after a moment he pulled back. "Tell me," he insisted, running his fingers up and down my spine until I shivered.

"I want it," I whispered back. I was unable to do anything but admit the truth. With him like this—sexy, confident, and demanding—I didn't have a chance. So much for breaking up. I was now about to let him fuck me right here on the desk.

What are we doing? My brain chimed in belatedly as I felt his erection pressing hot and hard against my cotton panties. My fingers found the buttons on his jeans an instant later. *We're in the bar! I'm supposed to be working. Someone could come looking for me any second...*

"Cole... the door," I moaned, rocking my hips forward against him without conscious thought. The thought of stopping was unbearable. My body was aching.

"It's blocked," he whispered back. His voice was a low, husky rumble against my ear. "It's busy out there. Loud. No one will know." He sounded sure, but I trembled under his touch.

"*Promise?*" I begged, working the button free and running my hands below the hem of his boxers to grip him with two eager hands. He arched into my touch with a low groan. His skin felt like molten silk under my fingers.

"Yes. I promise." The way I was touching his cock, he'd likely promise me anything at that moment, but neither one of us were able to care. This was eight years in the making and it was going to happen right here on Ward's desk. In that moment, I was fine with that. In that moment, I'd have been fine with the floor.

Cole sensed when my body relaxed completely against his, and he buried one of his huge hands in my hair and kissed me. The other hand tugged my panties off with enough roughness that anticipation made me clench deep inside. I was still wearing my skirt, but at some point, my shirt had been unbuttoned and Cole had lost his entirely. I ran my appreciative hands up along the smooth ridges of his abs. His body was perfection.

I leaned back on the desk, both to better admire him and to sort through the sensations of his hands on my body and the pressure where we touched. I felt myself smiling at my own irrational behavior. I'd wanted to protect myself from this? To drive Cole away? Why? All I could think about was getting more of the feeling of him against me.

And Cole looked similarly overwhelmed. He pulled my bra down with eager hands, and his eyes widened at the sight of me spilling free over the folded, satin edge of the demi cups. The look on his face was simple awe. When his hands cupped me, I felt safe, warm, and admired.

He touched me reverently, stooping down to kiss my chest and lavishing attention on one hardened nipple and then the other. I arched under him, soaking in the feeling of being worshipped like this. It felt incredible, but the ache between my legs was starting to become unbearable. I tipped my hips forward again, searching for friction and finding it against his hard body.

But Cole wasn't going to rush this. He'd said that he was done with slow, but that apparently did not apply to foreplay. He left my chest and petted between my legs, learning and exploring me with long, thick fingers. I stared up at the ceiling when he dipped one inside me, rubbing his thumb over my clit as he pumped his forefinger in and out in a slow, teasing rhythm.

At this point, I was in no mood to be teased. I wanted him. Now. I leaned further forward, grasping him and giving him with my hands what he wasn't letting me give him with my pussy. I pumped my hands down his length. He didn't take long to get the hint.

Cole produced a condom out of his pocket and rolled it on, giving me a look that could melt ice from across a crowded room. I leaned into him, gripping his shoulders and yielding openmouthed into the feeling of fullness and possession as he penetrated me. My head tipped back, and he cradled it with one hand, wrapping the other around my waist to draw me closer. I wrapped my legs tightly around his waist.

I wanted this. I needed this. We both did.

We stared into each other's eyes in a slow, shared exhalation once we were fully joined. I'd never felt so impossibly complete, but I still needed more. We moved together gently and then eagerly. Each stroke hit the ache inside me head on, not relieving it, but stoking it higher. I whispered his name instead of screaming it, but it took every iota of my control to stay quiet. The tightness and pressure inside me ratcheted higher and higher. My breathing grew labored and I leaned further back until my back was parallel to the desk.

Desperation took over. I wasn't being quiet anymore.

My control was gone and pleasure was overwhelming my senses.

"Please, Cole," I moaned, much too loudly, and Cole's eyes became huge. He shushed me, but I was having trouble keeping it down. He covered my mouth with his palm and grinned in obvious pride when I still couldn't stop my noises. I was no longer in command of my body's reactions. Having him forcibly keep me quiet to prevent us from being discovered was a dark, exciting thrill. The fear of being found out was more sexy than scary.

Cole pounded into me relentlessly, gripping my hips with his free hand and looking as lost and overwhelmed as I felt. When my climax hit—so sudden and explosive that I worried it rocked the bar's foundations—I saw stars and made a noise so loud that I doubted his heavy hand could muffle it. He came almost immediately after, collapsing on top of me and then pulling us both down onto the floor behind the desk.

25

COLE

THE OFFICE SMELLED LIKE SEX, but it was nothing a little Febreze couldn't fix. The bigger problem was the look that Kate leveled at me when she woke up after her fifteen-minute nap against my chest. She looked disoriented and her blue eyes went from drowsy to alarmed in the time it took to blink them once.

"Oh, my God," she whispered, suddenly becoming aware of her surroundings. "*What the fuck did we just do?*" Her tone had an edge of hysteria, and I wasn't sure if it was joy, fear, or shock that had a monopoly on her expression.

I arched an eyebrow at her and grinned. I was not about to let her spoil the afterglow with doubt or unhappiness. "Was I really so forgettable? Gosh, you know, that hurts my pride." I wasn't even willing to entertain the idea that she hadn't enjoyed herself. She could lie to herself, but her body couldn't lie to me. Those noises had definitely not been faked, and she'd clenched so tight around my cock when she came that I'd been pulled overboard right with her.

But none of that seemed to matter to her now. Kate got to her feet and righted her clothing in a hurry before looking down at me and pointing with wide eyes. I followed her gaze and shrugged.

I still wasn't wearing pants. No one had knocked on the door in all this time, so I saw no reason. Pants were over-rated in general. Plus, I didn't want to wake up Kate. She'd conked out almost as soon as we finished. I'd always heard that was what the man did after sex, not the woman. I'd never seen a woman do it before, but I found it absolutely adorable. She just switched off like a little light. Apparently, she could switch back on just as quickly. Reluctantly, I got up and dressed.

"Are you okay?" I asked Kate, reaching out to touch her hand and feeling better when she came and leaned against me affectionately. She was hot and cold tonight, but she was so, so worth it.

"I was going to dump you when you came in," she told me. Her voice was muffled against my chest. She looked up at me sheepishly.

"I really hope I fucked that terrible idea right out of you." That comment earned me a rare blush and a little giggle, both of which pleased my ego. Her grin, however, didn't last.

"I'm scared," she said softly, "and I just think you

should know. This could all go so horribly wrong." She'd buried her face back into my chest, but her body trembled slightly against mine. I wrapped my arms tighter around her.

"It's not going to go wrong," I told her, squeezing her as if I could make her believe it through hug strength alone. Kate might have her doubts, but I'd never been more sure of anything in my entire life than I was about her. This was meant to be. It maybe would have been six years ago if I just hadn't been an idiot.

"I really want to believe you," she whispered. There was still distrust in her eyes, but it was mixed with more optimism than before.

"I'm telling you the truth." The fact that she still doubted me hurt, but I knew I deserved it. I was damn lucky she'd given us any kind of second chance, even if it was a halfhearted one.

"You don't think anyone heard us, do you?" Kate asked, pulling away and pressing her ear flush against the door

"I really don't think so." I also really didn't care, but that would *definitely not* have been the correct thing to say. Still, even from where I was standing, the music of the live band in the main room was loud enough to vibrate in my sternum. Despite her enthusiastic vocalizations, it would take some superhuman hearing to have overheard us unless someone was standing right outside.

Kate looked at the door with a worried little line between her eyebrows, but nodded solemnly after a moment, apparently accepting that I was correct. "I had better get back out there," she eventually said. "I don't want anyone to come looking for me." She pulled the chair away from the door and was going for the handle when I pulled her back into my arms.

"Who would know if you just disappeared for a little while more?" I asked, kissing her again because I could, and because her plump, cherry colored lips were irresistible. She let me have a few seconds of her, enough to make me hard again. "Couldn't we just... go?" I'd go anywhere with her. Anywhere we could be alone would do.

She shook her head wistfully. "I wish we could, but I do actually work here you know. *I have to get back to work.*"

I sighed heavily in defeat. I knew when I was beat. Kate was too stubborn to convince, and although my cock disagreed, I knew trying to get her to bail on her job was neither nice nor cool. "You might want to brush your hair at least," I suggested, running one hand over her poufy locks. "Although the thoroughly just-fucked look really does suit you."

Kate rounded the desk and pulled her compact out, grimaced at her reflection, and then went to work with a comb. "You did this," she grumbled. "My hair looked nice before."

"*We* did this," I countered, coming up behind her and swatting her round, lovely rear end playfully. "And I really do think it looks nice that way."

She rolled her eyes. "You have no idea how long it takes to set pin curls in my hair."

"I know about how long it takes to destroy them now, though."

"You're way too happy about nearly getting me fired." Her attempt to look stern was weak. She was happy. Even if she hadn't been smiling from ear to ear, I could hear it in her voice and see it in every single movement she made. Just like me, she'd needed what we just did.

"Please. Ward wouldn't fire you over a little coffee-break sex in the office. Although he might murder me..." The thought of Ward was unwelcome, although Kate just rolled her eyes again. She was just full of sass tonight. "Can we tell him we're dating now?" I asked hopefully.

Her expression froze. "No."

"But—" I started to argue, going mute when a knock at the door caused us both to freeze.

Emma poked her head in. "Oh!" she exclaimed when she saw us both standing there with guilty looks on our faces. Her eyes narrowed knowingly, her little upturned nose twitched, and her smile was smug. "I'm sorry to interrupt. I just wanted to tell Kate that Ward and I are going to call it a night early because we're driving up early tomorrow. Bye!" Her words came out as one continuous rush. She slammed the door shut again as soon as she finished talking.

"Great," Kate said sarcastically, slumping down into the desk chair. "Well, now Emma knows."

I shrugged. I didn't see that as a bad thing at all. "So, does that mean we can tell Ward now?"

Kate looked at me like I'd grown two heads. "Why do you want him to know so badly?"

"Because he's my friend and I don't like lying to him." That much was true, of course, but it wasn't just that. "And because I want the whole world to know. I'm happy to be with you. I want to shout it from the rooftops. I hate skulking around like we've got some dirty secret."

A tiny smile tugged the corners of Kate's lips upwards. She nodded. "Okay. You win. I'll tell him, okay? Just let me do it my way."

Victory coursed through me. *Finally.* "When will you tell him?"

She thought about it for a moment. "Next Sunday."

More than an entire week from now? That seemed like a truly ridiculous amount of time to wait. I tried not to pout. "Why not tomorrow?"

Kate smirked at me. She shook her head at me like I was unreasonable. "Because Ward and Emma aren't going to be here tomorrow or for the rest of the week. They're going to visit my mom in Plano."

I bit back a sigh. "I guess that's okay then." I could wait a week. If I tried really hard.

Kate threw her purse back in the file cabinet she'd fished it out of, locked it, and laughed at me. "You're so impatient," she teased. I could tell she liked it though.

I'd waited years for this. Of course, I was impatient. "I just want everyone to know how hot my new girlfriend is," I told her. The g-word produced a wide-eyed, openmouthed expression on her face. She hid it a moment later behind a smug smile.

"I never said I'd be your girlfriend."

I paused, suddenly confused until I realized I'd forgotten to ask. "Oh. Will you be my girlfriend?"

She nodded, unexpectedly shy again. Only Kate could go from bold sex goddess to shy retiring flower and back again. She was a kaleidoscope of emotion, and I wanted to see every pattern, design, and configuration of her feelings, even if they were infinite. Especially if they were infinite. She was like a puzzle I'd never solve, but also never tire of.

I knew there was still doubt in Kate's mind about me. I knew that I should have told her about the pictures that Eddie had. I knew I should have told her that I'd been in love with her for years. But I was still afraid of blowing it, and I figured if I could just keep her interested in me a little longer, the time for total honesty would come soon enough.

26

COLE

My new realtor, Jolene Fairway, reminded me of my third-grade teacher, Mrs. Lockhart. Just like Mrs. Lockhart, Jolene was in that ambiguous range between forty-five and sixty where attempting to guess a number was asking for a slap. Just like Mrs. Lockhart, Jolene had that platinum blonde chin-length bob that used to be so popular among newscasters. And just like Mrs. Lockhart, Jolene wore sweater sets in pastel colors and sensible shoes. Thankfully, unlike Mrs. Lockhart, Jolene actually seemed to like me and had not yet suggested that I might be hyperactive (I was just a nine-year-old boy!).

"Oh, we'll find you something, sweetheart," she told me at our first meeting. "It's not going to be easy, but nothing worth having ever is." She'd looked at my budget, patted my arm excitedly, and sent me back to my hotel room with homework.

A few days later, Kate and I met her at the first property she'd lined up for me to visit. We'd met at a local coffee shop to game plan the tours, and when Jolene laid eyes on Kate and learned she was my girlfriend, she'd thrown out the entire plan and swore she knew exactly where to start.

"Damn!" Kate said as we drove up in her little Honda SUV. I could tell she really meant it because she let her accent turn it into a multi-syllable word: 'day-um.' I couldn't disagree with her assessment.

The three-story home in a fancy downtown neighborhood was buried behind a tall wrought iron gate that required a code before swinging open. Up the long drive, a stately red brick house looked more like something that would perch atop a hillside in New England than in Austin, Texas.

"Hey y'all!" Jolene said from the door, waving cheerfully as we walked up the manicured lawn. "I'm glad you two found it. Quite the place, isn't it?"

We both nodded in silent shock. The place was positively enormous. This was not what I wanted at all or had ever expressed an interest in. What would I do with a house this big?

"This house is five bedrooms, five bathrooms, four and a half thousand square feet. There's an attached garage apartment for a mother-in-law or nanny. It's got a lovely pool area too. It's been fully redone by the current owners and I think you'll be very pleased with the finish out. It would be a perfect home to raise a family. There are great schools in this neighborhood." She looked at Kate significantly. When neither of us could manage a word, she continued, "Well, go take a look around and I'll be down here if you have any questions." Her confident footfalls echoed off the marble as she went to go sit on the porch.

Kate and I stared at each other in the formal, extremely fancy entryway after Jolene disappeared. Kate laughed first, and I was quick to join her. This was just too ridiculous and too awkward not to laugh over it.

"Do I look pregnant with quadruplets in this dress or something?" she asked me, rubbing her flat stomach area and turning sideways to look at herself in a huge gilded mirror that hung on the wall.

"*You do not look pregnant,*" I reassured her, kissing her on the forehead before grabbing her hand and pulling her away from the mirror. "Come on, let's at least look at this place. Obviously, I'm not going to buy a damn mansion, but we're already here. It'll be fun."

She smiled back at me. "Okay. It'll be like House Hunters."

"Is that a game?" I asked.

She shook her head. "Not a game. It's a reality TV show. Picky couples look at houses and bitch about dumb, rich person things. Then they pick one."

I didn't understand. That sounded no more enjoyable than watching someone shop for groceries. Then again, football had occupied so much of my time in the past few years that I'd missed a number of popular cultural developments. My perspective was off. Still... "People just watch other people looking at houses for fun?" Kate nodded enthusiastically. I shrugged, still confused, but happy to play along.

Kate grinned and dragged me into the formal living room. "This is where you would serve the Queen tea when she comes by."

"Yeah, I do that a lot." This was wasted space as far as I could tell. The room was empty because the house was vacant, but formal living rooms were meant to be full of uncomfortable, stuffy-looking furniture. "Me and Lizzie are best friends, you know. She even named a corgi after me."

The first floor spread on and on. There was even a butler's pantry and a dumbwaiter to the second floor. *What the hell even is a butler's pantry?*

"Obviously you were kidding about the Queen, but who's the most famous person you ever met while playing football?" Kate asked as we strolled through room after unnecessary room.

I didn't have to think about it long. "I met Prince on an airplane once. And yes, he was wearing purple." From head to toe, no less. He pulled it off, too.

Kate looked appropriately impressed. "Prince? No way!"

"It's true. He had no idea who I was—I'm not sure he was a big football fan—but it was still really cool. He's so tiny though! I mean, he never looked huge in pictures or anything, but he was literally about Emma's size." I gestured to about waist height.

Kate looked wistful. "Prince was a national treasure. And living proof that it isn't all about size."

"That might be true," I agreed, drawing Kate closer as we climbed up the first set of stairs to look at the bedrooms. We paused in front of the gilded double doors leading to a truly opulent and enormous master bedroom. "But I think we can both agree that size is still very important."

Kate smirked at me and 'accidentally' bumped her round ass against my crotch when she paused to admire the bedroom's trayed ceilings. I was hard in an instant. God, the ass on her. It was obscenely perfect.

"You know it isn't polite to brag about your, um, generous endowment," she said.

I blinked innocently and gestured to the room. "What's that? I was referring to the bedroom."

Her little smirk grew into a full-blown, knowing smile. "So was I."

"You're a very naughty girl to talk like that," I whispered in her ear, enjoying her subsequent shiver far too much. We wandered into the master bathroom to find an enormous, couples-sized whirlpool tub. Kate proved me right by arching an eyebrow at me and pouting her full, pink lips.

"Do you think Jolene would be mad if we tested this thing out?" she asked. Her voice was a dirty whisper and I couldn't resist pulling her closer. Her soft, teasing lips were sweet torture. I could think of a thousand things that I would like to do to her in that tub. None of them would result in her getting any cleaner—my ideas were universally filthy. Downstairs, I heard a door open and close with a slam. Kate pulled away from me in surprise, breaking the spell. Jolene must have gotten tired of waiting for us on the porch.

Damn. I wish we were alone.

"She probably wouldn't like it very much at all," I admitted in disappointment, thinking I must have some kind of curse when it came to timing, "and while this house is clearly not for me, a hot tub is definitely going on my must-have list."

Kate smiled, but the awful, persistent doubt was back in her eyes. No matter what I said or did, no matter how serious I was about wanting a future with her, I couldn't seem to banish her fear that I was leading her on. I could only pray that she would still be around by the time I got that hot tub.

27

KATE

AFTER COLE'S lukewarm response to the gigantic, fancy mansion, poor Jolene reverted to her original plan. Her dream of an easy sale was visibly crushed, although her professional smile never wavered an inch. She assured Cole that there were loads of other options in his budget. The next property was in a modern condo tower downtown that looked much more like some place I could imagine Cole living. The lobby was incredibly sleek and futuristic looking.

"This is a really nice building," I told him as we ascended up (and up and up) to the fiftieth floor. My voice sounded high and scared in my own ears. Cole looked over at me with a concerned look on his face.

"Oh, it's a wonderful building," Jolene immediately added, producing a brochure from her big, pink, Prada tote bag and reading, "absolutely brand new, too. There are all the ordinary amenities here, of course: gym, pool, laundry, business center, rooftop deck. But they have some exceptional ones as well, including a full-service concierge, spa, and onsite massage therapist."

I'm sure I looked properly impressed under my newfound vertigo. My condo definitely didn't have any of those, not even the 'ordinary ones.' Cole merely shrugged. I supposed this sort of luxury was normal to him. I wasn't just out of my comfort zone because the building was fancy, though. The height—and the tiny elevator—were making me feel somewhat dizzy. I tried not to look out the window. It was a long way down.

The elevator door dinged when we finally arrived on the fiftieth floor, and I thought it sounded relieved. I knew I was relieved to be out of the small space. It was making me feel claustrophobic.

"You hate this already, don't you?" Cole whispered in my ear as we walked down the corridor. He looked worried. "Are you okay? You look pale."

I shook my head. "No, no, it's fine," I lied. "I'm fine. I think I'm just hungry or something." I smiled reassuringly at him and grabbed his hand to pull him forward.

He frowned, clearly unconvinced by my act. But then Jolene was talking at us again about the unit we were about to see and unlocking the door. We stepped inside to reveal a beautiful, furnished loft. It had tall ceilings, lovely wide-plank hardwood floors, and the most beautiful, open kitchen I'd ever seen in real life. Unfortunately, it also had an enormous wraparound balcony.

"Obviously the view is the big selling point," Jolene explained, pulling open the enormous glass doors to let the midmorning breeze in. "It has beautiful northeastern exposure, which means no hot afternoon sun."

Cole started toward the balcony while holding my hand, and I froze. There was no way I was going out on that flimsy little ledge. Rationally I could see that it was six feet wide and made of concrete and steel, but the frightened reptile me that lived in my brainstem wasn't buying it. Lizard-Kate didn't want to see the view. Lizard-Kate wanted to crawl down under a rock somewhere nice and safe. Somewhere at ground level or below.

"Oh, and you have to see the incredible double shower," Jolene was telling Cole excitedly. "It has unbelievable views."

"I'm sorry," Cole interrupted. He shot another look at me and shook his head. "This place just isn't going to work for me."

She froze mid sales pitch. "Really? You don't like it?"

I could feel panic rising in my throat. I'd never had a panic attack before, but I would bet that it felt something like this. Just exactly like this. My breathing had sped up like I was running a 5K, I was starting to sweat but somehow also freezing cold, and my vision was fading into a dark, narrow tunnel. If I didn't get out of there soon, I was going to fall on the ground and then melt down. I had maybe sixty seconds of coherence left.

"The unit itself is fine," Cole said, rushing through his words as he saw me deteriorating before his eyes. "I actually like it quite a bit, and the building seems great. But I don't want to live somewhere up this high. Are there any units on the second or third floor available?"

My condo was on the third floor. I could handle the third floor. I missed the third floor. I shifted uncomfortably on the polished wood floors I stood on and thought about how the many identical floors below me must look. All forty-nine of them probably had the same ash colored flooring. It was just layers and layers of ash colored flooring *all the way down*. The thought made me feel even more ill.

"I think I want to go sit down in the lobby," I heard myself saying. My feet were already carrying me toward the door. Jolene caught onto my distress at last. Her blue eyes widened, and she gasped, literally clutching at her pearls when she realized how uncomfortable I was.

"Oh, dear! The height is bothering you, isn't it sweetheart?" Jolene said comfortingly, pulling the doors to the patio shut and covering them with the electric window coverings. I felt instantly better. "Come on, let's get you out of here." She grabbed my elbow and maneuvered me out of the unit efficiently. Cole grabbed my other elbow and they urgently propelled me toward the elevator. Cole looked terrified for me. Jolene probably just didn't want me throwing up. The look on her face gave me the distinct impression that she'd seen clients have similar reactions before.

As we descended down the long elevator ride, I heard myself apologizing uselessly. "I'm really, really sorry. I've never had any issue with heights before." In fact, I'd flown on airplanes just fine. They didn't even scare me. But I'd never been up in a building this tall before, and apparently it had a completely different effect.

"Don't feel badly for one second, Kate," Jolene told me. Her constant talking was surprisingly comforting. "It can and does happen to anyone. Sometimes vertigo can come out of nowhere, you just never know. And if it is the height, you definitely aren't the first person to dislike high places. I've seen it many times with my clients. At least you aren't the type that gets nosebleeds or nausea."

"I guess bungee jumping is probably out for you too, huh?" Cole said, hugging my back to his front so I couldn't turn and see the city growing larger out the elevator's wide glass window. He kissed the back of my neck and held me the whole way. I shut my eyes tight and happily sank into his warmth and strength. We'd be down on the ground soon.

"Yeah, I don't think I want to do that," I agreed, still squeezing my eyes shut. "I think I'll just keep my feet on terra firma from now on."

I hated being the damsel in distress, but if anyone was cut out to play my heroic Prince Charming, it was Cole. Once we made it to the lobby, he scooped me up and carried me over to the adjacent Starbucks, bought me some tea and a cookie, and cuddled me until I felt better.

Ordinarily I would have fought tooth and nail not to be coddled, but I liked being doted on by Cole, and it was obvious that he wanted to take care of me. No man had ever wanted to do that before, at least, not sincerely. Not because they just cared. It frightened me how much I craved his comfort and affection, because the thought of somehow losing it—losing him—was a million times scarier than the fiftieth floor had been.

28

KATE

WE SAT in the Starbucks for a long time. Long enough for my tea to go cold. I didn't notice the passage of time until I looked around and realized it was now midafternoon instead of midmorning. I blinked in shock at my surroundings, only noticing most of the details for the first time.

"What happened to Jolene?" I asked Cole when I was nibbling on my second cookie and starting to feel normal again. "Did she leave or something?"

He'd been petting my neck and shoulders with his fingertips and paused in surprise. "Didn't you hear us talking in the elevator? We rescheduled the other showings for next weekend." His voice was very gentle, like he was trying to avoid frightening me more.

I shook my head. "Oh. Sorry. I was really pretty out of it." *For hours.*

Cole kissed my forehead. His amber-colored eyes were

huge and frightened. "I was so worried about you. I really, really didn't like that." He gripped my shoulders in his hands and stared into my eyes. "Are you alright now?"

I nodded. "Yeah, I think so. I've never experienced anything like that before." I was really embarrassed by the whole thing, honestly. "I guess I've learned something new about myself today. I don't like tall buildings. I am officially not a fan of skyscrapers." Not liking them was an understatement, but I didn't know what else to say.

Cole seemed incredibly relieved that I was returning to my regular personality and humor. His exhale sounded like a weight had been lifted and his smile was bright.

"You know," he mused, "Lucas told me that phobias are the result of traumatic experiences in childhood. Did you ever have something scary happen to you that involved heights?"

"You mean like Ward dropping me when I was little?" I smirked.

He flashed his white teeth at me. "I wasn't going to go straight to that, but sure. That seems like something he might do."

I searched my memory for anything that might qualify but didn't remember anything particularly scary happening to me when I was up high. I grew up in Plano, one of the flattest, most horizontally spread out places on Earth. It wasn't exactly an urban environment. "I don't think anything like that happened. Although maybe it was so terrifying that I've repressed it? We would probably need a real psychologist to help us with this. Not Lucas."

Cole's smirk became a bittersweet smile. "He enjoys psychoanalyzing people a bit too much. It's ironic really, because he doesn't really talk about his own feelings or seem to be terribly in touch with them. Last night was proof of that."

"Oh no. Did he run into Victoria last night?" I asked curiously. I figured he'd gone home well before she showed up.

Cole nodded. "Yeah, and it was brutal. The poor guy is still half crazy over her."

"Hey, I took Psychology 101. Maybe we just need to *condition* him," I suggested. "Like we show him a picture of Victoria and then shock him with a cattle prod or something over and over. That way he learns to associate her with something unpleasant and negative. In class I saw this one super messed up experiment with a baby and a rat, and it totally worked. Every time the kid saw the rat, the scientists would make a big, scary noise. The kid went from liking rats to being terrified of rats. It was really horrible actually."

"I think she did something unpleasant and negative to him already," Cole replied. His voice was dry, and I could tell he had no love for Victoria.

I'd heard the story from Ward and couldn't disagree. She had been pretty heartless. "That man needs a rebound. Or maybe a shrink. Maybe both."

"I'll suggest your cattle prod idea to him," Cole told me with a wry smile. "He might go for it."

"It would probably just result in a fear of cattle prods."

"Or pictures."

"You know, I think my DNA actually said I would be afraid of heights," I remembered.

Cole's surprise was obvious. "Wait, what?"

I giggled. It did sound a bit insane. "I did one of those DNA kits they advertise on TV. You know, the ones that tell you where you're from?"

"Oh sure," he said. "They tell you what you're likely to fear? That's in your DNA?"

"They tell you all kinds of weird stuff other than your ethnic origins. Mine told me I have a higher than average chance of being afraid of heights. I mean, they can't tell you for sure about very much, but they give you probabilities." It was all science I didn't really understand.

Cole looked mystified. "But they can tell you that by looking at your DNA?"

I shrugged. "I guess so."

"That's amazing!" His expression turned somewhat embarrassed. "My mom bought me one of those tests for Christmas and I still haven't done it."

"Why not?" I'd always been curious about my own origins. My dad hadn't been around in years, and his extended family had disowned us years ago. I just wanted to know where they came from. Ireland, as it turns out. My genetic results were a whopping ninety-three percent English and Irish. The other seven percent were so broadly distributed that they fell within the margin of error. I was basically an Irish peasant. It was no wonder I loved potatoes so much. Or whiskey. "Don't you want to know where you come from?" I asked.

Cole's embarrassment deepened. "I feel too guilty."

"Guilty?" I didn't understand.

Cole dragged a hand through his hair in what looked like chagrin. "Guilty," he repeated after a moment. His tone was hesitant. "I feel like I shouldn't look into my genetic origins. I don't want my mom to be sad or think that I don't feel like she's my real mom."

"But she gave you the test as a gift," I ventured. "Doesn't she want you to use it?"

"I know, but what if I tell her that I looked into my genetics and then get really into my 'real identity' and then make her feel like I don't think of myself as her son anymore?" He looked genuinely unsure of what to do. "I'm curious but it feels like I'm betraying her even to admit it."

"I'm sure she wouldn't give you the test unless she knew all that," I told him. It made sense that Cole would be conflicted when I thought about it. He wanted his mom to know that he still thought of her as his family, not whatever the genetic tests showed. "I'm sure she knows that you see her as your mom."

"She is my mom." His tone was defensive. I got the feeling I was treading on delicate ground. This wasn't really a conversation I knew how to have.

"Sorry. That's what I meant," I said carefully. I didn't want to upset him. "I just can't imagine any not-crazy mom giving her kid a gift that was really some sort of loyalty test. Even unintentionally. She probably just wants you to know your background for health reasons."

He nodded. "You're right. Sorry I'm weird about this," he said after a moment. "Being adopted comes with all kinds of strange, unhealthy complexes and insecurities." His admission diffused the tension between us.

I shrugged. "Don't worry. I'm weird about all sorts of things," I told him. "Like heights and feeling inadequate. We all have our issues, right? Lucas' is Victoria. Ward's is abandonment."

"Inadequate?" Cole asked. I instantly regretted admitting it. I toyed with my cup of cold tea, not answering. Maybe if I pretended to be fascinated with the paper cup, he would move on? When I looked back up at him a moment later, he was still staring at me intently. I sighed. No such luck.

"Yeah. Maybe inadequate isn't the right word, but it's always been Ward who was the talented one in our family. Not that our mom, you know, loves me less or anything. That's not what I mean. I guess I just struggle with feeling like the extra kid." I shrugged and stared off in the middle distance before continuing. "I mean, before I was born, our dad was still around. Who knows what would have happened if I'd never been born? Maybe everything would have been different for our family? Maybe things could have been better?"

I didn't mention the fact that not being good enough for Cole in college had also taken a huge chunk out of my self-esteem, leading me on a year-long journey of self-destruction and depression. He didn't need to know about that. I'm not sure I'd ever be ready to tell him.

Cole was silent when I stopped talking. He looked at me with a feeling that I couldn't imagine being anything but pity. It irritated me. The irritation was a familiar, welcome change.

"Don't," I told him sharply, and he blinked in surprise.

"Don't what?" He asked.

"Whatever pity you're feeling for me, just don't."

"I wasn't—" he began.

"Yeah, you were." I'd seen plenty of pity in my life. I didn't want it from him.

His eyes turned sheepish. "Sorry. I just think you've got it all wrong. I think you were probably the glue that held your family together. You're the one that saved Ward from himself by preventing the bar from going bankrupt. Ward was talented, sure, but he was also lucky. You're the one with the head for business. When everything was really at risk, you caught the hail Mary pass."

I chuckled at the idea. It was mostly wrong, but I liked it anyway.

"You're a good person," I told him, leaning forward to

lay my cheek against his shoulder. "I'm lucky to have you as my friend."

He brushed my hair back from my forehead and kissed me. "I'm more than just your friend."

I kissed him back, finally feeling better. "Yeah. That too."

I wanted to believe him. He said so many things that I desperately wanted to believe, but this was on a whole different level. I didn't admit my insecurities easily. I hardly did it at all. I wouldn't have done so now except that my panic attack in the condo tower had stripped off a bit of my emotional armor. The more time I spent around Cole, the more of myself I wanted to show him. But even though I adored him, even though I was starting to trust him, I knew there was a risk. Cole might not like what he saw.

29

KATE

THAT EVENING and all the following day I had to cover both Ward's and my shifts at the bar, but I invited Cole over for dinner the next night. I even cooked a meal for us. He arrived right on time, with a bottle of wine in one hand and more flowers in the other. Roses this time. They were lovely.

"This looks great," he told me when we sat down. I smiled nervously.

"I'm not exactly the world's greatest cook," I told him. "If you hate it, we can order pizza or something."

I'd made one of the few dishes that I knew how to prepare, could use a crock pot with, and thought was date-worthy: pot roast. It wasn't exactly fancy, but it was whole-some and good. As a bonus, it made the whole house smell good.

"I'm sure it's going to be great," Cole told me, happily

digging into his food. He was such a big guy, I was glad I'd bought almost three times as much meat as I would if I was cooking just for myself. Feeding Ward had always been a challenge for my mom—he was *always* hungry—so I'd learned to simply take what I thought was a reasonable portion and triple it. It seemed to work well.

"How do you like the dealership world so far?" I asked between bites. I'd nailed this pot roast. It was really tasty. I'd never been so relieved.

Cole smiled but his eyes looked somewhat panicked. "I like it, but I'm overwhelmed," he told me. "I'm glad I've got good general managers in place, but there's a lot for me to learn." He smirked. "In hindsight, I should have tried a bit harder in my business classes."

"You didn't have time," I replied, and he nodded. Ward and Cole were on the road almost constantly during football season, and then any remaining time was just as busy when they were training.

"That's true. I'm just going to be playing catch-up for the next year or so as I figure out what I'm supposed to be doing."

"You'll get the hang of it." I didn't have any doubt about Cole's abilities. He was loads smarter than Ward, and even he had caught on to business ownership eventually. It couldn't be that hard.

"I hope so," Cole said, smiling at me with a vague look that I interpreted as a mixture of exhaustion and excitement. "At least it's keeping me busy."

"Well, if that changes, you're always welcome to pull a shift or two at the bar," I offered with a wink. "I know the manager. I can hook you up."

"If I go bankrupt, I'll be taking you up on that offer." His tone was wry.

"Did you get my roadster yet?" I teased.

"You mean *my coupe*?"

I rolled my eyes. He grinned back at me.

We'd fallen into this relationship so quickly, and so perfectly, I could barely believe it. It was almost like we had been made for one another. His easy humor seemed to be a perfect match for my teasing sarcasm. His open optimism balanced my natural negativity. And maybe I offered him some perspective and honesty about the world that he never developed in his otherwise privileged life.

"I sent my testing kit back," Cole told me as we were washing the dishes together.

"That's great!" I was glad to see that he'd decided to figure out where he was from.

"Where in the world do you think your family is from?" I asked.

Cole shrugged. "Apparently I was born in the US," he told me. "In Michigan. My mom said she had a closed adoption through a private charity, so there's no real way to find out any information. I'm hoping that I'm part Samoan."

I smirked. "Samoan?" I'd never thought of that.

"Yeah, you know, like The Rock."

"Do you just want to be related to The Rock?" I teased.

He grinned. "He's a talented guy. And he has superior genetics." I couldn't disagree with that.

I squinted and turned my head to the side, searching Cole's features for similarities. "I guess I could see it, a little bit." It seemed like a bit of a stretch, but I didn't want to disappoint him. "Maybe?"

"What do you think I'll find out?" he asked.

I shrugged. I honestly had no idea. The amount of time I'd spent thinking about Cole's beautiful, symmetrical features was possibly unhealthy, but I truly had no idea where he was from. I didn't really care, either, except that I wouldn't mind going there and admiring the people.

"I hope you find out that you have a decreased risk of all the bad diseases," I finally told him. "That's the most important thing."

He nodded. "I'm nervous about that," he admitted. "I don't need to find out I have any genetic predisposition to Parkinson's disease or Alzheimer's diseases or anything like that. I've already had enough damage to my brain to spike my chances of having issues later in life."

"At least you retired before it could get any worse," I told him. I touched his arm in an attempt to comfort him. "Just think, ten years ago, no one really understood the risks."

"You're right." He shook his head in disbelief. "You know," he added, "if I had a kid in high school today, I'm not sure I would even let them play football."

"Really?" Even though there were real dangers associated with the sport, I couldn't imagine not letting a kid play. "Even if it was their dream?"

He sighed. "I don't know. It's a hard question. When I was sixteen there was nothing on earth that I wanted more than to play football in the NFL. I'm not sure I would have let anything stop me."

When I was sixteen, there was nothing on earth that I wanted more than you. I didn't say it. It would have probably just made him think that I was a crazy person. But here he was, in my condo, washing out my wine glasses. Patience had never been a virtue that I possessed, but somehow it seemed to have paid off in this case.

"Nothing did stop you." My voice sounded proud, even to my own ears. Cole smiled at me, but then his smile faltered. Something was going on in his mind, but he wasn't sharing it.

"What?" I asked, taking a step closer and pulling his hands around my waist. "What are you thinking about?"

He blinked. "You."

"What about me?" I didn't understand why he was frowning all of a sudden. But then he was kissing me, and I forgot my question entirely. There was only Cole and me, in my kitchen. The rest of the world could be burning to the ground, foreign armies could be invading, or it could be raining frogs, and I wouldn't care. As long as he kept on kissing me, everything was perfect in here.

30

COLE

SIX YEARS AGO...

After the disastrously bad date that I took Kate on, I avoided Ward for almost a week. It wasn't an easy thing to do. We lived together, trained together, and played together. The fact that I managed to avoid being in the same room with him in all that time was an achievement. One that backfired massively. Eventually he cornered me in our apartment. He closed the door to my room behind him and looked me square in the eye. Every muscle in my body tensed up.

"I know what you did," he said. His voice was serious, and his expression gave nothing away.

My heart was hammering in my ribs in a way that would probably kill poor Lucas if he got this worked up. Ward was actually going to murder me. Right here. Right now. This moment was the end of my life. There was a text-book in his hand, and he was probably going to bludgeon me to death with it. The coroner's report would say that I had my brains bashed in with an algebra textbook. What a humiliating way to die. *Death by math.* I hoped they didn't put that on my tombstone.

"I, uh..." There was really nothing to say. I might as well accept my fate. If he knew, there was no escape. "I'm sorry."

Ward sat down in the chair across from me. "You did the right thing."

I swallowed hard. What was happening? My fear was mixing with my confusion in a way that made me feel light-headed, weak, and unreal. I still wasn't able to speak, so Ward continued. I struggled to keep up with him.

"Kate's really upset," he told me. "It's for the best, though."

"How—" I stuttered, and Ward cut me off with a gesture.

"Lucas sold you out, obviously. He was worried that you couldn't keep a secret, so he told me himself. But I'd already figured it out by then anyway. Hell, I figured it out before either of you did." He smirked at me like I should find this as funny as he clearly did.

Ward had a bad habit of making his intelligence known at the most inconvenient times. It was great in football and terrible in person. He really was quite brilliant when it came to strategy. That's what made him such a good quar-terback.

"S-sorry?"

Ward's smirk turned into a full grin. "Did you really think I didn't know what was going on with you and Lucas? That you two could skulk around with your little top-secret plan and I wouldn't catch on?"

I made a noise that was not a word, but sounded vaguely like a denial, and Ward laughed at me. Being laughed at should have made me annoyed, but in that moment, anything that wasn't a beat down felt like a victory.

"Dude, I'm not mad at you!" He shook his head at me like I was a total moron. "Stop acting like I'm about to jump you with a tire iron again."

"You aren't?" I still wasn't sure I believed him. This could all be some sort of a trick to make me incriminate myself.

"No!" He laughed again. "I couldn't have planned that better myself. You did the right thing."

"I did?" My voice was an octave higher than usual and it broke halfway through. It was like I'd become fourteen again.

"Yeah." Ward sat back in his chair and regarded me with a look that did *seem to be* approving. "I'm glad you ran Kate off like that. She needs to focus on her school work, not chasing football players." He rolled his blue eyes at me. "I know my sister pretty well, you know, and not just because I read her diary once. She's had a huge crush on you *for years*. Ever since you gave her those daisies when you apologized for the glitter. She's convinced herself that she's in love with you."

Kate was *in love* with me? My heart hurt. I didn't deserve to be in the same room with her.

Ward couldn't contain his laughter. "*I know, right?*" He seemed to think the idea was simply hilarious. "She's just a kid though. Don't hold it against her."

"I don't think she likes me anymore," I managed to say. At least I could be honest about that.

"Well, that was the point, wasn't it?" He arched an eyebrow at me.

"Yeah. That was the point."

"So why do you still look guilty then?"

Because I want her. I want her so badly that I can't think of anything else. I think about her from the second I wake up until the moment I fall asleep, and then I dream about her all night long.

"I don't know," I lied.

"Lucas said you would be weird about this," Ward told me. He was still smiling. "I guess I didn't realize just how weird that could be." He was still smiling, clearly thinking I was still afraid. I wasn't. Fear had given way to a guilt so powerful that I wanted to crawl under a rock and die.

"Look," Ward was saying as he rose and turned to go. "Don't worry about Kate. She's tough. She'll be fine. She's going to mope around for a week or so and then she'll probably hate you forever, but she'll move on."

The thought made me want to throw up. Ward grinned and shut the door behind him, pleased as punch. I wished that he had just beaten me up. It would have been kinder than telling me the truth.

She loved me.

31

COLE

I held Kate in my arms and kissed her, wondering if anyone had ever been as lucky as me in the history of humanity. I was the living pinnacle of human luck. And I was fairly certain that I was about to get even luckier.

Kate's light blue dress was soft under my hands. It hugged her curvy figure, tightly around her perky chest to her narrow waist, and then flaring out again at her full hips. As pretty as the dress was, I was very ready to see what was underneath. I lifted the hem of Kate's skirt brazenly, running my fingers up along the back of her silky soft thighs to her round, perfect ass. She shivered up against me as I did, spreading her legs apart to grant me access and leaning into my chest. Her little sigh of satisfaction was sweet, but not as sweet as when I gave her plump ass a good squeeze. Her body was pure perfection.

"Can I see the rest of your house?" I asked her, kissing her plump lips again, and feeling them curve up into a smile against my own.

"You mean, the bedroom?" Kate asked me. Her voice had transformed into that low, sexy whisper that made me ache for her.

"We can start there, sure." I had every intention of having her in every room of her house. On every surface of her house. Up against every wall, on every floor. Against the doors, the windows. Everywhere. Hell, I'd fuck her on the ceiling if we could figure that out. But we could start with the bed. That was fine with me.

Kate's small bedroom was painted a brilliant eggplant purple, and everything inside it was ivory and white. The lamp in the corner washed everything with a warm glow. The room was neat, stylish, and lovely, but I didn't have the energy or capacity to appreciate it at the moment. The only thing I could think about was getting Kate out of her little blue dress.

She worked down the hidden zipper underneath her left arm, shrugging out of her dress and sending it down to pool around her feet. Underneath, she wore a tight, sexy bustier with laces in the back and a tiny thong. All her lingerie was in a light, blush pink, which just happened to match her heels perfectly. My lips parted in appreciation and surprise. Thought had definitely gone into this sexy ensemble, and it showed.

"Whoa," I managed. "You look--" I trailed off, looking

for an appropriate adjective but utterly hypnotized by what I was seeing. If I were a cartoon character, my eyes would have been bugging out and my jaw would be dragging along the ground.

Holy hell.

"You like?" she asked in her bedroom voice, spinning around to display her mostly bare, entirely fuckable, round ass for me.

"You're beautiful," I told her. I'm sure she could hear the awe in my voice. Saying that I merely 'liked' her in sexy lingerie was the understatement of the century.

Unable to wait any longer to touch her, I steered her by the waist to the bed, pressing her down into the coverlet and touching every inch of her long, smooth legs. Every time our skin touched, a little ping of electricity shot through me.

Although this wasn't our first time together, it still felt brand new for me. I was certain that it always would. She was unbelievable. Getting used to her would be like getting used to seeing a unicorn. It just couldn't happen.

Kate's big, blue eyes shone in the low light of her bedroom. My cock was hard enough to hurt, and when her mischievous fingers worked down my zipper and found me, I gasped and nearly came in her hands then and there like a teenager.

"I want you," she whispered up at me, stroking eagerly with one hand while unbuttoning my shirt with the other.

"I want to taste you." She licked her plump lips and stared at my cock eagerly.

That was an invitation I would never, ever turn down.

When she wrapped her lips around me, my hands shook from the intensity of the feeling. Her mouth was paradise. There could be nothing better than watching Kate suck my cock in her little corset and thong. She worked on me like I was a puzzle she wanted to solve or a game she wanted to win. I was more than willing to let her play with me, except that she was much too good at it. Every stroke was pure bliss. Her wet lips and smooth, hot tongue would make short work of me. I knew there was no way I could hold out for long.

"You're going to make me come way too quickly if you keep that up," I told her, grabbing her hair at the nape of her neck and holding her back. Her tongue flicked out to brush me one last time, and I shivered. I knew I'd have to get her back for that. "My turn."

We maneuvered a bit on the bed and then I worked her insubstantial little thong down those long, gorgeous legs. Did she really think she was too tall? It must have been the jealousy of other women that convinced her of that. She was all legs, and they were absolutely flawless.

But not as flawless or as perfect as the pink pussy that lay exposed between her white thighs. I kissed her there hesitantly at first, savoring the clean, sweet taste of her. She smelled like woman and sex. Her pussy tasted as good as her mouth had felt on my cock a moment before, and the noises that she made when I worshipped her there were my reward. I took my time, lavishing attention on her and hoping she knew that it gave me just as much pleasure to give as to receive from her. She arched her back and touched the back of my head to urge me on, and I happily complied, adding my fingers to the mix eagerly.

I gazed up at her while I tasted her, seeing her biting her lip and rolling her hips. She was getting close. "Fuck," she moaned. She was almost there. Her whole body was shaking as she fucked my face, and I used my thumb to press and rub her warm, swollen little clit. She came with a whimpering little moan. Her eyes were glassy and vacant when I dragged myself up to her level on the pillows, and her body was pliant under my hands.

"More," she whispered into my lips, probably tasting herself on my mouth. I was glad she wanted more, because at this point I needed to use her pussy. I'd waited as long as I physically could.

I turned her on her side to face me and hitched her left leg up onto my right hip. I rolled the condom on with shaking hands. Her pussy was dripping wet when I notched my cock against her. She moaned when she felt it. "Please," she begged. I penetrated her in one quick thrust, and it was only a few short strokes before she caught on, grinding her hips down against me and bouncing her tits against my chest. Neither one of us stood much of a chance of lasting very long.

Kate came again within moments, her mouth falling

open in bliss and her back arching like a bow. I pushed her flat onto her back and pounded into her a few hard and fast strokes more. Her tight little pussy was still pulsing around me when I came. When I finally climaxed, it was hard enough that I collapsed atop her a second later, then realizing that I was probably crushing her, and rolling—cursing—onto the side. We lay there, panting, side by side for a long moment.

"I'm in love with you," I told her a few minutes later.

"Hmm?" she replied, nuzzling into my side. She was about to fall asleep, I could tell.

This again? Poor sleepy Kate. What have I done to you?

"Nothing baby, you go to sleep," I told her, still completely charmed that this was her reaction to orgasm. She was so, so sleepy. It was fucking adorable.

"Okay," she mumbled, laying her head against my chest and wrapping one arm and one leg around me possessively. I carefully undid her little corset, not wanting her to have to sleep in something that looked so binding. By the time I got it off her, she was completely out cold, and I was all but trapped half beneath her. I was apparently going to be her body pillow tonight. There were much worse fates. I settled in and kissed her forehead. I could tell her I loved her tomorrow. There was still time.

32

KATE

Six years ago...

The weeks and months went by, but I barely noticed their passing. I was just marking time. Emails started piling up in my school inbox, professors were asking if I wanted to drop the classes I hadn't been attending, and classmates were wondering if I was ill. My calendar pinged with assignment due dates and missed tests. My coach was calling to ask why I skipped practice. I ignored them all. None of it mattered anymore.

I took up smoking cigarettes, even though I didn't have the money and knew it was an unhealthy habit. It looked cool, and my new friends did it, so I did it, too. And it gave me something to do with my hands while other people were eating. I no longer had any desire to eat. I'd lost probably fifteen pounds. It was the reverse freshman fifteen.

My new friends, a motley group of students that were

the opposite of a good influence, took me under their collective, tattered wing and showed me all the different ways to self-medicate my new depression. Some ways were harmless: I got two tattoos and a few new piercings. Some ways were harmful: I tried drugs I never would have touched before. I drank, and I smoked, and I flirted with anyone that gave me the time of day. But all the strategies I tried were pointless. None of it really made me feel better. Still, it didn't make me feel any worse, either. At least I was distracted.

Eventually I found myself at a house party, staring across the crowded room at Cole. He was staring back at me in shock, clearly not expecting me there. And why would he? Why would I be invited to a party filled with upperclassmen? Well, because I was the life of the party now. I'd make out with anyone. I'd dance on tables. This was the new, improved Kate. Kate 2.0 couldn't be rejected because Kate 2.0 didn't give a fuck about anything.

Except that Kate 2.0 was a lie. The moment I saw Cole, all my newfound bravado evaporated into nothing. I felt clearheaded for the first time in months. *And it hurt.*

I stole away from the frat boy I'd been flirting with and made my way outside to smoke a cigarette. I sat on the stairs of the back porch and prayed that Cole would leave me alone.

"You shouldn't be here, Kate," the low voice from behind me warned. I turned to face him reluctantly. He was still as goddamn perfect as he ever had been. It made me want to beg him to like me, and it just wasn't fair. He moved to sit next to me on the stair and I leaned away from him. The nearness made me feel lightheaded.

"You really don't need to babysit me, Cole. I'm a big girl."

"Is that why you're smoking cigarettes now? Because you're a big girl?" His voice was skeptical.

I frowned and took another drag. "I've always smoked," I lied.

He pulled the cigarette out of my hand and snuffed it out before going through my purse and confiscating the pack. "Don't make me tell Ward about this." He handed me a piece of gum instead. I unwrapped it and chewed it obstinately.

I didn't want to deal with Ward knowing about Kate 2.0. I could buy more cigarettes tomorrow. Still...

"This is blackmail," I told Cole.

"This is for your own good."

"What do you know about what's good for me?" My voice was bitter.

"A lot more than you think." The bitterness in his tone gave me pause. I turned to look at him to see him staring at his shoes. His face was unexpectedly sad.

We sat in silence for a while. I'd expected him to go inside and leave me alone out here, but he didn't. He just... stayed. He drank his beer and stared out at the lawn or his shoes. Every now and then he would steal a glance at me and then look away again. I stared at him unabashedly.

"What's the matter with you?" I questioned. I was bold enough to ask now that I knew he didn't like me. A guy like Cole had no right to be unhappy. He had everything. There was no girl at the party going on inside behind us that wouldn't be thrilled to go home with him tonight. And that included the ones that had boyfriends.

Cole arched an eyebrow. "Me?"

"Yeah, you," I laughed unkindly at him. "Why are you out here pouting with me? You should be in there," I jerked my head in the direction of the door.

"I hate parties."

"Really? I love them." That was another lie. I didn't mind parties, and I liked being social, but parties that were just about getting drunk and then pairing off made me depressed. This was definitely that kind of party.

"I hate the noise and I hate the crowds," Cole told me. He poked at the laces in his shoe with a bobby pin he probably lifted from my purse. "I hate flirting with strangers and I hate it when strangers flirt with me."

That was the entire point of parties like this. "Then why are you even here?"

He shrugged. Silence descended again. I thought he was never going to answer, but eventually he sighed and said, "I have to at least pretend to be normal."

"Why do you have to do that? I don't bother." Kate 2.0 didn't care about being normal, although Kate 1.0 hadn't been particularly concerned with fitting in either. I'd been the odd one out all my life, so I guess I'd just gotten used to it after a while. Being stared at for being tall, or poor, or strange, it just no longer mattered to me. The stares just rolled off my back like water off a duck.

"Otherwise Ward and Lucas will get suspicious."

My heart thumped in my chest. "Wait a second," I said, and Cole looked over at me with wide eyes. Scared eyes. *Holy shit.* "Are you gay?" I asked, stunned.

Cole's eyes got even bigger. Then he laughed. He laughed so hard that he started coughing from the left-over cigarette smoke and then laugh-coughed some more. When he finally stopped, he shook his head and chuck-led. "No. I'm not gay, Kate." His laughter bubbled up again and I scowled until it died down. "But thanks for the laugh."

He might not be gay, but he was hiding something. I was now one hundred percent sure of that. "Then what are you worried about Ward and Lucas finding out about?"

Silence. We sat there a little longer. I was banking that if I just sat here for long enough he would answer me, and he did. "I've got a problem."

"Is the problem that you're attracted to men in a sexual way?" I ventured. I was still not convinced. It would be the simplest solution. Plus, it would make me feel a whole lot better. I found myself seriously hoping he was gay. Maybe if he was gay, we could at least be friends.

He rolled his eyes at me. "No. I'm not gay. I promise you that." He sighed. "My problem is that I have an attraction to a woman who I shouldn't have feelings for. If I sit around and sulk all day, Ward and Lucas will eventually figure it out."

Oh no. He had a crush on someone else? Why couldn't he have just been gay?

I didn't know how to reply, so I didn't. Cole continued to poke at his shoelaces with my bobby pin. I stared straight ahead of me at the green grass of the backyard. This house backed up to a golf course and it seemed to go on and on.

"This woman you like, why can't you be with her?" I asked. It was a somewhat masochistic thing to ask, but I was too curious to protect myself. In fact, if I was smart, I'd have left this conversation a while back. But I'd never been very smart.

"It's complicated."

"We've got time."

He looked over at me and took a sip of his beer. "She's unattainable. Let's just leave it at that."

Unattainable? That could mean that she was already with someone. Or it could mean that she didn't like him back. Or it could mean that she was a professor or something. Or it could mean that she lived in Canada. It could mean a lot of things. But I supposed it didn't matter what the details were. He was in love with someone that he couldn't have.

"I'm sorry," I heard myself saying. "I know how that is."

He paused mid sip and then swallowed hard. He knew I was talking about him. "Thanks." He didn't sound all that thankful.

"Maybe you just need to get your mind off her," I suggested. "That's what I do when I'm sad about something. I find distractions." I was thinking about the boring frat boy that I'd been flirting with all night. I wasn't even sure I would recognize him if I went back inside. The only thing I'd really noticed about him was that he was wearing a polo shirt and boat shoes. That was pretty much the frat boy uniform though, so it didn't help me narrow it down much.

"Why do you think I'm at this party tonight? I'm looking for a distraction."

"Did you find one yet? There are plenty of pretty girls in there."

"I found you. You're pretty."

His amber eyes looked dark brown in the moonlight. I thought at first that I'd misinterpreted what he was saying, but then he kissed me. Electricity and emotion poured through my veins, making my heart pound furiously. His soft lips were everything I'd ever wanted, and I was captivated by the feeling.

"Are you asking me to be your distraction?" I asked him when he pulled away.

"Only if you want to be." His voice was the tiniest bit sad. It was almost like he wanted me to say no.

Instead, I kissed him again. We made out for a while and then walked out on the golf course together. We made love in the soft, green grass, under the full moon. Cole didn't know I was a virgin, but he was so gentle and giving with me that there was no pain. I came easily under his touch. He was so beautiful, and I was so nervous, but I gave myself to him completely. I could only hope that I was doing it right, although he showed no signs that I disappointed him. We lay for a bit in the grass, just breathing together in the dark. Then we walked back to the party, hand in hand, before going our separate ways.

My misadventures as Kate 2.0 continued until I got tired of her and then I had to bust my ass to catch up in my classes. I almost lost my scholarship, but somehow, I made it through my freshman year. I never saw Cole again during college.

33

KATE

PRESENT DAY...

When I woke up the next morning, the sun was shining but my bed was empty. Cole must have gone home. I drew my knees up to my chest and tried not to feel abandoned. Tears were starting to burn the edges of my eyes and I fought against the feeling of loneliness. Then I heard the front door open and shut and steps down the hallway. Cole came around the corner with two cups and a bag from the donut place down the street. Relief flowed through me.

"You woke up!" he said. "I hoped I would get back before you did."

I grinned at him, feeling foolish. Of course he wouldn't disappear on me. Cole was a gentleman. "All is forgiven if there's a glazed donut in that bag for me."

"There might be." His sexy smile was better than breakfast pastries.

I crawled out of bed and wrapped the bedsheet around me carefully at the same time. I'm not usually the modest type, but just springing out of bed naked was beyond even my exhibitionism. After all, Cole had clothes on. He looked disappointed at my modesty.

We ended up sitting on the couch to eat our breakfast. I snuggled up under Cole's arm and he squeezed me around the waist. "This is nice," I told him. "I like this."

"I could get used to this, too," he replied. "You look cute in the morning."

Considering that I hadn't taken my makeup off the night before, I probably looked like a greasy raccoon from the smeared mascara, but I decided to accept the compliment graciously. "Thanks. You look cute in the morning, too."

"Do you have to work today?" Cole asked.

I nodded. "I have to work twice as much when Ward isn't around."

"Can I see you tonight?" His expression was hopeful, and I hated to squash it.

"I have to work until close."

"After that?"

"Unfortunately, 'after that' will be about three-thirty a.m."

He seemed totally undeterred. "Do you want me to drop you off and pick you up?"

"I said three-thirty a.m. not p.m."

"Yeah, I know." He grinned at me. "I really want to see you."

My heart fluttered. "Oh. Okay."

I could hardly believe this was happening to me at last. Cole wanted me. We'd had sex and he still wanted me. This was real. I had to admit it to myself. I'd been holding myself in reserve for so long that it was hard to admit the truth to myself, but I couldn't help but see this for what it was. I was in love with him. And it seemed like he was in love with me, too. For the first time, I started to imagine a future for myself that had him in it. And it was beautiful.

* * *

RAE CALLED me around three that afternoon. She was back in New York after her quick trip to Austin, but I knew she wouldn't forget my news so easily.

"Alright, I'm going to need a full update on your new man," she said.

I realized the phone was on speaker a bit too late. A regular who was sitting a few seats down the bar, turned to look at me. I cringed, and then realized that had probably given me away even worse. He turned away again, hiding a smile.

Crap. Well, that's another person who knows.

Cole had shared with me the details of the conversation he'd had with Willie as well as the run-in with the obnoxious journalist, Eddie. Telling Ward the truth was pretty much our only option at this point, because it seemed like the entire rest of the world now already knew.

Rae was still hanging on the line expectantly. "Hello," she prompted, probably wondering if I'd hung up, "Kate? Are you okay?"

"Sorry," I replied with a shake of my head she couldn't see. "Let me grab a couple of drinks that need to go out and then call you back in about fifteen minutes?"

Rae made an affirmative noise. "Okay. Talk to you then."

"Okay." I spent the next fifteen minutes desperately trying to organize my thoughts. When I got on the phone to talk to Rae, however, all that came out was, "I'm in love." I had a giddy, heart-pounding feeling in my chest just to admit it.

"That's wonderful! I'm so happy for you." I could hear the grin in her voice. "I'd hug you if I was there," she told me, "and you know I'm not usually a hugger."

"I never thought it could be like this," I admitted to her. "I mean, I know I've liked guys before, but it's never been so... intense. All I can think about is Cole."

"His name is Cole?"

"Cole Rylander. He's actually a very good friend of Ward's."

Rae's voice turned from elated to guarded in a flash. "Wait a moment," she said, "is this...that guy? You know, from your freshman year?"

I'm not sure why it made me feel embarrassed to admit

that it was, but my "yes" was small and hesitant. Rae digested this new information with a carefully neutral quality to her silence.

"Does he know what he put you through back then?"

"It wasn't his fault."

"But does he know?"

I shook my head. "No. And I'm not sure that I want him to." I was still somewhat embarrassed by the whole thing. Both the fact that I'd been in love with him, and the fact that we hooked up in a way that probably meant nothing to him but everything to me. He'd been my first, and it had been special to me. Even if it was *only* special to me. I wasn't going to let anything tarnish that night for me.

"He doesn't know that he was your first?"

"I mean, maybe he figured it out back then and just didn't mention it."

"Please. He was what? Twenty-one? Guys that age fuck like rhinoceroses."

They fuck like rhinoceroses? That was an unpleasant mental image. Cole had not fucked like a rhinoceros. He'd been perfectly lovely, thank you very much.

"Huh?"

"They lack finesse," she clarified. "He wouldn't have known if you didn't tell him. It's not like he could see your hymen or anything."

"He didn't hurt me." I probably sounded defensive.

Rae's doubtful silence was her reply.

I amended my reply to be clearer. "He didn't physically hurt me. I swear."

Rae took a second before replying, and the tone of her voice was resolute. "I think you need to tell him everything. You need to tell him how much you cared about him back then. You need to tell him how much he hurt you when he rejected you. You need to tell him that you had a seriously downward mental health spiral. And you definitely, *definitely*, need to tell him you were a virgin when you slept together."

I hung my head. "Why?" The guilt had begun to eat at me already, but telling him meant admitting so much weakness on my part. I'd gotten this far without telling him. Why rock the boat?

"Because if you love him, you owe it to him to be honest. Don't you think?"

I sighed. Rae was right, as usual. My head had started to hurt, and I pinched the bridge of my nose. I was definitely going to need an aspirin to make it through this entire shift. The next twelve hours were going to be hard.

"So, will you tell him?" Rae pushed.

"Yeah."

"Okay, good," she said, brightening, and the happiness came back to her voice. "I'm glad you've found someone that you really like."

I had been walking on air, but heading back into the busy bar, I now felt like my feet were made of lead. I wanted to tell Cole the truth, I really did. I just wanted to protect myself from humiliation and hurt more. The thought of telling him everything was terrifying. At least I had twelve whole hours to figure it out.

34

COLE

Six years ago...

When I woke up the day after the party, I felt more conflicted than I'd ever been in my entire life. I wanted to talk to Kate so badly that I found myself composing texts to her and then deleting them all morning long. A cold shower didn't help. A cup of coffee didn't help. Sitting alone in my room, staring at the wall for an hour definitely didn't help. Eventually I had to talk to someone, or I was going to go crazy. Ward obviously wasn't an option, so it would have to be Lucas.

"I need to talk to you," I told him, barging into his room and closing the door behind me. He looked up from his book in surprise and alarm.

"Ward ate it," he said instantly. "It was Ward and not me."

"What?" I was confused.

"Whatever it was that you had in the fridge, Ward ate it," he repeated.

He thought I was angry with him over leftovers?

I shook my head at him and laughed. "No, man. This... this isn't about food. At all."

Lucas' defensiveness faded. "Oh." He smirked. "What's up then?" His voice was much friendlier now. I sank down into the free chair next to his desk.

I took a deep breath and opened my mouth. No words came out save a strange, strangled noise. Lucas blinked at me, visibly confused. I frowned and tried again. Silence. Lucas' confusion turned to worry. "Are you having a stroke?" he asked, looking around like he was wondering if he should call 911.

On my third try, I was able to speak. "I had sex with Kate Williams at a party last night," I managed to whisper. "On the golf course." I don't know why I felt like that detail was important, but it was.

Lucas closed his book with a surprised pop. "Dude," he whispered back.

"I know."

"*Duuuude.*"

"*I know.*"

We communicated a surprising amount with such insipid conversation. Lucas stared at me with disbelief and concern in his hazel eyes. There was a small ring of white all the way around his pupils. Finally, he shook his head at me, sending his too-long sandy hair flying around his face.

He set his book down on the table in front of him and swallowed hard.

"*Why?* Why would you do that?" He spread his long-fingered hands in front of him.

"Because I like her." My reply was quiet. It was the truth. I did like Kate. I adored her. She was incredible and beautiful, and I wanted nothing more than to make her happy. She'd looked so sad when I saw her at the party, and I remembered that Ward said she loved me and then my hormones got the better of me and... it just happened. I didn't say all that to Lucas. I probably couldn't have even if I tried. Expressing my feelings had never been easy and Lucas and I didn't talk that way with each other.

"You shouldn't have touched her." Lucas looked completely horrified by my impulsive behavior.

"It's too late to change anything now." I felt compelled to at least defend myself a little bit. "I didn't take advantage of her in any way. I didn't pressure her. I'm not going to regret it." I was making up my mind as I was talking, but I couldn't bring myself to regret my time with her on the golf course that night. I still had her pack of cigarettes and lighter in my jeans pocket. They were disgusting, and I'd never smoke them, but there was no way I could throw them away either. They were the only tangible things I had to remind myself of Kate. Unless you counted the grass stains on the knees of my jeans. Or the hickey on my neck.

"You can't see her again," Lucas said. His voice was firm, and I knew he thought he was right.

"I don't plan to," It hurt to admit it, but I knew that it was probably the only way forward. Nothing had changed. Not really. I dragged a hand through my hair in frustration.

"You're falling in love with her," Lucas realized in a shocked whisper. "With Kate-fucking-Williams. This isn't about sex, is it? *This is about love.* That's so fucked up." His expression turned to genuine pity and he paused for a long moment when I didn't deny it. "God, I'm really sorry," he told me, "but don't let this destroy everything. You have a shot at the NFL. If Ward breaks your kneecaps, or if you fall in love with some girl and get distracted, or both, you'll blow your shot. You know I'm right."

Our coaches were always telling us versions of the same thing. Sleeping around was expected although not encouraged, but falling in love was a distraction we could not afford. Rationally, I knew that the advice was solid. My future was at stake.

Because rationally I knew there was no chance that I could date someone while giving one hundred percent on the field. Maybe some guys in different situations could, but not me. Football demanded everything I had to give. My time. My body. My concentration. Everything. There was no room in my life for anything or anyone else.

Now that I was close to graduation, and closer every day to the NFL draft, I couldn't waiver in my commitment. Right now, I needed to be at the gym. Not here, talking to Lucas, but lifting or running on the treadmill. Ward was already there, I was sure of it.

"But maybe—" I started, and Lucas interrupted.

"No!" He barked. "You aren't going to see her again. You aren't going to talk to her again. You have a shot at your dream. *You have a shot at my dream.* I'm not going to let you wreck it—or your friendship with Ward." His voice was venomous.

Lucas hadn't mentioned his heart murmur or his aborted sports career in a long time. I'd thought he was completely over the disappointment. But the bitterness and anger in his voice proved that wasn't remotely true. He was still resentful over his misdiagnosis, even now.

I didn't know what to say after Lucas' deeply out-of-character outburst. We just stared at one another in what I think was mutual disbelief. Lucas looked surprised at himself, too. But he didn't apologize for it. Instead, he continued.

"If you don't promise me right now that you'll leave Kate Williams alone, I'm going to march down to the gym and tell Ward everything," he threatened. "I'm doing this for your own good, and you know it." He looked as determined as I'd ever seen him. Usually Lucas followed up anything serious with a sarcastic remark or a joke. Not this time. This time his ultimatum was final.

The sad thing, the frustrating thing, the worst thing, was that Lucas was one hundred percent right. He was doing this for my own good. Not for himself, because his hope of football greatness was gone forever, but because he knew it was my dream and didn't want me to lose it. Fundamentally, Lucas was a good friend and a good person. I was lucky to have him in my corner, even though at that moment, I hated his fucking guts and wanted to murder him.

But I wasn't really the violent type. I was the reasonable type. The realistic type. The type that listened to good advice when it was given to me. So, with reluctance, I hung my head and promised Lucas that I wouldn't see, talk to, or touch Kate Williams again.

35

COLE

I HADN'T EXPECTED to hear from Ward that day, since he was supposed to be in Plano, so I was really surprised when he showed up at my hotel about halfway through the afternoon.

"Hey man," I said guiltily from the door of my hotel room. "What's up?"

Ward was carrying a football in one hand and a newspaper in the other. He threw the paper at my chest. I caught it with a sinking feeling in my stomach. I barely even needed to look.

"Take a peek," he said, and waited a moment while I obediently turned the paper to see the text. It was the social page of a local paper called The Community. The headline read 'Breeding the Next Generation of Texas Football?" The picture that accompanied it was unpleasantly familiar.

Eddie had found another job or at least a buyer for his salacious story. I swallowed hard.

"Oh," I managed.

"Oh, is right," Ward replied snidely. "Put on your shoes," he ordered me. "We're gonna' go play some catch and talk."

Catch and talk. That wasn't threatening. Right?

I complied, because I wasn't sure what else to do. In uncomfortable, absolute silence, I put on my socks and shoes and followed Ward out of the hotel and across the street to the small park. My head was spinning the entire time. This wasn't how I wanted Ward to find out. I'd taken steps to ensure that it wouldn't be. If I'd thought I was the luckiest guy in the world last night, now I was fairly sure I was the world's most unlucky. This situation was going to be very difficult to explain.

Ward threw the football at me from about thirty feet away and I caught it before returning the throw. We were too close to really stretch either of us from a physical perspective, but at least at this distance we could talk— well, yell at one another.

Whoosh. Thud. Whoosh. Thud. We weren't doing a lot of communicating.

"How long?" Ward asked eventually. Whoosh. Thud. Whoosh.

"Not long." Thud. Whoosh.

Thud. "How long?" Whoosh. Harder this time.

Thud. I stumbled back a foot. He still has a hell of an

arm on him, and he knew it. He smirked in satisfaction. "Only about a week," I answer. Whoosh.

Thud. "Why didn't you tell me?" Whoosh.

Thud. "Kate didn't want to." Whoosh.

Thud. Ward looked surprised. "Why?" Whoosh.

Thud. He was throwing quite a bit harder now. He was showing his strength on purpose. I backed up a few feet to soften the blow on my hands when I plucked the ball out of the air. I should have worn gloves. "She didn't want you to be angry." I threw the ball gently, barely hard enough to make it to Ward.

He caught it with as much disgust as a person could catch a football. "Why would I be angry, do you think?" Whoosh. He used way too much power. The ball flew above my head and I had to jump about two feet off the ground to grab it.

"I think you need to ask her that." I was starting to get annoyed with Ward. He might be able to throw a football a lot harder than me, but he couldn't run and jump worth shit any more. Whoosh. I threw it with all my strength.

Thud. Ward grabbed the ball like I'd fucking rolled it to him. How was he still in such good shape? "I'm asking you," he said. "The guy who's spent the last few years banging model after starlet. Never getting serious and never settling down. Playing the field like he was *playing the field*. I'm asking you." Whoosh.

Thud. "I was just doing what my publicist told me to do.

I was never into those women. It was all just casual and more business than personal. Even so..." Whoosh.

Thud. "That's really irrelevant." Whoosh.

Thud. "I agree. You brought it up." Whoosh.

Thud. "Well, why would Kate want to keep it quiet then?" Whoosh.

I considered throwing a long pass and seeing if he'd go limping for it, but that would be cruel. Instead, I threw the ball on the ground. "Kate wanted it to be a secret. I wanted to tell you from the start." *Fuck it*, I thought to myself. *Might as well be honest.* "I wanted to tell you back in college. I've been in love with her forever."

Ward paused. "You... what?" He blinked at me and seemed seriously like he was wondering if he'd misheard me. His blue eyes, so much like Kate's, had gone wide in shock. He couldn't raise a single eyebrow, so he had to raise both. My answer came spilling out of me in a crazed rush.

"I'm in love with Kate. I've been in love with her since I saw her again when she was a freshman. Obviously, we couldn't be together back then, but that didn't mean I wasn't crazy about her. I'm not going to give up on her just because you don't like it, either." I was practically begging him to believe me, and from the look on his face, he knew it.

"Hold on," Ward said, rubbing his temples with both hands as he struggled to adjust to the information I was laying on him. "Hold on." He shifted uncomfortably from foot to foot. "You're in love with her? With Kate? My sister, Kate."

I nodded. "Yes. And I've never been surer of anything or more serious about anything in my whole life. I'm in love with her."

Ward stared at me and I could see the second when he became convinced that I was telling the truth. His shoulders relaxed a moment later, not all the way, but a little bit. "Does she love you back?"

That was more complicated. My stomach cramped. "I don't know." I paused and stared at the ground between us. "I really hope so."

Ward didn't say anything for long enough that I thought we'd just stand here in uncomfortable silence until one of us fell over in exhaustion. "I was seriously considering beating you up when I came over here. I wasn't sure if I could do it, you know, on account of my knee, but I figured I could get a few swings in before you got away." He grinned at me and I didn't smile back at all. He was disturbingly serious. Ward smirked at my face and continued, "I saw this paper in Waco and drove me and Emma back immediately. I yelled at Emma when she told me that she knew, too. She's angry with me." He looked guilty.

"Don't be mad at Emma. Kate swore her to secrecy."

Ward sighed. "I'm not mad at Emma. Not really. I was mad at you, but now that's gone too."

"Wait. You're not mad?" It was true that he didn't look mad, but I still didn't totally trust it.

"No. I mean, I'm not exactly fucking pleased to learn that you're nailing my sister, but at least you love her." He shook his head. "How can I be mad at you? *I want Kate to be with somebody that loves her*, and it's obvious that you do." He seemed as stunned by his answer as I was to hear it.

I didn't want to talk about the fact that I was 'nailing his sister,' but I was grateful that he wasn't angry at me. Ward was being surprisingly reasonable about all this, actually. It was not what I expected, although of course he'd matured since we were in college. I wondered why Kate had insisted on the secrecy in the first place if it wasn't about Ward.

"Sometimes I wonder if I even really know Kate at all," Ward said eventually, waving me over to the nearby park bench. I left the ball sitting on the ground and joined him on the bench. I could tell Ward's knee was seriously bothering him today. He was limping pretty badly. I didn't mention it, but he probably shouldn't have been out here playing catch with me. He should have probably been icing the damn thing and keeping it elevated.

"What do you mean? You probably know her better than anybody."

Ward shook his head. "That's true in some ways," he said. "But she's got secrets she doesn't share with me."

I shrugged at him. "Everybody's got secrets." I was a fat kid until I was about ten. Nobody knew but Jimmy and my mom. And if I had my way, nobody ever would.

"Yeah, I know," Ward agreed, "but it's different with Kate. She's my sister but she's also become pretty much my best friend now that we're grown up. But I think she knows me better than I know her."

It was beyond strange talking about Kate like this with Ward. "She pretty much thinks that you hung the moon."

Ward smiled thinly. "Maybe that's the problem."

"How so?"

"I don't know. I just worry about her sometimes." He was holding something back, but I didn't push him. This conversation represented a fairly massive shift in our relationship, so I wasn't going to test the boundaries just yet.

"I'm going to treat her right," I told him. "You don't need to worry about that."

Ward looked at me for a long moment. "I know." He smirked. "I've never known you to be in love with anybody before, but I'm sure you can figure it out."

"I'll do my best."

Ward nodded at me. He wasn't smiling at me, but he wasn't beating my ass either. That was a victory as far as I was concerned.

My head was starting to pound from all this talking about feelings with Ward, but what really worried me was Kate. If Ward was so damn reasonable now in his old age, why had I been sworn to secrecy? What was Kate trying to protect? There was only one place I could go for answers.

36

KATE

Six years ago...

My new roommate was a drag. The pint size blonde named Emma Greene just transferred in from freakin' Yale and had a stick up her butt so big that it was amazing that she could comfortably sit down. I'd told her I was trying to stop smoking, but still stole outside for a cigarette now and then. Emma had said it was fine, but her housewarming gift to me was a bunch of Nicorette patches and a passive-aggressive hallmark card reminding me to clean up any cigarette butts since they were bad for the environment.

Emma seemed so unbelievably uptight that I worried she'd shatter into a million pieces if I cursed in front of her. Every interaction with her left me walking on eggshells. I got the feeling that she thought she was better than me with her girly-girl style and super-organized everything. Her room was spotless and everything in it looked expensive. In our bathroom, all her meticu-lously organized stuff smelled like flowers. Even her books were alphabetically organized. She was unlike anyone I'd ever met before, and not necessarily in a good way.

"Hey, Emma?" I knocked on her door carefully. "Can I come in?" I needed to talk to her about the utilities at our apartment. I'd been putting it off, but I was afraid the city was going to cut our power.

"Sure," she responded. Her voice sounded weirdly high and thick. "Come on in." I cracked open the door to her room and was surprised to see her blotting away tears. She stuffed the crumpled-up tissues into her trashcan as soon as she saw me. "What's up?" She asked, putting on a thin, fake-looking smile.

My overall irritation with her faded when I saw how upset she was. "Emma are you okay?" The utilities could wait. "Do you need anything?" I didn't like seeing anyone cry, not even her.

Emma's doll-like face, so delicate and pretty, was visibly torn. She looked like she wanted to talk, but she didn't know me well. We'd only been living together for two tense weeks and were still learning one another's personalities. So far, it seemed like we were pretty incompatible. She pushed her long, shiny blonde hair out of her eyes. I saw the second when she decided to trust me.

"My boyfriend and I broke up right before I moved here," she told me after a moment, "and I just really miss him. He was a complete raging fuckwad, but I miss his dumb ass."

The fact that Emma had just called anyone a 'raging fuckwad,' even if it was her ex-boyfriend, made me start to reevaluate her in a more positive way. "That sucks," I told her. "Why'd you break up?"

Her porcelain white cheeks turned a bright pink. "He was my professor and he dumped me to marry somebody else. He was cheating on me the whole time we were together. And he was my first. What do I do? I feel so lonely." She looked at me with wide, green eyes, as if expecting dismissiveness, judgement, or laughter.

It turned out Emma was human after all and came complete with a past and everything. All I could do was gape at her. I never expected Emma to open up to me like this. I honestly thought she looked down on me. Although she didn't know I came from a trailer park, I figured my manners gave it away. But there she was looking for *my advice?* Did it really look like I had my life together enough to advise anybody?

Oh shit. Emma's ex was way worse than my sob story.

"I'm really sorry," I told her, sinking down on her desk chair before remembering what I had in the fridge. "He sounds like an ass. Hold on, I know what you need. I'm gonna' go grab us the sparkling rose and chocolate cake I have in the fridge. This might take a while."

And from that first night bonding over bad relationships and a shared love of cake, our friendship was born.

Emma and I started hanging out more, and over time I cut ties with most of the so-called friends I met during my freshman year. I realized that they were more interested in seeing me fail than succeed, whereas Emma actually cared about my wellbeing and happiness. Unlike some of the people I'd thought were my friends, Emma wasn't looking for someone to validate her own poor life choices and share in her bad decisions. She challenged me to be a better version of myself and wanted me to do the same for her. My health improved, I gained back the weight I'd lost, and I started doing better in my classes.

But it was still months before I told her about Cole. We were putting away groceries one evening when I slipped up and started telling her about it as we were talking about losing our virginities.

"Yeah," I was saying, "my first time was actually really amazing. It wasn't painful at all. The funny thing is, the situation itself was completely messed up. So, the fact that the sex was good is sort of shocking. See, it wasn't with a professor, but it was almost as bad. I ended up losing my virginity on the middle of a golf course, to a guy that took me on a date to an Applebee's and a strip club."

Emma paused from where she was lining up the boxes of macaroni and cheese in our cupboards. "I'm sorry, what?" She turned to look at me with huge eyes. I couldn't imagine Emma in either an Applebee's or a strip club. She'd probably spontaneously combust with rage if a guy brought her to either.

I winced. It really didn't seem so great when I said it like that. "It's not quite as bad as it sounds."

"Considering that it sounds *tremendously bad*, I should very much hope not." Emma was the only person I knew who could say something like that and not sound like a conceited asshole. That was just how she talked.

"Well, it turns out that the whole date had been planned to make me hate him. He's my brother's friend, and he didn't want to get involved with me."

Emma tilted her head to the side like a confused cocker spaniel. "So, why'd he ask you out in the first place?"

"He didn't. I asked him." That day had marked the pinnacle of my self-confidence. It would never be that good again.

"But if he didn't like you, he could have just said no."

"I think he wanted to make sure I didn't continue to hold out hope. I'd had a thing for him for a long time. Since high school, actually. He isn't a bad guy at all. He was just trying to discourage me."

Emma's face was skeptical. "So, he took you on the world's shittiest date on purpose to make you hate him?"

"Yeah, basically." Now that it was more than a year in the past, I was able to laugh about it. But it had taken a full twelve months to get there.

"That sounds like a load of bullshit."

"It does," I admitted, "but it's true."

"And then you still slept with him?" Her question was direct, but her face was nonjudgmental. Emma was a surprisingly openminded person when it came to sex. She didn't sleep around, but if other people wanted to do it, she didn't care one bit. In fact, Emma was the person you could rely on to high-five you the next morning after you got some.

"Not right then, no," I told her. "I was pretty unhappy, obviously. We hooked up almost six months later when we ran into each other at a party."

"Hmm. He sounds like kind of a jerk." Emma looked angry at Cole on my behalf.

"He's not, I swear. He's really, really nice." Even I could hear the longing in my voice. I crumpled up the paper bag I'd just emptied with a bit more force than necessary.

"And he's one of Ward's friends?" Emma asked carefully. She rarely mentioned my brother. It was more than a bit of a sore subject for her.

"Yeah. His name is Cole Rylander. He graduated last year with Ward. He's playing professional football now." I tried my best not to spend my free time cyber stalking him and was mostly successful at it. Not seeing him regularly had helped me move past my feelings for him, at least a little bit.

"Do you think you'll ever see him again?"

I shrugged and pretended to be casual. "Probably not." I cracked open a can of diet Dr. Pepper and looked anywhere but at Emma.

"If you did see him, would you sleep with him again?" Emma seemed skeptical of my entire story. I got the feeling that she was fishing for some kind of detail that would help her make sense of it. I couldn't really help her with that. The situation was what it was. I'd come to terms with it eventually, even though I still had a lot of unresolved feelings for Cole.

"Probably," I told her. "I really like him. Even after everything."

Emma shook her head at me. "I'm sorry things didn't turn out like you wanted with him. You never know though, maybe someday you'll see him again."

"I don't know if I could take it," I admitted. "It was because of him that I started the whole smoking and drinking and running with the wrong crowd thing that I was doing when you met me."

"Oh." Her response was little, but her reaction was big. I'd told her a bit about the risky, not-so-smart stuff I'd done during my freshman year, and I think it had blown her pure, squeaky clean little mind. I hadn't even told her the worst of it yet.

In reality, I was very lucky that none of my antics had resulted in anything worse than a few bad hangovers and a fairly expensive coverup tattoo on my hip (what had I been thinking when I got that stupid rainbow taco?). Considering all the sketchy parties I went to and the drugs I experimented with, I could have ended up in a shallow grave somewhere.

I was proud to have put that chapter of my life behind me. I never wanted to feel that low again. "I'm working on learning to protect myself," I told Emma. "Don't worry about me. The next time I see Cole, if I ever see him again, I might sleep with him, but I'm not going to let him turn my life inside out. Nobody deserves to have that kind of power over me."

37

KATE

PRESENT DAY...

Cole picked me up at three-thirty a.m. on the dot. He was driving the i8 Coupe. It looked like something that had driven right out of the future. The door opened upward, revealing an interior made of leather and chrome. The new car smell was absolutely divine.

"I really like the blue!" I told him, slipping down into the low seat and marveling at all the luxurious, pretty finishes inside the car. There were so many shiny buttons! Some of them even lit up! My fingers itched to push every single one and find out what they did. I ran my hands up and down the smooth, wonderful smelling leather.

Cole's smile was proud. "I was going to go with the silver, but when I saw the blue, it was all over. It was just total love at first sight." His excited smile widened, revealing his white teeth. "It's the exact same color as your eyes."

It wasn't. My eyes were an unremarkable cornflower blue. This was a vivid, electric blue. The sort of blue that was so saturated that it looked like it might glow in the dark. Such a corny line shouldn't have made me blush, but this was Cole. He could use the corniest pickup line ever and it would still work on me. I smiled shyly back at him.

"You're really sweet," I told him before leaning over for a kiss.

He turned my gentle peck into a real kiss, claiming my mouth like he'd been away from me for a week, not a day. "Are you in a good mood?" he asked when he pulled back.

I nodded breathlessly, suddenly wary. "Why?"

He sighed. "Because I've got to tell you something and I'm afraid you're going to be angry with me." He reached behind himself into the back seat and deposited a newspaper onto my lap.

"What's this?"

Cole switched on the overhead light. "Read it," he told me. His face was still, and it made me nervous. I looked down.

The picture of Cole and me making out pretty much said it all. There wasn't a whole lot of point in reading the article, but I did anyway. According to the author of the article, "Speculation is wild that Cole Rylander and Kate Williams, the sister of UT football star Ward Williams, have become an item."

Shit. Shit. Shit.

"Ward knows," Cole added. "He showed up at my hotel room this afternoon."

I shook my head, not remotely understanding. "Ward and Emma went to visit my mom in Plano."

"They did, but they never made it north of Waco. Ward saw this, went ballistic, and insisted they come home immediately."

"Emma didn't tell me." *Why hadn't she warned me? She should have warned me!*

"I think she might have been busy. Ward was pretty angry with Emma about it. She admitted that she knew about us of course."

My anger evaporated. *Oh no. That wasn't what I wanted. I never meant to create trouble between them.*

My heart sank. "I have to talk to Ward. Tell him not to be mad at her. I was the one that wanted to keep it a secret. I made her keep it from him. It wasn't her idea. This is my fault." Guilt rose up in my throat, making me feel ill.

"I already told him. I told him everything, Kate. I told him that I love you."

My mouth fell open, effectively cutting off my next statement. I stared at Cole in the dim overhead lighting of his space car. "I...you...what?" Not my finest response by any means, but this was a lot all at once.

"I love you, Kate," Cole looked at me with such intensity that my guilt over Emma and my shock over the newspaper couldn't compete. All I could think about was the fact that Cole—the man I'd waited for, dreamed about, and pined after—was here, next to me, saying that he loved me.

I'd dated plenty of good men. Bad ones too, a couple of unfortunate times, but mostly good ones. Nice ones, smart ones, good looking ones. Guys that had great senses of humor, guys that could cook, guys that liked kids and animals, guys that were in touch with their emotions, guys that weren't afraid of commitment. Ambitious, kind, handsome men that would make good husbands and fathers one day. None of them, *none of them*, had ever meant *anything* to me compared to Cole. There were other guys and then there was Cole. He was in a league all his own.

The fact that I'd been in love with Cole since I was sixteen years old wasn't something I could lie to myself about. Not anymore. Ever since he showed up on my doorstep with daisies and showed me what a gentleman could be, I'd been holding a torch for him.

Which was why it was so hard to do what I did next. My instinct for self-preservation might be rusty, but it worked. And my instinct was telling me to run.

"Cole, I'm not the girl I used to be." I looked down at my hands, twisted into one gnarled knot on my lap. "I can't do this. I can't keep seeing you."

I felt the change in the atmosphere of the car, like all the air had rushed out. But I kept my eyes on my hands. I couldn't look at Cole.

It was a long time before he replied. "Why?" he asked softly. There was pain in his voice.

Telling him the truth was too painful. But I was going to do it—at least halfway. "Because I don't want to get hurt by you again. I can't go through that again. I don't think you know what you did to me during college."

"Tell me." His voice was so soft, I wondered if I almost imagined it. "Please tell me, Kate," he repeated, and I swallowed hard.

"I'd been in love with you for two years by the time I asked you out. Crazy, obsessive, teenage love. I wanted to be with you so badly, and then you took me on that date and it really messed me up for a while. It wasn't your fault. You didn't know how crazy I was about you. I know you were just trying to run me off. But after that I had a small-scale breakdown. I stopped going to my classes, I started smoking, drinking, hanging out with a bad group of people. I made out with drunk guys at parties. I danced on tables, accepted pills from strangers, got depressed, went wild."

"Kate..." His voice was full of what sounded like shock and horror, but I wasn't finished yet. This wasn't even the worst part.

"Look, I'm not telling you all this because I want you to feel guilty or pity me. That isn't what this is about at all. I just want you to understand. When we met up at that party and ended up having sex, I was still a virgin. You were my first. And I knew what I was getting into. You told me I was just a distraction, and I knew that was true. But my self-esteem didn't recover for a very long time. And I'm not going to risk myself like that ever again."

Cole was silent. I finally looked over to see that his face had gone blank. I wasn't sure if it was horror, pain, or just shock that had forced those walls to come up, but I couldn't tell what he was thinking. Maybe it was a blessing. It made it easier for me to say what I had to say.

"This is why I can't be with you. I didn't want Ward or anyone to know about us, because I'm not going to go through pain like that again. Ever. I won't do it. I don't think I would survive it."

"But I—"

"*No. Don't tell me you love me. Because I don't care. I can't trust you. I loved you once, and it nearly killed me.* You can't love me already, it's much too soon. I don't believe you..." I trailed off. My voice was bitter. What did it matter if he loved me? He could still rip my heart out, and I'd barely survived it the first time around. "I'm not going to make the same mistake twice."

Then I was shooting out of the car so fast he couldn't stop me. I didn't look back.

38

COLE

I'd never been heartbroken before. I thought that I had, after sleeping with Kate on the golf course that time, but I was wrong. That wasn't heartbreak. That wasn't anything.

The morning after being dumped, I awoke in pain. Everything hurt. My bones ached. My muscles throbbed. My eyes burned in their sockets. My soul felt like it was being torn in two. If this was how I made Kate feel, it was no wonder that she drove me away rather than risk this again. I wouldn't wish this feeling on my worst enemy.

The next three weeks passed in a haze. I think that I managed to go about my daily business in an ordinary way. Errands were completed on time, bills were paid, meetings were conducted. I continued to live a regular life on the outside, even though I was rotting on the inside.

Ward called me to let me know that he'd made up with Emma. Kate had come by his place and the two women talked for a long time. Ward told me that he knew that Kate had ended things with me. He told me that it didn't change anything between us. I was still his best friend, and best man. He promised to be in touch soon.

I must have said the appropriate things at the appropriate times in that conversation, but for the life of me, I couldn't remember what they were. Maybe I just grunted like an ape. Either way, Ward was left with the impression that I was okay or at least alright to be left on my own.

The dealerships kept my days busy. I threw myself into work, and into learning the minutiae of selling BMW's with so much enthusiasm, eagerness, and focus that I think everyone around me thought I was some kind of idiot savant. In reality, I just had nothing else to occupy my time during the days.

The days were fine or at least bearable, but the nights were total torture. The revelations about Kate that I'd learned in front of the Lone Star Lounge at three thirty in the morning haunted my dreams. She'd been a virgin when I'd walked with her out onto the dark golf course that night. And then she hadn't been a virgin when we returned an hour or two later.

How could I not have known? Shouldn't I have been able to feel it somehow? Well, I hadn't. In the dark, on that cool and quiet spring night, with the amount of beer I'd consumed, somehow, I hadn't realized that I was deflowering the woman I loved. I didn't think I was particularly rough. I knew I'd been careful, but I hadn't necessarily been gentle. I would never have hurt her during sex, not on purpose. *Never.* But maybe I had hurt her unintentionally. Even if I hadn't hurt her physically, however, it was clear I'd inflicted other, more lasting damage.

She didn't trust me, and I didn't blame her. I didn't deserve her trust. I never would.

After three weeks, I got a text message from Lucas. I'd been starting to wonder what he'd been up to. He asked to meet me, and I agreed to come over to his place. He sounded excited.

When he opened the door, his hair was uncombed, and his shirt was wrinkled. "Hey! Come on in." He looked and sounded somewhat manic. "Beer?"

"Sure." I hadn't touched alcohol since Kate dumped me. I was half afraid that I'd enjoy it a bit too much in my current state. But Lucas' super-hoppy beer was still as disgusting as ever. I was safe from any risk of alcoholism if I was drinking this crap.

"Sorry about Kate," he told me. He shook his head at me. "I really am."

I didn't reply. There was nothing to say. I hoped this wasn't what Lucas called me over here to talk about. It was going to be a very one-sided conversation. Lucas cleared his throat uncomfortably.

"Anyway," he told me, "I wanted to tell you about something I've been working on."

"Oh yeah?" I brightened a bit. Talking about Lucas' work was much easier than talking about me. Anything to avoid thinking about Kate, though. I would be happy to talk about the weather for a few hours if it helped distract me from Kate.

"Yeah, I think I'm finally onto something big." Lucas had been keeping his latest project under a veil of secrecy for the last few years. His first success—an app that connected a wide variety of other apps in a complicated way that helped advertisers target consumers—had sold for a solid seven and a half figures. That nest egg had been enough to fund his one-man startup for the last few years.

"It's a brand-new project?"

Lucas shook his head. "Not exactly. It's something that I've been toying with for a long time. But it was actually seeing Victoria that made me realize that I've been doing everything all wrong. She was the key."

Oh no. Not fucking Victoria. I looked around his apartment for any sign that she'd been here. There was nothing. Lucas' place still looked as threadbare and bachelor pad-like as ever. I prayed she wasn't lurking in the bedroom.

"Victoria?" I asked him carefully.

Lucas smiled a tiny, cold smile. "Victoria," he repeated. "When I saw her, I realized what was missing in all my prior algorithms."

"You have algorithms now? Why?" I remembered algorithms, at least a little bit. They were used frequently in statistics, although the applications were broad. Algorithms could be complicated or simple, but at their core they were just methodologies for problem solving. Anyone who has ever solved a crossword puzzle or a sudoku puzzle has used an algorithm.

"Yes. For my new, amazing, *dating app*." Lucas' voice was as proud as if he were introducing his firstborn. Despite my depression, I found myself getting excited for Lucas.

"Okay, lay it on me. Let's hear your pitch."

He grinned. "Most dating apps focus on the premise that you can match two people by asking them to rank their preferences about life and love and then using some percentage of objective criteria that the two people have in common to predict the likelihood of them liking one another. People tell you what they think they want and who they think that they are, and then the app matches them with other people that say they meet those criteria. But it's all fundamentally bullshit, right?"

"Um, is it?" I'd never tried dating websites. My publicist did try to get me to sign up for a season of The Bachelor, but I refused.

"Yes!" Lucas was excited. "Total bullshit. These websites say that they have all these proprietary algorithms that match people at the deepest levels of compatibility or some shit. But really, it's a complete crapshoot. Just because someone says that they like long walks on the beach and puppies doesn't mean that they're going to like some rando that also likes long walks on the beach and puppies, will they?"

"I assume it's more complicated than that."

"Not really. I mean, the thing that the more successful

dating apps appear to be doing, at least from my research, is that they match people primarily by age, race, and location. They group similar types together. Attractive people get matched with attractive people. Successful people get matched with successful people. That's all there is to it."

"That's... actually really depressing." I knew people that had met and married on dating websites. I guess opposites didn't attract?

Lucas shrugged his shoulders. "Yeah, maybe," he said, "but the thing is, they're simple. There is nothing that's actually very proprietary going on behind the scenes."

"And you're going to improve on this broken system how?"

"By creating something that is actually going to be innovative. I've found a metric that can actually be used to determine compatibility."

"Well, don't keep me in suspense over here."

Lucas spread his hands wide. "Musical preference."

I arched an eyebrow. "Unpack that for me."

"Musical preference as a compatibility indicator is pure genius because it isn't based on similarity. It's waaaay more nuanced than that. Statistically, someone who likes the Pixies isn't necessarily that likely to like someone else that likes the Pixies."

"Really?"

"Really. In fact, someone that likes the Pixies is statistically five times more likely to be interested in dating someone that likes Taylor Swift than someone that exactly matches their own musical preferences."

"Okay?" That didn't make a ton of sense to me.

"I've got the data that support it. I mean, there's still work to be done, obviously, but there's a lot of promise here. There's a ton of potential if I can get a large enough sample to do real beta testing to make sure that my algorithms are sound."

"So how do the algorithms actually work?"

Lucas gave me his best Mona Lisa smile. "I'm sorry, that's proprietary information."

"You mean it's bullshit?"

"No. I mean, for once, *it isn't bullshit*. Because I'm not matching like with like, it's much more complex. I can't even tell you how it works if I wanted to, because it's way too complicated. I could draw flowcharts for hours and still not be able to summarize it."

I looked at Lucas to see if he would divulge more information, but he just continued to smile his secret little smirk.

"Okay, I think I understand. It sounds like a good idea. So, what's next?"

Lucas was practically vibrating in his seat from excitement. "Testing. Testing. And more testing. Want to help?"

"Help how?"

"By creating a profile and then rating some females."

"Rating some females? That sounds very sexist." Also, unless Kate was on there, I was going to rate all the women at zero. There was no competition. To me, all other women looked like water buffalo.

"This is a dating app remember?" He laughed at me. "The female testers will be rating you back if that makes you feel better. And women are super harsh when it comes to dating apps. They usually reject nine out of ten guys that match with them."

"I'll think about it." I wasn't sure I wanted any more rejection right now, even if it was the theoretical, beta-testing type.

"You're no fun."

"You're definitely right about that." I'd probably never been less fun in my entire life than I'd been since Kate dumped me. Lucas was the first person that I'd spoken to in a halfway normal, personal way in weeks. I'd basically become a hermit who only emerged to work and then went back to his half-darkened cave of a hotel room to mope each evening.

"You should go and talk to her," Lucas offered. He'd shifted gears now and was looking at me with what I interpreted as well-meaning sympathy. "Did you end up telling her everything?" That had been his initial advice. I should have followed it.

He wanted to know if I'd told her how much I'd cared about her. Not just now, but always. I knew that I should have told Kate that I'd loved her from the start.

"I never got the chance." My admission was sad.

"You could still tell her. It's not too late."

"What do you mean? It is too late. She already dumped me." I sounded pathetic, even to my own ears. It grated on me to be so damn weak.

Lucas took off his glasses, cleaned them, and slid them back on before replying. When he did, his voice was mild but serious. "Do what you want. But if it were me, I'd go find her and make her listen. That's what I should have done with Victoria. But instead I let her go on tour and disappear. I lost my chance to win her back. I had to wait almost two years just to get in the same room with her again."

I wanted to tell Lucas that his experience with Victoria was completely and totally different from my relationship with Kate. Victoria was a freakin' energy vampire. Kate was perfection made flesh. Comparing the two was just beyond ridiculous. But I didn't. Not only would it hurt his feelings when he was trying to help me, but it might get me injured if he felt the need to defend Victoria's honor. I was fairly certain that I could take Lucas in a fight—the guy was only six-one—but I didn't want to fight him over something as stupid as Victoria. She certainly didn't deserve it. And she definitely didn't deserve Lucas' loyalty.

"I'll think about it," I mumbled. I thanked him for the beer and went home, but not before Lucas had installed his new dating app—Notable Match—on my phone. I looked it over and then promptly forgot about it. My depression was waiting, and it required all of my time and attention.

39

KATE

"Hey, darlin', can I get another old fashioned?"

I nodded at the man who thought I was his darlin'. The fact that I was still standing, walking, and talking was a miracle. But my miraculous ability to continue my normal life after breaking up with Cole had somehow also robbed me of my ordinary reactions. I made the drink with practiced hands and barely a thought in my head. I felt like a robot or a sleepwalker.

"Thanks, sweetheart," the guy said when I slid his drink across the bar to him.

I nodded again, mute.

"Smile, sweetheart," he told me. His tone was petulant. "A pretty girl like you shouldn't frown."

I forced myself to smile at him, drawing my lips away from my teeth with effort, and then immediately turned away. It probably looked more like a sneer than a smile, but only because I didn't feel anything. I didn't have the heart to tell him off. I didn't have a heart at all these days. I found something to busy myself with and tried not to think.

The days had been sliding by around me, turning into lonely, long nights. Most of those nights I dreamed about Cole, and it was only then, in dreams, when I felt like I was real. Then I'd wake up and go through my waking life in a haze. I'd gone through this before and my response had been to internalize my pain and go wild. This time I was smarter. This time, at least, I was numb.

"Hey, Kate," Ward asked a bit later, approaching in my peripheral vision with a frown on his face. "When you get a second, I need your help on the payroll." He had a handful of rumpled papers in one hand and a calculator in the other.

In anticipation of finally, *finally* doing something other than working at the Lone Star Lounge, I'd been working to get Ward up to speed on some of the business processes at the bar. Of course, I didn't say that to Ward. Not yet. Instead, I told him that I was sick of it and he had to do it.

"You've only been at it for fifteen minutes."

"I need help."

"So, Google it."

"Come on, Kate." He made puppy dog eyes at me. That might work on Emma, but it would never, ever work on me. Especially these days.

"What would you do if I got hit by a bus?" I asked, arching an eyebrow at him. Even through my heartbroken haze, I could scrape together enough feeling to be annoyed at my brother. "You'd be totally unable to pay Willie."

Willie, who was next to me at the bar, looked over in mock horror. "We can't have that," he chimed in.

"Yeah, but *Willie knows how to do payroll*," Ward argued. "If you know, and Willie knows, why do I need to know? You can both just cover for each other."

"Oh, I dunno, maybe because you own this place?" I countered. "*What if both me and Willie got hit by a bus?*"

"I'd probably just shut down." Ward's face was unexpectedly serious. He had taken the joking suggestion literally. I bit back a comment. Ward might be annoying sometimes, and he might be helpless when it came to payroll, but he loved me.

But this was also exactly why I was worried. Ward relied too much on me. Surprisingly, it was Willie who answered Ward.

"You had better not," he told my brother. His voice was chiding, and he looked unimpressed. "I sold you this place specifically so you would keep it open. You'd be breaking your word to me if you closed it. I'd have to rise from the grave and come haunt you until you reopened."

Ward and Willie exchanged a significant glance, and whatever passed between them was beyond words. Ward nodded after a moment and Willie glanced away, seemingly satisfied. Whatever that had been about, Willie had obviously won.

"Then we're good," Ward said to me a second later. "Ghost Willie can do payroll if you both die." He shrugged.

I sighed. "Come on," I told him, rounding the bar and heading towards the office. "Let's go take a look at it. I'll walk you through everything again."

* * *

LATE THAT EVENING, when the bar had gotten quiet just before closing, I caught Lucas and Ward talking in the corner. They fell silent when I came close, and I instantly knew they were talking about either Cole or me. I cringed but curiosity got the best of me, as always.

"What is it?" I reluctantly asked. "What are you two talking about that you don't want me to hear?" I pulled up a chair and sat down with them, waiting on the answer.

Lucas looked at Ward, who was staring resolutely at the ground, and then at me. I saw indecision flit across his face before he decided to answer. "Cole's not doing so great these past few days," he told me. His voice was uncharacteristically soft. "I think he misses you." After a moment, Ward nodded. He wasn't looking at me, and his face was blank, but I could tell he was listening carefully.

Cole misses you.

Cole loves you. Deep down, you know he does.

My heart throbbed in my chest, telling me lies just like

Lucas was. I shook my head to clear it from the surge of memories and thoughts. The numbness descended again, cool and cleansing. Once again, I felt remote and distant, like I was watching a movie of myself.

"He'll get over it," I told Lucas. My voice was totally unemotional. "Cole's a great guy. I'm sure he'll find someone new soon."

It should have hurt to say those words, but it didn't. I wasn't feeling a thing. If I didn't let anything around me be real, I didn't have to imagine him in another woman's life. Or her arms. Or her bed. Hysteria rose again, along with bile in my throat. I took a deep breath and pushed the images down and the jealously away.

Don't melt down, I ordered myself. *Breathe. Keep it together.*

"I don't think he wants someone new." It wasn't like Lucas to talk about feelings—his or anyone else's—so I should have been shocked. Yet in the moment, I couldn't muster the appropriate disbelief or grasp its significance.

"Are we still talking about Cole? Or is this about you and Victoria?" I asked the question to distract him. As usual, mention of Victoria did the trick. His eyes filled with the same helpless emptiness I saw in my own every morning in the mirror. The fact that he'd been dealing with this emptiness *for months* penetrated my haze enough to make me feel a bit guilty. "Sorry, Lucas," I told him. "I'm just not up to talking about this right now."

Lucas shrugged. Like me, he'd gotten good at wearing a

mask that made him appear like a normal, functioning person. It was only now that I was broken that I saw it for what it was. Lucas was still suffering over Victoria all this time later. He hadn't recovered at all. I could only hope I would heal faster from Cole than he had from Victoria. I wasn't sure how long I could keep this act up.

40

KATE

I'D ONLY BEEN TRYING to protect my heart. By being smart and mature, I thought I could spare myself from pain this time. My plan had been solid and my execution had been good, but I had still miscalculated. It turns out that you can't protect your heart from being broken if it was never yours to begin with. My heart had always been Cole's, and he took it with him when he left. My chest was just an empty void. Again.

It's funny how things turn out. You think you can control things, and fate will find a way to prove you wrong. I'd never been more wrong in my life.

Experience had made me stronger than the last time Cole stole my heart, however. This time I was able to keep up a semblance of normality. As the weeks rolled by, I went to work, I learned to smile, and I fooled the world. Even Emma and Rae seemed to buy my act. They knew I wasn't thrilled that my relationship had come to such an early and decisive end, but neither was going to question my decision. They respected my ability to make decisions for myself. They were on my side, even when my side was stupid and lonely.

Even your closest friends can be fooled if you're willing to outright lie to them. They didn't see, couldn't see, that I was empty on the inside. Every day was a struggle to seem whole when I was hollow. My emotions rattled around in the empty cavity in my chest, but everything felt muted and fake. I couldn't feel anything without my heart.

I put my condo on the market. I hadn't wanted to move, but after I drove Cole away, I couldn't look at my house the same way. It felt haunted by him. I could smell him in my sheets no matter how many times I washed them. I could see him in my kitchen. I could hear him down the hall. It was unbearable.

The condo sold within days, and for much, much more than I expected. A bidding war between two all-cash buyers drove the price up well above asking—well above market price, really. Not that I was going to complain. Because all of a sudden, I had enough money to open my boutique.

Emma helped me to scout out the right location. We drove all around central Austin looking for the right shopping center. We ended up choosing a trendy district in east Austin, where the rent was still reasonably low, but the vibes were good. It was even right next to my absolute favorite coffee bar and bakery. I signed the lease on the storefront with shaking hands, with Emma by my side. Even the badass red power suit I was wearing—complete with oversized 1980's shoulder pads—couldn't quell the feeling that I was an imposter when the landlord handed me the keys.

"Do you have your business plan completely worked out?" Emma asked after we left the property management office. We'd gone around the corner to the bakery and were celebrating over cupcakes and caffeine.

My cold brew had no bitterness, but my face still twisted. "I think so." It was a daunting thing, writing a real business plan and then having to execute it. I was going to be a one-woman show for a while, although Emma had already promised to help man the register when I needed help. "I've got to start selecting fixtures and inventory next."

"I'm so proud of you," she told me, smiling brightly from ear to ear. "This is what you always wanted and you're making it happen. When are you quitting the bar?"

I looked down at my cupcake and bit my lip. I had no answer for that. "I haven't even told Ward about selling my condo yet."

Once again, I'd sworn Emma to silence on something that I knew her husband-to-be would want to know about. I hated doing it, but having my best friend engaged to my brother wasn't easy. I still needed my friend. Emma promised me that she and Ward had discussed that Emma would occasionally keep things about me to herself, but it still worried me.

"You should probably tell him soon," Emma prompted me gently. "He needs to find a new manager." Her expression was supportive and kind, but I knew that she wouldn't stay patient forever. Ward's business depended on me right now.

"You're right. I'll tell him tomorrow," I resolved. "When I go in for my shift."

Emma nodded approvingly.

All my professional dreams were coming true, and in a bizarre way, it was because of Cole. If he hadn't come back into my life, I might have continued on the way I was forever. I'd have just kept working in Ward's bar, under his shadow. I loved my brother dearly, and I appreciated and valued everything that he'd done to help me over the years, but I needed to be independent from him. I needed my own career and my own life. And now, finally, I was going to have it because of Cole.

"Did you get Lucas' new app?" Emma asked me, drawing me back to the conversation at our table.

I'd been avoiding Lucas and Ward because they talked to Cole. "No, what is it?"

"It's a dating app. Here, let me show you." Emma grabbed my phone off the table and installed something (she knew all my passwords). "It matches people based on musical preferences."

"Musical preferences?" It sounded kind of lame to me.

I'd never found taste in music to be particularly tied to whether I found a guy attractive or not.

Emma looked excited though. "Yeah. It's cool. The app grabs your social media profiles and your streaming music data and feeds it together into some kind of an algorithm. It's very counterintuitive, but he showed me some of the beta testing data and the early results are really interesting."

"Hmm. I don't really want to answer a bunch of questions and sort through a bunch of losers." I wasn't really sure I understood anything Emma had been talking about with the algorithms, but I could just delete the app later.

"Don't worry," Emma added, "you don't have to answer any questions or sort through losers. The app does all the work for you. The first test group had all the ranking and sorting stuff you're used to, but Lucas just put out a new version. Now, if the app detects someone it thinks you might be compatible with, it will alert you and show you their picture. That's it."

Considering that my musical taste was eclectic in the extreme, I doubted it would ever find me anyone. "Well, I hope he makes a billion dollars with it." I shrugged.

"It matched me and Ward together without knowing who we are," Emma said. I raised an eyebrow.

"Well, then he probably will make a billion dollars with it," I admitted. If anyone could be described as having the golden touch, it was Lucas. He was smarter than was good for him some of the time, but I didn't begrudge him for it.

Unlike a lot of super smart and super successful guys that I'd met in my time, Lucas was still very down to earth. At least, he was unless his ex was involved. Then he was unbalanced. Hopefully he would eventually find someone nice. Victoria certainly didn't know what she had with Lucas. He would have done anything for her.

Thinking about Victoria and Lucas made my head hurt. I was as lovesick for Cole as Lucas was for Victoria. At least Cole deserved to be heartbroken over, I told myself as I picked at my cupcake. That wasn't much, but it was something.

* * *

THE NEXT MORNING, I found Ward behind the bar as always. We weren't open just yet, so we could actually talk.

"Hey, I have something important to tell you," I told him, kissing him hello. He didn't reciprocate my greeting and I paused. "Are you okay?"

He stared straight ahead like a zombie until I waved my hand in front of his face.

"Ward?"

He blinked and shook his head slowly from side to side. His eyes were wide. "Willie's retiring. He's leaving."

My jaw went slack. "What?" Of all the things that Ward could have told me, that was one of the most shocking. Willie had frequently said that he planned to work at the bar until he either died or won the lottery. Sometimes he threatened to come haunt it after he was dead, too. I wouldn't put it past him.

"He's moving back to Lubbock with Nancy. They're getting remarried." Ward delivered the news with as much sadness as Willie's death would have warranted, although it should have been happy news. He stared down at the note I hadn't seen clutched in his left hand. "He gave me his two weeks' notice." I was worried that Ward was actually going to cry.

Willie had started this bar in the early seventies. It had been his pride and joy, second only to his son, Willie Junior. Considering that his son didn't speak to him, the bar was his life. Willie sold it to Ward not because he needed the money or wanted to be out of the business, but because he wanted to see it go on to the next generation. He continued working here, day after day, year after year, because he really, truly loved the Lone Star Lounge.

But Willie wasn't just a professional mentor to Ward. He was a friend and a father figure. Willie had helped Ward through a number of personal and professional struggles over the years, mostly just by listening. Willie was a tremendous listener. And he never judged anyone. Ever. Losing Willie, and having him move away, was going to be an enormous life change for Ward.

"I can't believe it," I told him, hugging Ward tightly. "It's all gonna' be okay."

He hugged me back for a long moment. Even though

we were siblings, we didn't hug very often. It felt nice. When he drew away, his face looked a bit less horrified.

"At least I've got you," he told me. My heart twisted. I had to tell him now, it wouldn't be right to wait another moment.

"Ward, I—"

Bang. Bang. Bang. Someone slammed a heavy fist against the front door. "Hey!" Lucas' voice was muffled, but it was definitely him. "Ward! Kate! Willie! Let me in. I know you're in there."

Ward rolled his eyes and headed toward the door. "I'm coming!" He hollered. "Keep your wig on, Lucas!"

"I've got something really important to talk to you about, Ward," I called out. He nodded at me seriously.

"Later okay? Let me see what's got Lucas all worked up."

Ward unlocked the door and let him in. Lucas was grinning from ear to ear.

"I've got news!" He announced. Lucas was wearing a suit jacket at noon. That never happened. The man lived in worn-out jeans and T-shirts.

Ward and I exchanged a worried glance. It seemed like everyone had news today.

"What?" Lucas said, his enthusiasm dimming for a second. "What's wrong?"

"Is your news good?" Ward asked. Lucas nodded enthusiastically. I prayed he hadn't eloped with Victoria or something similarly crazy.

"Tell us your good news first," I told Lucas. "Then we'll tell you our bad news."

"I've found a buyer for my app." He was grinning from ear to ear.

Holy shit. That was fast.

"Congratulations!" Ward and I said in unison. Ward shook Lucas' hand and I gave him a little hug. I knew the guy had been working night and day on his project, even if I'd only learned what it was yesterday.

"This deserves a toast," Ward told Lucas. He fished a bottle of champagne out from the cooler.

"No!" Lucas cried, causing Ward and me to jump. "No toasts yet," he continued in a more normal tone. His eyes went wide, and he looked around fearfully. "We don't want to jinx it."

Ward laughed and slid the bottle back in. He rolled his eyes at Lucas. "Alright. Fine. Be superstitious. We'll drink it when you formally sign the deal."

"Who's your buyer?" I asked Lucas. "Are you allowed to tell us or is it all still super-secret?"

He bobbed his head up and down. "It's super-secret but I trust you two. It's a private equity group out of New York. They have a number of similar companies in their portfolio, so this is a natural acquisition for them. Hopefully we can come to an agreement that has me staying on as CEO for at least five years—that's what I want. They're going to be sending down their valuation team in a week or so with a small army of due diligence lawyers."

I couldn't very well pretend to know what that meant, and nothing involving 'an army of lawyers' sounded good, but he was smiling. It sounded like Rae's new job, actually. Wouldn't that be a weird coincidence? I just smiled and nodded along. "That's exciting," I told him. "I'm really happy for you!"

Lucas looked like he was about to explode from excitement. "I can barely believe this is happening." He shook his head in total disbelief. "If I can pull this off, everything is really going to change."

Lucas meant this in a positive way, but when I looked over at Ward, I could see that he was not nearly as enthusiastic about all this change. His face was smiling, but it was a brittle, frightened type of smile. It was a panic smile. I hated knowing that I was about to make it that much worse.

41

COLE

Lucas called to invite me to his victory party at the bar that evening and I couldn't very well tell him no, even though it meant I might see Kate. It had been almost an entire month, but I wasn't sure I could be in her presence without falling to my knees and begging her to take me back. Needless to say, it took me a long time to work up the courage to drive to the Lone Star Lounge that evening.

The bar was unusually busy, so I had to park a few blocks away. I sat in my car for a while before going in, just trying to work up the nerve. While I was sitting there trying to find my strength, my phone pinged. I looked down to see that my genetic results had been processed and uploaded. Curious, I opened up the app and took a look.

It took me a moment to process the pie graph I was seeing. I was from... everywhere. The little pie chart was divided into dozens of slices. I had genetic ties to every continent except for Australia. The majority of my ancestry seemed to be around the Mediterranean, especially Spain, Italy, and Northern Africa. That would explain my tan skin and dark eyes. The chunk of my ancestry that came from northern Europe helped explain my above-average height. The part of me that was—score—from the Polynesian islands helped explain my heavy build and more almond shaped eyes. I was Samoan just like The Rock! I mean, I was lots and lots of things, but Samoan was one of them.

My fingers were dialing up my mom before I realized what I was doing. She answered on the first ring, as usual. My mom practically lived with a phone in her hand at all times. She always had friends calling and hated missing the latest gossip.

"Hey sweetie!" her voice was a comforting, twangy southern balm.

"Hi, mom. I just got my genetic results. I wanted to tell you I'm from everywhere." I sounded excited even to my own ears.

She laughed. Her laugh was light, airy, and happy. I could see her smiling face in my mind. "Tell me all about it, darlin'," she ordered me.

I carefully explained the pie chart I was seeing, telling her how the genetic markers showed that I'd probably been the product of two extremely multiracial parents. There must have been a lot of interbreeding in my family over generations, possibly indicating that my family might have been merchants, or lived in cities that saw a lot of international trade. There was no one country that had a majority on my ancestry. I was, literally, from the entire world. Except Australia. And, I supposed, Antarctica.

"You're the future of humanity, aren't you?" she mused. She sounded impressed by my motley background.

"I guess so." We were a long way from a world without race or racism, but it was a nice thing to think about. I'd never come across as being any particular race, so I'd never encountered any real racism. Sometimes people just assumed I was from their race, whatever that may be. Black people sometimes thought I was mixed. White people sometimes thought I was just swarthy. Usually I just got a lot of second looks and questions I couldn't answer about where my family was from. Until now. Now I could tell people confidently that I was from everywhere.

"Well, the future is going to be very handsome just like you," she told me. "And very smart and talented. Oh, and probably very tall if they're all like you." My mom, who was five-four in her church shoes was very glad that I'd turned out to be tall. She made good use of my height whenever I was around. I felt like I spent a lot of my time getting things down from high places for her.

"Thanks, mom." My mom was never light on her praise of me in general. She'd always been that way, even when I was a fat kid with bad skin, bad grades and low self-esteem. Back when I'd had a face only a mother could love, she did.

"You're welcome, darlin'. They certainly took long enough to give you your results though. I thought they said it would only take a few weeks." She made a disapproving clucking noise. It was the same noise she used on the cat when it jumped on her kitchen countertops.

"Well, I didn't turn the test in right away." I hesitated. "Actually, I was kind of worried about it if I'm honest."

"Why's that?" She sounded mystified and I relaxed. Kate was right.

I felt silly now, but I wasn't going to keep the truth from my mom. "I was worried you would think that I was rejecting our family if I looked. I didn't want you to feel rejected or anything. I just wanted you to know that I don't want any other family than the one I've got."

She was quiet for a minute. I heard her sigh over the phone. "Jimmy said you would feel like that. He said I was putting you in a situation where 'you'd be as lost as last year's Easter eggs.' I told him he was being overly sensitive. I guess he was right. I never wanted you to feel like that. I just wanted you to know it was okay to look into your birth family if you wanted to."

"I liked learning about where my biological family came from in the world," I said carefully, "but I don't really want to know anything else about them. I know who my real family is."

I could almost hear my mom smiling into the phone. "I know, honey. I know. But you can always change your mind and I won't be mad. You can look into your birth family whenever you want. I won't be offended. I know you're always gonna be my son, and I'm always gonna be your mom."

Talking to her made me feel a lot better. I ought to call more often. "How is Uncle Jimmy?" I asked.

She made an unladylike noise. "Getting into trouble as always. Yesterday I thought I heard some squirrels up in the attic. I told him about it, and instead of calling the exterminator like a normal person, he went on the internet and found out that if you put a radio up there it will run them off. So, he decided to climb up in the attic during the heat of the day and damn near killed himself. But you know him. If he isn't as busy as a one-legged cat in a sandbox, he thinks he's going to seed."

I laughed with her, feeling my spirits lift. "I miss you guys."

"We miss you too, sweetie. What are you doing tonight?"

"I'm going to a friend's celebration party. He just had a —" I didn't know how to express the concept of selling an app to a private equity investor in a way that my mom could easily grasp. She didn't do technology. "—a good thing happen to him at work."

"That sounds like fun. I don't want to keep you. Besides, I've got book club."

"Okay, mom. Thanks for talking to me. Have fun with your friends! I'll talk to you soon."

"Bye sweetie! Love you."

"I love you too, mom."

When I hung up I had a smile on my face, but it didn't last very long. I was glad that my mom was supportive of whatever I wanted to do with my life, and supportive of me seeking out my birth family if that's what I wanted to do, but talking to her had also reminded me how lonely I'd been lately. Not having any real social interaction for weeks was beginning to take a toll on me both physically and psychologically.

I'd lost weight—something that I knew was going to happen and needed to happen based on my conversations with my nutritionist—but at a rate much faster than intended. I just wasn't hungry. I was also much sleepier than usual. Both were symptoms of depression.

But the physical symptoms paled in comparison to the psychological ones. I was still holding things together well, but the more functional I seemed to become, the more real the loneliness at night was. The haze that had settled in front of my eyes had started to lift up like mist burning off in the morning, and all I could see ahead of me was loneliness.

My mom had raised me to believe that it wasn't necessary to be in a romantic relationship. She was happy with her friends and her family. She didn't have or want a mate. There aren't that many people out there who actually admit that they are asexual. Due to social stigmas and all sorts of stupid prejudices that people hold, it isn't always easy for them to be honest. But my mom was honest from the start. She was happy and complete just the way she was. Jimmy was the same, although never in so many words.

But me? I didn't feel happy or complete by myself. From an early age, I knew that I wasn't destined to be like my mom. I saw my friends' parents and thought that I wanted what they had. A little family and a partner to help run it. I'd never imagined that I'd find myself looking down the barrel at thirty and still be single. In my childhood dreams for myself, there had always been a wife at my side. Someone to care for and to care for me. Someone that I could protect and cherish and love. Someone who would be there in the mornings when I woke up and in the evenings when we went to bed.

These fantasies of mine were never sexual in any way. I was too young for that. I just thought that it would be nice to have a partner that I could live my life with. Like a best friend, but better.

Now, I feared that I'd met the woman that I was supposed to have as my partner in life and failed to make her mine. I wasn't worthy of her, and I'd made too many mistakes, and she'd figured that out. So instead of having a partner in my life, I was going to end up like my mom after all, only not because that was how I wanted it. I would be alone forever, because no one else would ever be as perfect for me as Kate.

Reluctantly, I made my way down the block to the Lone Star Lounge. It was twilight, and the sound of happy people in the bar carried down the street on the evening breeze. It sounded like people finding their partners to me. That sound was the music of people finding love. I feared if I failed tonight that there was nothing but silence in my future.

It occurred to me then that I had nothing at all left to lose. Kate had already dumped me. It was time for me to go all-in. I might not be able to win Kate back tonight, but I wasn't going to let indecision or fear get in the way of trying. It was time to tell her the whole truth, and I still had one ace up my sleeve. I loved her.

42

KATE

WARD and I were working through the evening rush when my phone pinged. The whole day had been nonstop madness, and I hadn't had a break in hours, let alone managed to tell Ward I was quitting. It was the busiest we'd been in months. I wasn't used to the noise since it wasn't my usual alert tone, and I looked down at it in confusion. An icon I had almost forgotten about was demanding my attention. Lucas' app.

I frowned at my phone. What did the app want? I hadn't messed with Lucas' dating app at all since Emma installed it on my phone the night before. She was at the bar tonight, across the room, laughing with Lucas and Rae at a table. Too far away. I would just figure it out myself. I clicked the app.

A little chime played and then Cole's face appeared on my screen. *You have a new match*, my phone informed me in animated blue text on a cheerful, cartoon background. *Cole Rylander is within two hundred feet of you.* A tiny cartoon heart turned in a circle and then exploded into a thousand more rainbow hearts.

I froze. *Lucas' dating app matched me with Cole? And he's here?* My heart immediately started banging in my rib cage. The noise and commotion of the bar receded around me in an instant. I felt hot and cold, like when I'd had a panic attack on the fiftieth floor. I had not expected to see Cole tonight. He hadn't been to the bar all month, and I thought that we had an unspoken arrangement that this was my territory and not his.

How dare he come here? How dare he—

"Hi, Kate." The voice ripped my attention up from Cole's image on my phone and to the real thing. He smiled at me confidently, wearing that same look that he'd worn on the day of Ward and Emma's engagement party. The one that said, 'I know you want me, Kate.' In that crisp blue button-down and sexy, slouchy jeans, he was absolutely right.

And absolutely wrong.

"Can I get you something?" I asked blandly, putting on my patented bartender smile. Inside I was shaking, but at least on the outside, I was all business. My smile, tone, and demeanor were not too warm or not too sweet. I'd carefully designed and practiced this act to discourage the guys who thought I wanted to date them when I really just wanted a good tip. I never thought I'd need to use it on Cole.

He was totally undeterred by my professionalism. "How about fifteen minutes of your time?" he asked. Cole's amber-colored eyes were full of that same, familiar heat. The kind that made me restless, flushed, and wanton. Even now, all I could think about when he looked at me that way was rolling over and spreading my legs for him. And I suspected, from the way his grin widened a bit and crinkled the edges of his eyes, that he knew it.

I cleared my throat and shifted from foot to foot. "Sorry, that's not on our menu. Anything else?" I wasn't trying to be rude, but there were about ten people trying to get my attention at the moment because they wanted beer, and my poor battered heart couldn't handle seeing him yet.

"Kate..."

"Cole. Just... please," I begged. My cool bartender attitude slipped, and my voice cracked. I sounded heartbroken, because I was. I hated that it happened. I hated even more that he saw it. And not just him, either. In this busy bar, a dozen people got to see me fight back tears.

"Fifteen minutes, Kate. That's all I'm asking you for." I was going to tell him no, of course, but then he added, "and if you want me to leave at that point, I will. And I won't come back." His tone was self-assured, but his eyes held a vulnerability I wasn't used to seeing.

Despite my better instincts, I softened. "I'll meet you in the office in five minutes," I told him, trying to maintain my bland persona as best I could. "I still have a few orders to get out."

He nodded and wandered off, leaving me with six drinks to make and a lot of anxiety. My hands had already been pulling beers as fast as I could, but I kicked it into overdrive. I was shaking a martini shaker, garnishing, and refilling waters at the same time to buy those precious fifteen minutes.

"Can I get a margarita over here?" A customer snapped down the bar at me. "Or do I have to watch your entire relationship drama play out first?" She tapped her long nails along the bar like Cruella De-Ville and mumbled something about me being a lazy slut.

Oh hell no.

"Go fuck yourself," I snapped right back. "Just for that, no drink for you." A couple of regulars laughed. Just because I was heartbroken didn't mean anyone got to push me around. I was still me, and I didn't take shit from anybody. The woman slunk away from the bar, flushing purple. I turned to another customer that had been waiting even longer and much more patiently. "Sorry about the wait. What can I get for you?" I asked him with a smile.

I FOUND Cole seated at Ward's desk, looking more like the CEO of a dealership empire than a pro athlete. He'd either adjusted surprisingly quickly to the business life, or he had been born for it, because the man looked good behind a desk. I left the door open, fearing trouble if I let it close. We'd gotten to trouble on that desk before.

"Okay, here I am," I told him, darting my gaze at the clock on the wall. "Your fifteen minutes start now."

"I'm lucky I work well under pressure," Cole said coolly, "because a lesser man wouldn't be able to handle this sort of stress." If I didn't know him, I would have thought he was perfectly at ease. His smirk was sexy, but I could still see that there was vulnerability in him.

Outside in the bar I could be tough, but in here I was still an insecure little girl. I didn't trust myself to say anything, so I just arched an eyebrow, crossed my arms, and stared. Maybe if I looked tough, I could convince myself I was tough. Maybe I could even convince Cole.

"When you asked me out all those years ago, I was crazy about you," he told me. He shook his head with some emotion I couldn't place. "I lied to you. When you asked me if I liked you, and I told you that I was just being polite, I lied. I was stupid and young. I was trying to make sure I had a future, and I was trying to make sure you had a future. I knew that there was no way for us to be together back then. So, I drove you off. But I was in love you. Even back then. It was always you." He fell silent and looked at me.

My heart hurt. Before I couldn't trust myself to find words to say, but now I couldn't find any. I'd been rendered completely mute. *He loved me? Even back then he cared?* Cole glanced at the clock nervously and continued.

"I didn't know you were a virgin that night. I've got absolutely no excuse for how I behaved. I'm sorry. I hope I didn't hurt you, I... Please believe me that I never, ever would have hurt you like that on purpose. I probably wasn't as gentle as I should have been and if I hurt you..." His voice broke painfully. He looked down at the desk in front of him, and all his former confidence seemed to drain out of him.

Rationally, I knew he was still the same man, but he seemed to shrink into himself from guilt. He tried to meet my eyes and failed before burying his head in his hands. I melted in an instant, coming over to touch his shoulder with a shaking hand. "You didn't hurt me," I whispered. "It's okay. I swear you never hurt me. Not at all. It's okay."

He looked at me, wide-eyed, and shook his head. "How could it possibly be okay? I told you that you were *just a distraction to me.* You were—"

"Willing," I interrupted. *"Cole, I was willing.* I was a grownup making a grownup, sober decision about my own body and my own life." No matter what, this was the truth and he needed to believe it. I would make him believe it.

"But I—"

"No!" I wasn't willing to let him hate himself over a decision made a half decade ago at a college party. "Stop it. Stop feeling sorry for yourself and don't you dare pity me. You know how much I hate it." I stared at him so obstinately, he had to smile, even if it was a humorless, tiny smile.

"Kate, why don't you hate me over how I took your virginity?" he asked after a moment. He was looking at me like I was nuts. "I would understand if you did. I would deserve it."

"Because you didn't take shit from me," I snapped. "*Virginity is not a commodity*. Anything we exchanged that night was freely given. This isn't the middle ages. It's not like I was expecting you to marry me or something. We were two kids at a party who had one night of meaningless sex on a golf course. The end."

That shut him up. The seconds ticked by as we stared at one another across a chasm of misunderstanding, recrimination, and guilt.

"Meaningless?" he finally asked. "It wasn't meaningless to me. I loved you then. I love you now." His voice was low and earnest.

Now I was the one to regret my words. I took a deep breath and let it out slowly. My whole life was revolving around this moment. "It wasn't meaningless to me either," I admitted. "I loved you. That night was special to me, really special. I thought you would never feel anything for me like what I felt for you, but at least for that little while, you were mine." Emotion was making my words sound thick in my own ears. I wanted Cole to believe me so badly that I wanted to shake him by the shoulders and scream at him. The idea that he would think I'd not enjoyed every second of our intimacy was criminally wrong.

"You don't know how much I wanted to call you the

next day and confess everything. I almost did." His eyes were begging me to believe him, too. "I should have."

Despite everything, I giggled. "Don't be ridiculous. Of course, you shouldn't have." He looked up at me in disbelief. I shook my head at him, wondering what sort fantasy world he thought we lived in. This wasn't a fairy tale. "You did the right thing. You were about to graduate to play in the NFL. I'm..." I laughed again, feeling ridiculous. "I'm not good enough for you. I never was."

There. I'd said it.

Now he knew the truth. The whole, ugly truth. The real, secret truth.

The thing I didn't want to admit even to myself.

I wasn't good enough for Cole.

Why else would he not want me? He was perfect, but me? I was ordinary. Average. Disposable.

I stared at him, shocked at myself for admitting the truth, and there was an equal amount of shock in Cole's eyes. *Then he laughed.* I stepped back, astounded and instantly offended. Before I could lash out, Cole grabbed my hands and pulled me back to him. He swept me up in a hug so powerful that I could barely breathe. I squeaked in surprise.

"*You're* not good enough for *me*?" His voice was totally and completely appalled. "That's so fucking off-base it's not even funny. *I'm not even fit to be in the same room with you.* I love you though. Please, *please* take me back. Will you, Kate? Will you give us another shot?" He had both of my hands and stared up at me with so much affection and tenderness that it hurt to see.

All my childhood, I struggled with not being good enough. My family was poor, I was the second, less-talented child, and my dad took off like my brother, my mom and I were all disposable. As a young woman, I learned that men who seemed to care could easily cast me aside. Even the good guys, like Cole, might not want me or stick around. But knowing that he loved me—that he'd always cared and wanted to be with me—it changed everything I thought I knew about the world. It changed what I thought I knew about myself.

I don't cry a lot. I'm not a very weepy girl in general because my usual response to feeling pain is to lash out and cause some of my own. But now I was fighting big, fat, hot, ugly tears. They crawled down my face in ecstasy while I nodded yes. My response to realigning my worldview in a positive way was a good, old fashioned, ugly cry. I smiled and laughed through my tears.

Cole pulled me into his arms and laughed, rocking me back and forth like a baby. I could feel the relief radiating off him in waves. We were two real pieces of work, him and me. Neither one of us seemed to believe we were worth a damn thing. At least we each had the other to remind ourselves that it wasn't true.

A familiar call of a distant "*Kate, where the hell are you? We're slammed out here!*" followed by a much closer "*What the fuck?*" made me lift my head off Cole's chest. Ward was standing in the doorway. His face was a mask of total, dumbstruck horror.

Cole and I were both red-faced balls of emotion, clutching at one another in the desk chair. This was not a flattering way to be caught by my brother (although it could be worse, all things considered). His eyebrows were so high they were about to be swallowed by his hairline and his jaw was slack. I could see a white ring all the way around his blue pupils. He backed up and out of the office without another word. Clearly, he did not want to deal with whatever very private, extremely emotional thing was going on in here between his sister and his best friend. He disappeared around the corner, still walking backward.

"You know, I feel like I should have taken a photo of your brother's face just now," Cole said to me after Ward had gone. Humor had returned to his voice, and I knew that we were going to be okay. "I don't think I've ever actually seen Ward be struck truly speechless. That was a first."

"I know. We'll probably never see it again, either, since he's gonna be too busy bitching about seeing us like this for the rest of his life."

43

KATE

WHEN I FINALLY PEELED MY body off of Cole's and went back to work, I kept moving nonstop until close. It was hours before the bar even remotely began to settle down. This night had been one for the record books. At least we were making money, because my feet were definitely going to pay for the effort the next day.

The good thing about being so busy was that except for the occasional, disgusted glance from my brother, we didn't discuss what he'd witnessed in the office. Neither one of us had time to think, let alone talk. The bad thing was that my news about quitting the bar, let alone sharing news about my reconciliation with Cole, had to wait for almost four and a half hours.

Ward was taking the last tray of glasses to the kitchen when I finally had a chance to drop my tired ass into a chair around the table where Lucas, Emma, and Cole were already sitting.

"Mazel tov!" Lucas said to Cole and me, toasting us with his last sip of beer. "Glad you two idiots figured it out." He was grinning from ear to ear. He'd been celebrating all evening.

"Thanks, Lucas," Cole said, brushing my hair back from my tired face and kissing me on the forehead. "Tonight is a night for all kinds of victories. You have your deal, I got my girl--"

"And Kate has her new business!" Emma chimed in. "Don't forget about that."

Neither Lucas nor Cole looked surprised. "Wait, you guys know?" I asked. "How?"

"I learned from Wille who hears all," Lucas said, shrugging. "Why, was it a secret? I think it's great you're opening a lingerie boutique. I've seen too many beautiful women wearing ugly panties in this world. Life is much too short for ugly knickers." He said this as if it were a very profound insight. Some genius he was.

"What about you?" I asked Cole. His answering smile was mysterious. "Tell me!" I squealed. I looked at Emma, but she shook her head innocently.

"I know how to keep a secret," Emma insisted. "Unlike Willie, *apparently.*"

"Well then, how did you figure it out?" I asked Cole. I frowned at him until he cracked.

"Jolene," he finally admitted. "She heard that you'd

listed your condo. I put two and two together. Who do you think helped drive up the price so high on your place?"

My jaw dropped open and Cole and Lucas both snickered at my expression. "You bought my condo?" My shock was complete. Not that there was a thing in the world wrong with my condo, but it didn't exactly scream millionaire athlete bachelor pad. Even on its best day, my little condo was several hundred thousand dollars below the very bottom of Cole's budget for a place to live. We were on totally different planes of existence when it came to finances.

Unexpectedly, Cole shook his head. "I tried to buy your condo," he corrected. "Somebody outbid me." He looked annoyed. "I had this whole plan to buy it and give it back to you if I managed to get you back, but now it's ruined."

"You know that you drove the price up way beyond what it was worth," I told him. "You're lucky that you didn't win."

Cole looked unconvinced. "I wanted to buy it for you. I knew that you didn't really want to sell it. You were only selling to fund your business."

"I'm glad you didn't buy it," I told him. Secretly I was sad that I'd come pretty close to having both my beloved condo and my business seed money, but it didn't really matter. I had Cole. He was better than anything that money could buy.

"At least it was some other dumb shmuck that overpaid for Kate's condo," Emma said. "I wonder who it was?"

A familiar voice cleared his throat, and all four of us turned to see Ward approaching with a fresh pitcher in one hand and something small in the other. "Emma, my love, that dumb schmuck would be me," he announced. All four of us stared at him in shock.

It took the entirety of the pitcher, but we eventually pieced together what happened.

"I can't believe you outbid me," Cole groused, looking at Ward with annoyance.

"I'm not as dumb as you thought I was, huh?" My brother was preening disgracefully. "I called Kate's friend Tiffany and had her do a little extra reconnaissance on my part in exchange for a small, off-the-books commission. Let's just say that I made extra sure my final offer was higher." That sounded vaguely unethical, but given the circumstances, I'd let it slide.

"How come your name wasn't on any of the closing documents?" I asked. "I thought I was selling it to some real estate company."

"You did. My new holding entity bought your condo," Ward said matter-of-factly. "I needed to reorganize all my rentals anyway, and some expansion was in order as well." Sometimes I forgot that Ward had business savvy buried deep in skull beneath all the brain damage. He was doing pretty well financially, though, so I supposed it made a bit of sense that he'd want to invest in the booming Austin market.

"So, you're going to rent it out?" I asked, wondering if I could rent it back from him. Having Ward as a landlord was not exactly ideal, but since he was already the person I called in the middle of the night if the toilet broke, at least he was used to it.

He gave me a disbelieving look. "No."

"Oh, are you going to flip it then?" I'd thought I'd done a fairly good job with the improvements to my condo, but what did I know? Ward was the property guru here. Maybe he was going to paint everything beige and turn a huge profit. HGTV was always telling people to paint shit beige. Apparently, that's what normal people liked.

Ward shook his head at me. His grin was wide. "Wrong again." He was enjoying this way too much. Teasing me had always been one of his favorite games. I'd venture he liked teasing me even more than he liked football, and he liked football far too much.

Lucas, Cole, and Emma were all hiding smiles at this point. I hated being the last one to figure something out. It made me feel dumb.

"Well then, what are you going to do with it?" I asked Ward, annoyed. It wasn't my fault I didn't have the same level of real estate knowledge as the rest of them.

"*I'm going to give it back to you, you dummy!*" Ward looked exasperated that he had to spell it out, but he was also fighting chuckles. "I swear, you telepathically seem to know if I change my brand of breakfast cereal, or need some life coaching, but you are not very self-aware. If someone wants to *help you*, or God forbid, *cares about you*, it's just freakin' mystifying to you, isn't it?" After his outburst, he shook his head at me in a mixture of affection and annoyance that I was very used to seeing from him. He and Cole exchanged a look that bordered on camaraderie and I wasn't sure if I could handle that. The last thing I needed was those two bonding about how hard I was to deal with.

"Shut up. I'm plenty self-aware," I snapped. It wasn't true, but I had to defend myself anyway. Otherwise Ward would think that he could just walk all over me. "So, you knew I wanted to start a lingerie boutique?" I'd never told him about my ambition. I hadn't even told my diary, since I didn't keep one anymore after that time Ward read it when I was in high school. The only people who were supposed to know were Rae and Emma (although I wasn't surprised Willie figured it out).

He shrugged his massive shoulders. "Nope. I had no clue about that. Sounds like you though. You have good taste. It'll be successful. I'm sure of it."

His support was welcome, and I smiled a shy little smile at him. Then another thought intruded, and I wrinkled my nose at him in confusion. "Ward, you were going to buy my condo just 'cause? That hardly seemed like a good investment of money, even if it would be nice for me to have it."

Ward chuckled at me and clearly thought he was very

clever. "I knew you weren't going to work here forever. I'm always monitoring the local real estate listings for good investments, so when I saw your condo come up for sale, I figured that you were going to do something big with the money. You've never been irresponsible with money. I knew it had to be business related. So... I decided to help." He glanced over at Cole in clear annoyance. "*I didn't expect to help quite so much,* but some *asshole* decided to bid against me and run the price way up. Thanks buddy."

"Oh yeah, blame me," Cole said sarcastically. "All I was trying to do was win the love of your sister by helping her achieve her dream the same exact way you were. That Cole. What a gigantic, fucking asshole."

Ward's reply was typically childish. "You said it, not me."

Their exchange was funny, but another piece had just fallen into place for me. "Hold up. So, you knew that I was going to quit the bar today?" I asked Ward. His face was guilty enough to tip me off.

"Well... not today, but I figured you would soon." *Oh, he definitely knew.*

"But you let me worry all day long about how you were going to handle it? I was seriously concerned you were going to have a nervous breakdown if you lost me and Willie at the same time." My voice had become annoyed. Ward smirked at me. What an ass. Lucas and Emma were highly entertained by this entire exchange between Ward and me. They watched the two of us fighting like it was a movie.

"You made me witness whatever the hell you and Cole were doing in the office in *my desk chair*. Let's just call it even, how about that?" His face betrayed how traumatic he'd found the experience. Emma reached over and patted his arm comfortingly.

I looked over at Cole and we both nodded. Considering that Ward didn't know what Cole and I had done *on his desk* a few weeks back, I was willing to let that statement stand. There were things my brother just didn't need to know, and the fact that I'd been fucked within an inch of my life in the exact spot where he signed my paycheck was one of them. "Okay. Fine. You win."

EPILOGUE

KATE

"PLEASE STAND FOR THE BRIDE." Willie's voice shook just a little bit, and I found myself blinking away tears.

Emma was the most beautiful bride that I'd ever seen in my entire life, and I'd watched every single episode of every single season of 'Say Yes to the Dress.' Her dress wasn't the one I would have intuitively picked out, but it just went to show that I didn't know *everything* about fashion. I would have put her in something slinky and tightly fitted, but Emma? She wanted to be a princess.

And I'd learned over the years that although she might be shy, in the end nobody gets between Emma and what Emma wants. Especially on her wedding day. So, Emma was a princess. She was wearing a gigantic, blush pink, bedazzled lace and satin ballgown, complete with a tulle petticoat and full, cathedral length, lace train. Atop her golden braid sat a rhinestone encrusted tiara and a massive, bedazzled lace veil. Her bouquet was a barbie pink spray of roses, each of which had a rhinestone glued in the center of the blooms. Even her shoes were barbie pink and covered in crystals. Objectively, this entire look shouldn't have worked. Not only was Emma too petite, it was just too damn much. She should have looked like the unholy spawn of a ridiculous cupcake and a gypsy bride, but she didn't. She looked perfect.

Emma had such natural beauty, grace, and poise that when she walked down the aisle on her father's arm, she looked as elegant as any runway model. She was breathtakingly, heartbreakingly beautiful. Her beaming face, full of adoration for my lucky dumbass of a loveable brother, made everything work. Cole and I shot flirty looks at one another from opposite sides of the makeshift altar, and I knew that my turn wasn't far away. Secretly we were already engaged, but I was wearing my ring on a long chain around my neck for the time being. The ring was fully hidden behind the many rhinestones encrusting the bodice of my ridiculous, barbie pink bridesmaid gown. It wouldn't be right to announce my own engagement so close to my best friend's wedding.

Today, all attention was on Emma and Ward. My brother looked surprisingly calm and happy to promise himself away for all time. I never thought I'd see the day, but I was happy to be wrong. I couldn't be happier for him. Beneath all the annoyance and irritation he caused me on a daily basis, I loved Ward and wanted him to be happy. And if my amazing friend Emma was willing to be the one to make him happy, well then, he'd better take care of her and I wished them both well.

Willie fiddled with his Bible as Emma finished her slow, careful walk down the aisle we'd created in the bar. He was officiating today, and really, he was the only appropriate person to do so (even if he got ordained online). He'd been Ward's unofficial confessor for so long that he was basically a saint anyway. He definitely had the patience of one. It seemed weirdly right that Willie should be the one to marry Emma and Ward, here in this bar. Next week he'd be moving back to Lubbock with Nancy, so this was as much his goodbye party as their wedding.

This wedding was both the ending and beginning of an era at the bar, and the tears I'd been blinking away started to escape as Ward and Emma exchanged their vows. By the time they were kissing their I-Do's, I was all out bawling. I hope everyone there enjoyed seeing me cry, because I'd already threatened the photographer that if I looked like shit in the pictures, it was his head. Thank God for waterproof mascara.

"Was that you I heard sniffling over my shoulder?" Emma asked me during the post-ceremony photos.

"I don't know what you're talking about," I lied, "It must

have been someone else. Your great-aunt was looking really weepy though. It must have been her."

Emma arched an eyebrow. "Ethel?" She looked around carefully and then whispered, "I don't think Ethel even knows this is a wedding. She thinks it's 1998. She gets very upset if anyone suggests otherwise, because then she remembers that her favorite cat, Buttons, is dead. *Then she will cry*, at least until she forgets again."

I hoped Emma's Aunt Ethel didn't run into my second cousin Bill at this wedding. He could easily supply her with a new cat or ten. Or some goats. He had animals to spare and an order from the county to cut their numbers down or the animal control folks would do it for him. Weddings had a wonderful way of bringing all the *really fun relatives out of the woodwork*.

"Groom and groom's parents, please," the photographer requested just then, unintentionally proving me right.

My mom and dad hadn't been pleasant to one another in years, but they were being civil today for Ward's sake. I was half shocked that Ward had even wanted our dad to come to his wedding, but he was getting sentimental in his old age. Either that or he'd just caved to Emma's request to meet him. My mom and dad stood on either side of Ward and smiled, and they looked pretty convincingly like a happy family.

"Groom's whole family, please," the photographer called, and I grinned at Emma before obediently stepping forward to be posed. I ended up standing next to my mom with my dad at my right shoulder.

"I hear things are going well for you, Katie," my dad said cheerfully in between snaps of the camera. I resisted the urge to cringe and kept smiling for the pictures. I still couldn't stand when he called me Katie.

"Mhmm," I said without turning my head. I smiled toward the camera and hoped he wouldn't insist on talking to me. I really had nothing to say to him. Other than supplying the sperm for my conception, he hadn't done much in my life but cause pain and suffering. This was actually the first time I'd seen my dad in several years. He'd made parole just in time to attend the wedding.

"You opened a store here in town, didn't you?" he asked, and I could feel my mom and Ward shifting at my side. My dad was taking an interest in me? That could only mean one thing.

"Mhmm," I answered. I kept smiling at the camera.

"And you're doing well? Your store, I mean?" His voice had taken on a warm, friendly tone that I knew better than to trust. I saw my mom roll her eyes.

"Yes," I told my dad simply. Business couldn't be better, actually. In the few months I'd been open, I could barely keep my inventory in stock long enough to meet demand. It was insanity what women would do—and in some cases had to do—to get the right lingerie. I frequently had customers that drove all the way from San Antonio, Dallas, and Houston, only to cry when they put on their first properly fitted bra. Some of them had been wearing the wrong size for decades. It felt good to know I was helping people, in addition to making mad cash.

"And you're dating one of Ward's friends, too? Cole Rylander? I bet he's doing well financially, too."

Ward and I made eye contact. Our communication was wordless, but clear: *here it comes.*

I turned to my dad, unwilling to make this painless for him. "Yes, I'm dating Cole Rylander. He is doing well financially, too." His dealerships were thriving, although they kept him busier than I'd like. Getting enough of Cole was a constant struggle for me. I was addicted to his humor, his mind, his body, his personality, his everything. Everything except his money. I didn't really care about that. I wished my dad could say the same.

"Do you think you could spare your old man a few thousand dollars, Katie? I want to start a scrapping business and need a little seed capital if you know what I mean. I'm thinking no more than five grand ought to start me up."

The fact that he was asking this of me at his son's wedding, while we were taking pictures, and in front of all the rest of our immediate family, was not surprising. It was annoying, however. And sad. It was especially sad because I knew, if he was given the money, he'd spend the whole lot on whatever his most pressing addiction was at the moment. In between the alcohol, the gambling, and the small-time con jobs he liked to run, he had no shortage of expensive vices.

I didn't reply, and after about thirty seconds or so he eventually figured out my answer. The photographer moved on to the next group and we dispersed. My mom and I headed over to the nearest champagne. We'd earned it. Being this close to my dad was physically exhausting for us both.

"You know, sweetie, in his highly unique way, your dad just paid you the greatest compliment on your achievements that he possibly could," she told me.

I rolled my eyes. "How?"

She smirked at me. "He's never asked you for money before, has he?"

I frowned. "No." I shrugged. "I've never had any money to give him before. He's asked me to ask Ward for money and then give it to him, though."

My mom's smirk widened into a real smile. "Exactly."

"I don't get it. How is begging for money a compliment to me?"

She brushed my hair back behind my ear affectionately. "He thinks you've got your life under control. You've got your successful business, you've got your boyfriend, and you're living a completely independent, adult life. I mean, not that he would know what that is except to mooch off of it. But still. He now sees you as an adult."

My mom was right, although it was bittersweet to admit it. The clearest indicator that my dad thought I had my shit together was that he thought I might be an easy mark. I found myself giggling. "Hooray for me!" I told my mom, lifting my glass in self-salute. "I'm mooch-able!"

She hugged me, and I hugged her back happily. My life wasn't perfect, but it was pretty damn close. I may not have the world's best father, but I had the world's best mom, the world's best boyfriend, and the world's best brother (but don't tell him that).

"Hooray for you," my mom repeated. Real joy lit up her eyes as she smiled. "I really am so proud of you, Kate."

EPILOGUE

COLE

KATE LOOKED like a million bucks in her pink bridesmaid dress. She'd been nervous about it, but it hugged every curve of her in pink satin. It fit her perfect body in such a way that she had every male eye in the house following her around longingly. It was even worse than usual. I was actually a bit surprised that Emma let Kate look so hot at her wedding. If I were her, I'd be worried about the competition. Actually, I was the one who was worried about the competition. The many men who were ogling my fiancée were welcome enough to look, but only I was allowed to touch.

And I couldn't seem to keep my hands off her (not that I was really trying). I'd never danced so much in my life as I did at Ward and Emma's wedding reception, and it was all because I never wanted to stop touching Kate.

"I love you," Kate said blissfully, kissing me when we

took a short break from the dance floor at our table. Other women sweated, Kate glowed. I, however, was sweating. Apparently being a professional athlete had not been adequate physical conditioning for dancing in a tuxedo.

"I love you too," I told her feelingly, "more than you know. But do you think we could take a song or two off?"

Unexpectedly, she nodded. "Sure," she answered. "I've got to go powder my nose anyway." She sashayed away, and I savored my few moments of idleness with a deep sigh of relief.

"You two make me sick," Lucas joked from my left. "I mean, I'm happy for you. And I'm happy for Ward and Emma, but still. Could you maybe try not to be so revoltingly cute, in love, and happy all the time?"

"Get out there and find someone to fall in love with," I suggested, pointing at the crowded dance floor. There were lovely single women out there. Probably. Lucas had told me once himself that this town was full of them. In fact, I was fairly certain that he'd brought a date, but she was now nowhere to be found.

"I have," Lucas said unexpectedly. My attention snapped from the dance floor to his face in surprise. "Her name is Victoria," he continued to my annoyance, "and I've got a plan. I'm going to win her back."

I resisted the urge to dissuade him, roll my eyes, or display any emotion that might get my head bit off. Instead, I just asked, "How?"

Lucas nodded his head toward an elegant redhead who

was approaching our table from across the room. She looked vaguely familiar. One of Kate and Emma's friends, maybe?

"See her?"

"Yeah."

"Her name is Rae. She's my date."

"Okay." I failed to see the point of Lucas taking this attractive woman to a wedding when hung up on Victoria. I'm sure my confusion showed on my face. Lucas smirked at me and leaned forward conspiratorially.

"She's not really my date. She's Emma's old roommate and part of the valuation team that's performing due diligence on my app."

"You brought her to the wedding as your date?" I was confused. "What does that have to do with your app?"

"Nothing. But Rae is the key to winning back Victoria. Step one was establishing that we're in a relationship to mutual friends."

Oh no. A sinking feeling started in my stomach. Maybe I was wrong.

"And step two?" I barely even wanted to ask.

Lucas smiled. "Jealousy. Step two is jealousy."

"Step three?"

"I let Victoria destroy the 'relationship' between Rae and me and get back with her."

This plan was not good. This plan was going to backfire. I looked at Rae, who was still trying to fight her way through the crowded dance floor and over to our table and winced. Lucas was off his rocker. Somebody was gonna get hurt.

"You're an idiot." I told him. I could already see there was no way to slow this train down, but I felt obligated to at least try to talk sense into Lucas.

"Actually, I'm a genius," Lucas replied. He took a sip of his champagne. "This is my plan. Therefore, it's a genius plan."

Rae was looking annoyed. She'd attracted several men who clearly wanted to dance with her, but she obviously wanted none of it. She said something to a man who'd placed a hand on her arm. It was inaudible to me, but it caused the entire group to step back and then scatter. The one who touched her ran off faster than a one-legged man in a butt kicking competition.

"You know," I told Lucas seriously, "my uncle Jimmy has a saying about geniuses."

"Oh yeah?" Lucas wasn't really listening to me. He was watching Rae cut through the rest of the crowd like a knife through butter.

"Yeah. He told me one time that he'd met a few geniuses in his life. The problem, according to him, was that outside of their realm of expertise, most geniuses were so dumb that they couldn't pour piss out of a boot with the instructions written on the heel."

Lucas smirked. "Thanks, but I'm not sure your uncle Jimmy's hillbilly wisdom applies here. Don't worry about me, Cole. I've got this all figured out."

Sure you do, Lucas. Sure you do.

* * *

THANK you so much for reading 'Kiss Me Like You Missed Me'! Keep your sweet and sexy binge going with the next book in the Lone Star Lovers series, available now!

Lie With Me features the fake-then-all-too-real relationship between Rae and Lucas, plus Cole, Kate, Emma and other Lone Star Lovers characters. It's full of big secrets, big drama, and witty banter. Turn the page for an exclusive teaser!

SPECIAL TEASER - LIE WITH ME

"I don't feel so good."

Cliff didn't look good, either. In fact, he looked awful. My boss' round face was always ruddy, but right now he was puffy, beet red, and his ordinarily beady eyes were bulging out of his swollen eye sockets. Throughout the short drive downtown from the Austin airport, he'd only been getting puffier, itchier, redder, and grumpier. I was starting to get genuinely worried about him.

"I think you're having an allergic reaction to that bee sting," Annie said from the backseat. This was the third time she'd said it, and I was fairly sure she was right.

Cliff dug his thick fingers beneath his collar, scratching at the hives that were spreading over every inch of visible skin. He loosened the tie that had grown too tight around his neck and groaned.

"I wonder if I might be having an allergic reaction," he mumbled as if he'd just had some kind of spontaneous insight. "What kind of rental car company lets their cars be infested with fucking bees?"

Infested was probably a stretch. There was a bee. One. It probably flew in the open window looking for a sugary taste of Cliff's soda. Cliff just happened to be unlucky enough to swallow it—or attempt to swallow it—and then spit the front half of the bee out, getting stung on the inside of his mouth in the process.

Cliff wiggled in his seat uncomfortably. "Rae, do you think you could drive any slower? I swear, this is why I usually don't let you *girls* drive. You drive like my grandma. And she's been dead for just about thirty years."

I made eye contact with Annie through the rearview mirror. Her expression was more uncertain than offended by Cliff's blatant, casual misogyny. For once, I was willing to excuse it, too. Although the joke in the office among my female coworkers was that Cliff was so named because his mother took one look at him when he was born and wanted to jump off one, I'd never seen him like this. He was often obnoxious, sexist, and generally dismissive of women's ideas, but not usually *totally unreasonable when we were obviously right.*

"I think we should get you to an emergency room just to rule out anything serious," I said, attempting a reasonable tone.

Cliff harrumphed. "Don't be hysterical Rae," he snapped at me. "I'll be fine in a second. We can't be late to this meeting."

Hysterical? You ate a damn bee!

"Cliff—" I tried again, but he cut me off with a rude noise.

"Hush! Now why is it so hot in here? You *girls* always want it to be so damn hot."

Annie and I exchanged another glance through the mirror. Somehow everything was always our fault. Soon he'd probably be blaming us for the bee.

"I'm not hot Cliff," Kyle volunteered from the backseat. The poor guy always tried to be decent, despite being naturally more of a quiet person. His kindness earned him a glare from Cliff.

Kyle wasn't hot because the car wasn't hot. If anything, it was cooler than comfortable. Cliff cranked up the air conditioner anyway. He was sweating profusely, and he'd begun wheezing a bit with every breath.

I was driving us to a preliminary meeting with a new target company. Usually I didn't get to drive, and we were all subjected to Cliff's hatred of safety norms, but today just kept getting weirder. We all needed to get back on track.

This was a crucial meeting, and the first of many in which we would try to convince our target that he wanted to sell his business to us after letting us investigate every square inch of it. Since I was the second most senior person here, Kyle and Annie, the technical members of our evaluation team, were looking to me to do something about Cliff. Annie was painfully shy, and Kyle had just joined our team six months ago; if something was going to get done, it was up to me to do it.

In my three years working for the Azure Group, I'd never led an onsite acquisition team before. I'd worked my way up to second in command, however, and I was well aware that my only chance of moving up further was by replacing Cliff or someone like him. As hard as Cliff was to work with, I had no desire to take his place because *he'd died from a simple bee sting*. Still, I sensed that a battlefield promotion might be near.

And that wasn't the only thing near. "We're here," I told the group. I shifted the car to park in front of The Lone Star Lounge and turned to Cliff. "You need to go to the emergency room," I ordered him. "You're not well. You can't meet with the client like this."

Cliff, who was fighting a coughing spell, shook his head furiously. His mouth framed an obvious "no" but no sound escaped, even after his coughing sputtered to an end. When he finally did manage to make a noise, it was a small panicked wheeze. He clutched at his throat in a panic.

Shit.

I'd seen *My Girl.* I knew how this ended. Not willing to waste another second, I threw my door open and prepared to sprint across the parking lot.

God dammit Cliff. Don't you fucking die you pompous, chau-vinistic pig. Not before you recommend me for a promotion.

"Kyle, call 911!" I shouted over my shoulder. "Annie get his jacket and tie off."

"On it," came the in-unison reply.

I'd run track in high school. Even in the three-inch heels and pencil skirt I was wearing, I was fast. I dashed across the asphalt, garnering stares from other patrons who were making their way to happy hour. I threw open the door to the bar and marched into the middle of the room.

"Does anyone have an EpiPen? There's a man in the parking lot going into anaphylactic shock. He was stung by a bee. It's an emergency."

I wasn't using my inside voice, and when I want to be loud, *I am LOUD*. It comes from being a born New Yorker, telling off catcallers in a big city, and working in a heavily male-dominated business. I was no shy, retiring flower at the best of times. When I needed to be scary and pushy, I could be terrifying. As expected, the room fell instantly silent. People stared at me like I'd just announced the rapture.

Lucas Stevenson was somewhere in this bar, but I couldn't spare more than a passing thought about this possibly being our first interaction. The tech wunderkind had created what was probably another brilliant innova-tion, one that the Azure Group desperately wanted to acquire. I would focus on that later. Right now, my annoying boss was potentially going to die if I didn't make a scene. So, I would make a scene.

"Please! Anyone! I need an EpiPen right now! Please!" I repeated. I stared around me at the faces of strangers, entreating them to listen. In New York, people are good at ignoring strangers, but when there's a crisis, a real emergency, strangers will help. I prayed it was the same here in Austin, Texas.

"I have one." The bartender, an extremely petite blonde, extended the slim injector to me.

My breath slid out in a relieved rush and I flew over to grasp it. "Thank you," I managed. "Thank you so much." I looked at the device in confusion. I'd just realized that I didn't know how to administer it. The bartender was already rounding the bar.

"I can show you how to use it, if you need me to," she was saying. "Did you call 911?"

I nodded. "Yes, and yes. Follow me."

The blonde and I ran back outside to where Kyle and Annie were desperately trying to assist Cliff. My trip back to the Four Runner was a lot slower than my trip from it. My new, tiny blonde friend had very short legs by comparison.

"I'm Rae Lewis," I told her as we ran. "Thanks for your help. Seriously."

"Emma—" she panted, "Emma Williams."

"Ok, so what do I do?" I asked when we got near to Cliff.

He was still in the passenger seat, clutching at his throat and obviously struggling to get enough air. His reddish color had turned a deep, ugly purple. He was still making noises though; that had to be a good sign.

"Pull off the blue cap and then hold the orange end against his thigh," Emma explained as I unwrapped the injector. She was shaking slightly, and her voice was tremulous, but I tried to ignore it. "Keep the injector there until it clicks and then count to five."

"I'm going to inject you with this," I told Cliff, in a loud, clear voice. I shook the EpiPen in front of his purple, swollen face. "Your airway is closing up. We have to stop your reaction from getting worse."

He shook his head furiously as soon as I said the word 'inject'. What a baby. Did he want to suffocate? Too bad. He wasn't allowed to die.

"This is happening," I told him. "Don't test me."

Cliff tried to bat my hand away when I did as Emma directed, but Kyle and Annie helped me hold him still. The click of the needle was tiny, but I felt it. Cliff definitely felt it. He made a noise somewhere between a whine and a moan, jerked a bit, and then glared at me like I'd just poisoned him. Then, as I removed the needle from his skin, he started to shake violently. I blanched.

"What's he doing?"

"That's normal," Emma said when my gaze snapped to her delicate features. She looked nervous. "It's good, actually. It means the medicine got in him. He'll shake for a while, and may feel frightened, cold, or paranoid. But he won't die, and he'll be able to breathe better soon." She paused. "I've, um, I've never done this before, but that's what the instructions said." Her expression was sheepish.

I'm glad she didn't tell me this was her first time before I injected him.

All four of us stared at Cliff anxiously while he shook like a leaf. He shook and jerked, but just like she said, he *was* starting to breath more normally. He took deep, grateful gulps of air. His plum color began lightening into a healthier, but still unnatural pink. He wasn't able to speak, but over the next ten minutes he became increasingly responsive, though he was also clearly confused and dizzy.

"I—I just don't know how to thank you," I stuttered at Emma, and she patted my arm comfortingly with her little hand. I'm not used to being touched by strangers, but somehow, I found myself appreciating her contact rather than resenting it. I managed a small smile and she returned it.

"You don't need to thank me," Emma told me. "It's all ok." Whether she knew it or not, she was my angel this afternoon. I could not imagine what I would have done without her help. I wasn't sure how long Cliff would have been able to wait for help.

I relaxed a little bit at her words, and then relaxed a lot more when the high, familiar squeal of an ambulance began to grow closer. The white and red vehicle peeled into view around the corner with the squeal of brakes, bringing with it flashing lights, lots of questions, and professional help. The next hour was a bizarre, dizzy whirlwind.

"No, no. You stop that," the paramedic—Vanessa—told Cliff when he tried to rip the IV out of his arm. Both her tone and the way she grabbed his hand and held it was just like one would do with a kid, not a fifty-something-year-old who just acted like a child. "Be still now," she chided. He continued to mumble something, and she pushed a syringe into his tube and depressed the plunger. "There you go," she told him. "That'll help you relax."

A moment later, Cliff nodded incoherently, and his eyes slipped closed.

"Is he going to be ok?" Kyle asked for all three of us.

Vanessa and her hunky partner Sam exchanged a glance at one another. Then they both shrugged.

"He needs to be seen by a doctor," Vanessa said after a moment. She'd clearly been trained to dispense the minimum amount of information necessary. I knew she couldn't make us any promises. "He's stable now and that's what's most important. We do need to take him to a hospital though. I know they will want to run some tests on him."

The two of them had instantly taken over when they arrived. I'd never been so glad to suddenly *not to be in charge.* The truth is, I had no idea how to treat Cliff. Other than the EpiPen, I knew next to nothing about allergies, especially the dangerous, life-threatening kind. Vanessa and Sam clearly saw it every day. They knew exactly what to do, and even more impressively, they knew how to comfort and contain us at the same time.

"One of you is welcome to ride with us," Sam offered as they finished getting Cliff ready to transport. "But only one. For insurance reasons."

"I'll do it!" Annie volunteered instantly. She was looking at his impressive biceps and big green eyes longingly. There was no denying that the paramedic was easy on the eyes. Unfortunately, for Annie, I was pretty sure that Vanessa and Sam were partners in more ways than one. I usually have pretty good instincts for knowing when a man was taken. The way Vanessa eyed buxom Annie with thinly veiled suspicion told me it was true.

"Kyle, you follow the ambulance. I'll go meet with Stevenson and explain things," I told him. "I'll meet up with you later."

I expected Kyle to argue, but he didn't. "Ok." He seemed really shaken by the entire experience and kept looking around at everything with worried eyes. He usually spent his time pouring over financial records, so this was way out of his wheelhouse. I patted his arm comfortingly. Vanessa and Sam loaded Cliff's gurney into the back of the ambulance, and Kyle slid into the driver's seat of the rental SUV to follow.

"See you soon," he said. "I'll call you if anything important happens."

I nodded.

"Thank you so much!" I cried to the ambulance, waving goodbye to the paramedics and letting them take my entire team away. Vanessa gave me a thumbs up through the open driver's side window. She had confirmed that we'd done the right thing injecting Cliff with the EpiPen, possibly even saving his life. Getting an airway open during an allergic reaction apparently became exponentially harder the longer you waited. Even Cliff, although he was in and out of consciousness and who's tongue was several times larger than normal, admitted that he appreciated what I'd done. Annie and Kyle called me a hero.

I didn't feel like much of a hero. I felt utterly exhausted and drained. More than anything, I felt like I'd just been in a fistfight. I slumped down on the curb and put my head against my knees, thoroughly depleted of energy. Now I had to meet with our client alone, and there was nothing that I wanted to do less. Meeting with Lucas Stevenson in my current rumpled state was not ideal, and I was already horribly late. I figured taking a moment to collect myself while sitting on the curb was allowable. I wondered if I could slip inside and make it into the bathroom to touch up my makeup first. It had been hours since I looked in a mirror, but I had a feeling my hair was doing bad things atop my head. It had been in a sleek bun, but that was hours ago.

My phone beeped in my purse, and I checked it wearily. There were a number of things waiting on my attention. Fourteen new emails, dozens of texts, and interestingly, the app belonging to our client. The app that we were here to acquire. It chirped that it had a notification for me.

Curious, I pressed a button and the minimalistic interface of Notable Match popped up. I'd installed it on my phone during the flight from New York, but hadn't had a chance to really mess around with it yet. The new notification had come in about the time we arrived at the bar, but I was just now seeing it.

You have a new match, the app informed me in cartoonish text. *Lucas Stevenson is within two hundred feet of you.* A man's face, square jawed, hazel-eyed and devastatingly handsome, blinked on my screen. The man in the photo looked a lot more like a model than a tech guru. *That's Lucas Stevenson?* I doubted it. He probably used a fake photo. A small heart icon spun, grew and exploded into dozens of smaller hearts.

His app had matched us as a couple? I was still staring at my phone while sitting on a curb, dumbfounded, when someone cleared their throat behind me. I twisted around, looking up and into the face of Lucas Stevenson. He looked just like his picture. I closed the app as quickly as I could, but I could tell he'd already seen it.

"Can I buy you a drink?" he asked with a smile.

* * *

"So, is Cliff going to be ok?" Lucas asked me a few minutes later. We'd snagged a table out on the patio of the Lone Star Lounge, and I'd been explaining why our meeting was an hour late.

"I think so," I told him, sipping at the beer he'd recommended. It was a Hefeweizen from a local brewery—Live Oak. I liked it. I liked it even more with the orange slice he'd insisted I add. "I apologize. This isn't at all how our initial client meetings usually go. I can't even show you the PowerPoint, since my coworkers took the rental and all my stuff to the hospital."

I could already tell that this meeting wasn't going to get more normal, either. He wasn't a normal client. About the only similarity between Lucas and our average client were the thick rimmed glasses he wore. He was young, at least thirty years younger than usual—possibly only a handful of years older than me. He was also wearing a Metallica t-shirt and beaten up jeans rather than a suit. Lucas was well built, too, broad shouldered and with defined muscles visible beneath his clothes. Most of our clients were potbellied, middle aged CEO's. Honestly, I had to do my best not to stare. The man was gorgeous.

"Well I would hope not," he laughed, drawing me back from ogling him. It was a good-natured, pleasant laugh that made the corners of my mouth turn up. "I'm glad your boss is gonna' be ok. I'll take a rain check on the PowerPoint." His sandy brown hair was tousled in a way that was either totally unintentionally sexy or carefully coiffed to look unintentionally sexy. Either way, I wanted to touch him. It. I wanted to touch it.

Get it together, I told myself firmly. *You're in a business meeting, not on a date.*

"So," Lucas continued, "tell me about yourself, Rae."

I blinked at him. *Me?* No. That couldn't be what he meant. He meant the firm.

I launched into the canned answer: "The Azure Group was established in 1996 at the beginning of the tech boom. Our portfolio is excess of sixty billion dollars and we specialize in acquiring the best in emerging software. We've got a full service—"

"Management and consultancy team, as well as an in-house evaluation and due diligence operation," Lucas interrupted with a smirk. *He knew my pitch as well as I did.* "I read all about the Azure Group before accepting this meeting," he admitted. Clearly, he had a photographic memory, too. The consensus in the office was that he was a genius, and I had a feeling that I was about to find out if it was true. "Of course, I'm familiar with your firm. *I was asking about you, Rae.*"

My lips parted in surprise. "I'm part of the evaluation team. I help investigate new prospective portfolio companies, like yours."

Lucas smirked at me and arched an eyebrow. "And?"

I fought the urge to shift uncomfortably in my seat.

Why did this feel like a date? "And I work with a technical and financial subject matter team to determine whether we should make an offer to acquire those companies."

If Lucas already knew all about the Azure Group, he probably already knew all about the team that had been sent to meet with him. Actually, I was certain that he did. I wrote him an email myself explaining about each of us, although Cliff had been the one to attach his name and send it. He loved to take credit for another's work. He called it 'delegating'.

"What about you, Rae? I want to know about you." His hazel eyes were an incredible color, green on the inside near the pupil, and golden brown on the outside. I couldn't help staring deeply into them.

"Me?" I was feeling very out of my depth. I thought I was ready to conduct one of these meetings by myself. I'd seen Cliff do it dozens of times. But none of those meetings had been anything like this. I took another nervous sip of my beer. "Ok. What do you want to know?"

"Where are you from?"

"Um, I'm from Flushings." Then I remembered we were in Texas, and that Lucas probably didn't know what that was. "It's a neighborhood in Queens. I've lived in New York my whole life. How about you?" It seemed only fair to turn the tables on him. After all, he was asking me personal questions.

He smiled. "I'm from the west coast. I was born in LA

and moved to Texas for school and just... stayed. I like it here. So how'd you get into the private equity business?"

That was easy enough. "I went to NYU and double majored in business and economics. I worked at a hedge fund for a year after college and the pay was good, but I hated every second of it. So, when a former classmate of mine told me about an opening at Azure Group, I jumped. I've been portfolio building ever since. I finished my JD this spring and am waiting to find out if I passed the NY bar exam."

"Do you like working for Azure Group?

What sort of a question was that? That wasn't what this meeting was about. And how could I answer it honestly while still being professional? I tried. "I enjoy puzzles. Deciding whether to acquire a company and pricing our offer fairly and appropriately requires a lot of the same skills that I enjoy."

"That's not an answer. If I say that I like water, and then say that sharks also like water, that doesn't mean I also like sharks." His tone was challenging. My heart fluttered. I loved a good challenge.

"Cum hoc ergo propter hoc," I answered. I took logic in college too. In Latin, the fallacy translated to 'with this, therefore because of this'. It was also known as the correlation-causation fallacy.

His incredible hazel eyes widened, as did his smile. He was clever. Probably much cleverer than me. "So, you don't like it?" His question was teasing.

"Assuming that conclusion would be a logical fallacy too," I told him, still feeling like I was being evaluated.

"That's a fair point. Post hoc ergo propter hoc." Lucas grinned. I'd clearly just won a point. The Latin translated to 'after this, therefore because of this' and it was also called the questionable cause fallacy. "Do you like your job, Rae?"

What I really enjoyed most about my job, and what was still incredibly rare, were conversations like this one. Times when I was able to match wits against someone who was my equal, or better. I lived for negotiations and the chance to be challenged. But I didn't say that to Lucas. It would reveal too much.

"I like a lot of things about my job," I told Lucas, deciding to be halfway honest. He was quick to display his intellectual ability, but he was a genius. I could hardly blame him for acting like one. "I like learning about companies and distilling what makes them profitable. I like making the argument for or against their acquisition. And then, once I've learned everything I can, I like moving on to the next one. Obviously, there are some things that I dislike about my job, too. But on the whole, I can't complain."

That answer didn't seem to satisfy him. "Why do I get the feeling you're only telling me the positives?"

I smirked. "Because you're a client, of course."

"And if I wasn't?"

I didn't know what he was getting at, but if he had reservations about the company, I could maybe do something about that.

"If you weren't a client, I'd tell you that Azure Group is a gigantic faceless corporation that has more yearly profit than some countries have GDP. Employees like me are cogs in wheels within wheels. Our lives don't matter to the machine. It can be hard to work for a big bureaucracy sometimes, especially if you're like me." I shrugged.

"What do you mean, like you?"

I shook my head. This was getting too personal. How could I tell him I was dissatisfied with my job but too afraid to ever complain? That wasn't professional.

He was looking at me carefully, as if weighing two alternatives. We sat in silence for a moment.

"I have a proposition for you, Rae."

"Isn't that my line? And a bit premature?" I arched an eyebrow at him for a change. We were nowhere near the negotiation phase of this process. There were weeks of investigation and due diligence that needed to happen first. I wasn't authorized to make an offer, and I definitely wasn't authorized to accept one.

"It's a proposition for you, Rae. *Personally*. Not for the Azure Group. I find myself far less interested in them than I am in you."

My lips parted in surprise. This conversation was wildly out of control. Still, I couldn't help but wonder where it would go. This was fun. "What's your proposition?"

"Are you single?" His hazel eyes were bright.

I blinked at him. "What... um, I mean yes, I am. Single, that is." I felt another hot blush on my cheeks.

He likes me? He must like me!

"I want you to pretend to be my girlfriend."

Oh.

Find out if Lucas and Rae find love in their sexy, secret-filled fake relationship now!

SPECIAL TEASER - ADMIT YOU WANT ME

"Come on, Emma!" Kate cried, banging on my bedroom door for the fifth or sixth time. "You can't hide in there forever. I'm sure you look fine. People are going to be here soon."

I glanced at the clock. She was right. It was almost go time. I slid into my green, marabou trimmed boudoir slippers and straightened my sheer tights. I had a bad feeling that I looked more than a little bit like a stripper.

"Just a second," I yelled. "I'm almost ready."

I frowned at my reflection in the mirror, poked at my fake eyelashes, and adjusted the mesh and wire wings strapped to my back. The wings were already annoying me, but not as much as the length of my dress.

My Tinkerbell costume was much sexier and more revealing than I'd thought it would be when I bought it online. My boobs were threatening to spill out of the bright green satin bustier, and the nearly transparent matching skirt just barely made it halfway down my thighs. This is what I got for trusting the photographs on eBay. It would just have to do. The only other option at this point was cutting a couple of eye holes in a sheet and going to our Halloween party as a ghost.

"Wow," Kate stammered when I opened the door a second later. "You look *amazing!*"

I smiled nervously. "It's not too slutty?"

Kate shook her head. "It's the exactly right amount of slutty. The fact that it's your real hair up there in that silly bun is what makes it."

Kate was blonde for Halloween too, but her flowing, gold Rapunzel hair was a wig. Our Halloween party was Disney themed and our apartment looked a bit like a five-year old's birthday party (but with way more booze). I grabbed myself a cup of the pink punch and tried to work myself up for being social.

My current pair of wings notwithstanding, I was not a natural social butterfly like Kate. If it wasn't for her, I probably wouldn't have any friends. Moving in with Kate at the beginning of my sophomore year was the best decision I could have made for my social life, even if it meant living inside a kegger one night a week. This Halloween party promised to be no exception.

Costumed people began to trickle into our apartment, armed with beer, smiles, and excitement. I struggled to fit in. After the disaster that was my freshman year at a school back east, coming to the University of Texas had been a case of serious culture shock. They don't call it a party school for nothing, and I'm a natural introvert and a bit of a nerd. Before coming here, I'd never had a drop to drink.

Unluckily for my liver, I was also a quick study. I'd determined that I hated most beer, most wine, and anything with a harsh liquor taste, but I loved anything sweet and fruity. Thankfully, Austin had a number of local breweries that specialized in ciders, shandys, and even sour beers.

"Are fairies supposed to be drinking, Tinkerbell?" someone asked me when I went to grab another apple cider from the fridge. I spun around and straightened, surprised.

Kate's brother Ward was leaning against the door. I hadn't realized that he'd followed me. I straightened abruptly, hoping my ass hadn't been totally exposed by my tiny skirt when I bent over.

My breathing sped up and I felt myself biting down on my bottom lip nervously. The hand not clutching a bottle sent fingertips to my hemline and found that my skirt had ridden up a bit. Yeah, he'd definitely just seen my ass. His cocked eyebrow and even cockier smile told me that he had appreciated it, too. I felt a hot flush burn my cheeks.

It didn't help that he seemed to know exactly what he did to me every time he came around, although this was only the third time I'd met him since Kate and I moved in together in August. I couldn't hide my attraction to him at all. He teased me mercilessly at every opportunity, and it felt like he did it just to see me blush. He clearly found how bookish, quiet, and prone to embarrassment I was simply hilarious.

I wasn't shy for his entertainment. I *wished* I could be different. But I would never be an extrovert like Ward, or his sister. Even dressed up like Tinkerbell and pumped full of alcohol, I was still just doomed to be a wallflower.

Ward and I stared across the kitchen at each other. Usually, I turned into a stammering mess whenever he was around. Thanks to the magic of alcohol, that wouldn't be happening tonight.

I flicked my gaze up and down his figure and then did my best to tear my eyes away again. It was all I could do not to sigh dreamily. Broad shoulders and an obviously muscled chest narrowed to a slim waist and long legs. Powerful, sinuous arms ended in large, strong-looking hands. But it was his classically handsome face, with fair skin, dark blue eyes, an aquiline nose, and dark curly hair, that made my heart pound against my ribs.

"Who are you, the morality police?" I smiled at him confidently and floated across the kitchen floor toward him. I was buzzed and feeling good. Brave. For once I was brave. "I might be underage, but at least I follow directions. You're not even wearing a costume." I leveled a finger at his chest and pushed him back an inch. He laughed lightly.

Ward was dressed up as a football player, which was not a costume, because he *was* a football player for the

Texas Longhorns. He'd actually graduated last May, but was in town for Kate's birthday, which was two days after Halloween.

"Sure, I am," he replied, grabbing my hand and tracing the logo with my finger. "This is the wrong team."

I thought that red color looked unusual. I shrugged and smiled up at him. "You can't expect me to know that. I don't have much interest in sports." We were still almost holding hands. His enveloped mine completely. I liked the feeling.

"Hmm. What do you have an interest in, Tinkerbell?" His voice was soft, and there was something hot and heavy in his gaze.

"Emma," I corrected automatically, still not pulling my hand away. I didn't want him to get in the habit of calling me that.

Ward laughed at my answer. "Oh, so you're self-obsessed?" He shrugged. "At least you're honest. Most girls really try to hide that, at least at first."

I giggled at him and my tone turned teasing. *"Don't call me Tinkerbell.* And I have lots of interests. But what about you? Do you have any outside of football or is it all just visions of sweaty men with balls in your head?"

He smirked and set the beer he was holding in his left hand down on the counter with a decisive clink. His response was slow and suggestive. "Well now, I just have all sorts of interests beyond that." His native, Texas drawl gave the words a few extra syllables we didn't have in Connecticut. I smiled shyly up at him and listened as he

353

continued. "For one, I'm finding myself very interested in you, Emma."

My lips parted in surprise. Ward was *interested* in me? As in, *romantically* interested? Interested in sexy-fun-times with me? The fact that we were standing alone, basically holding hands in the darkened kitchen suddenly percolated through my alcohol-soaked brain. He seemed to realize it too and straightened. He blinked like he'd just been awoken from a trance, releasing my hand which I pressed to his chest. I could hardly believe I was touching him. I stared at the hand like it belonged to someone else, and then looked up at him.

The look in his eyes suggested that he was thinking us through, just like me. He was Kate's brother, no longer a student, and definitely not going to stick around. I was on the rebound from the world's worst relationship, painfully shy, semi-drunk, and essentially wearing lingerie in public. We'd spent all most all of our time at this party until this point trading pointed jabs. But now I had a very different sort of exchange in mind.

Before I could overthink anything, I leaned up and up —he was much taller than my five-two—and kissed him. He wrapped his arms around my waist, crushing my stupid wings and then mumbling an apology against my lips. I could hear his heart beating hard as he pressed me closer into his chest, and he teased my tongue mercilessly with his until I was breathless. A dull, throbbing ache was starting in my core, and any silly things like consequences receded in importance. I only needed to fix that needy ache. The sound of someone laughing in the room beyond pulled us back to the moment. We needed to get out of this kitchen.

"Come on," I told him, pulling him towards the hall. "My room is this way."

He hesitated. "Emma, in three days I have to go back to —" he started to say. I shook my head and cut him off with another kiss.

"I know," I told him when I pulled away. I leaned up to play with the soft tendrils of dark hair that curved around his ear, and then leaned up to whisper. "I'm not asking you to go steady." He shivered and squeezed my waist.

"Are you sure?" he asked again. Distantly, I admired his willingness to be honest about what he was offering me and obtain my consent. He wasn't offering love, or friendship, or even companionship. Just... right now. Just tonight. Impulsively, I decided it could be enough.

In that moment, I didn't care that this would be very, very temporary. I was taking a risk and part of me knew I'd pay for it later, but at that second... I wanted to be the sort of girl who did fun and spontaneous things. I wanted to be brave. I wanted to be the girl who could recover from the last asshole I'd been with and come out swinging. I'd never done anything remotely like this before, but I found myself more excited than scared. Maybe I was channeling my inner, plucky Tinkerbell. Or maybe I was just dumb, drunk, and horny.

Whatever the reason was, my desire was simple. My answer was simple too.

"I know when to admit what I want, Ward. Do you?"

He smiled a slow, crooked smile, and then followed me back to my room.

Go to www.taylorholloway.com/email.html to sign up for My Mailing List for the **exclusive, extended epilogues** and the latest news!

HOW TO GET YOUR FREE EXTENDED EPILOGUES!

IF YOU'RE LOOKING for more **free** bonus content, including exclusive extended epilogues and check-ins with your favorite characters go to www.taylorholloway.com/email.html to sign up for My Mailing List! If you're already a subscriber check the last newsletter you received, the link is always at the bottom of the email.

XOXO
Taylor

ALSO BY TAYLOR HOLLOWAY

LONE STAR LOVERS

1. ADMIT YOU WANT ME - WARD
2. KISS ME LIKE YOU MISSED ME - COLE
3. LIE WITH ME - LUCAS
4. RUN AWAY WITH ME - JASON
5. HOLD ON TO ME - RYAN
6. A BAD CASE OF YOU - ERIC
7. TOUCHING ME, TOUCHING YOU - CHRISTOPHER
8. THIS ONE'S FOR YOU - IAN
9. BAD FOR YOU - BRANDON (COMING SOON)

FOR FANS OF EXCITING, ROMANTIC MYSTERIES FULL OF TWISTS AND TURNS, CHECK OUT MY SCIONS OF SIN SERIES!

PREQUEL: NEVER SAY NEVER - CHARLIE

1. BLEEDING HEART - ALEXANDER
2. KISS AND TELL - NATHAN
3. DOWN AND DIRTY - NICHOLAS
4. LOST AND FOUND - DAVID

76991540R20219

Made in the USA
Columbia, SC
28 September 2019